# WILD HEARTS

## JULIE CAPULET

**He's wild, brutal and dangerous. Against my will, he's also my new husband.**

The first time I saw Wolf Ramsey was at his family's estate in Kauai. He was huge and imposing. Armed to the teeth. When he looked right at me, fascination wasn't my first reaction. It was fear.

His outrageous good looks were shadowed only by his wild intensity. You could tell he would be reckless and brutal. Even from a distance, his dark, dangerous energy made my heart beat faster in a way I wasn't expecting. I knew he would take me places I've never been and ruin me, body and soul. I was relieved when it was time to leave.

But before I could escape him, one single announcement changed my entire life. Because it's not going to be my sister who secures the family alliance between the Ramseys and the Fitzpatricks.

It's going to be me. And my new husband-to-be, Wolf Ramsey.

*WILD HEARTS is a steamy new adult arranged marriage romance, set in paradise.*

**Please note:** Wild Hearts is the second book in the

Paradise Series. While it can be read as a standalone, this book contains spoilers to Book 1, so it is recommended that you read the first book in the series before reading this one: **<u>Devil's Angel (Paradise Book 1)</u>**

## JULIE CAPULET ROMANCE

**WILD HEARTS**
Copyright © 2023 by Julie Capulet

ASIN: B0BQHDV9MX
ISBN-13: 979-8374634358

WILD HEARTS is a work of fiction. The characters and events portrayed in this book are fictitious. Any resemblance to actual persons, living or dead, events, or locales is entirely coincidental.

**www.juliecapulet.com**

**Note to readers:**

Some of the places described in this book are real locations
on the Hawaiian islands of Oahu and Kauai. <u>Most are
reimagined</u>. The settings and locations have been
redesigned to fit the story.

# THE FAMILIES

| RAMSEY | FITZPATRICK | KING |
|--------|-------------|------|
| REMINGTON | SILAS | ENZO |
| BLAISE | MALACHI | RAVEN |
| KNOX | TATUM | STONE |
| WOLF | PERRI | JAGGER |
| ECHO | VIVI | AURORA |

# 1

# Vivi

"GIVE her more of that kohl eyeliner. Really lay it on. She needs a smokier eye. And for god's sake, get rid of that insipid pink lip gloss. Are you serious with that bullshit? We want a siren, fuck-me red. For lips *this* naturally perfect, it would be a crime not to pimp them out to every hot bachelor with a heartbeat. Think sultry, people. *Sexy.* It's time to get this girl some goddamn action."

*Okay, wow.*

My head stylist, whose name is Lana Lee, is at it again. Micromanaging me to within an inch of my life, meanwhile endlessly pointing out how nonexistent my love life is. Which isn't entirely my fault, but it's true enough. She's obsessed with shining a high-beam spotlight onto the obvious at every available opportunity.

I have limits. Sure, I've never *acted* on my limits but

they're there. I'm not sure exactly where my line is but I know I'm getting dangerously close to it.

They call me sweet. Shy. Quiet. I'm the good girl, the one who always does what she's told. But simmering just under the surface of my obedience is a wild heart. Some little spark in me is biding its time, craving … something. Freedom. Rebellion. Danger. I can feel it coming. Which is both daunting and sort of thrilling, to be honest.

I *know* I'm going to do something reckless that no one sees coming. I just don't know when.

I guess Lana has reason to be full of herself. Every A-list actor, model and influencer wants to work with her, from here to L.A., Aspen, the Hamptons, Manhattan, London, Paris, Milan, you name it. Even so, she spends most of her time here at Seven Mile Beach, my family's compound in Waikiki.

This is because my sisters pay her astronomical amounts of money to dress us and basically manage our lives—or at least the part of our lives that involves fashion, which is most of it. She also lives in one of our guesthouses as part of her employment package. Which has a cute, Juliet-style balcony that overlooks its own secluded sugar-sand beach.

Lana is in such white-hot demand, she sometimes gets caught up in her own hype. Like now, for example. And I'm tired of her non-stop commentary about my so-called "innocence." It's her favorite topic.

For a brief moment I think about getting up and walking out. Just standing up without saying a word to anyone and walking through our huge, busy fashion studio

—with its racks of garments, walls of mirrors, expansive windows that overlook the ocean, teams of stylists and tables strewn with designs and patterns and sewing machines, where ten or more dressmakers are finalizing tonight's looks for us, along with all the outfits we'll need for the rest of our weekend. Not to mention all the other upcoming photoshoots and events on our jam-packed schedules.

I picture myself silently making my way down the grand staircase of my family's estate, under the giant crystal chandelier, right out the front door, down the driveway and out the gate. Just walking away into the big, wide-open world where no one knows me and I can do whatever I want.

I won't, of course.

I'd probably be kidnapped within minutes. For … reasons.

We're famous. We own the most expensive piece of real estate in Waikiki, along with many others.

I understand why I'm guarded. I know why it's necessary and I'm used to it.

Mostly.

I'm watched like a hawk. My team of bodyguards protects my every move. My phone calls, posts and texts are monitored and filtered. My schedule is lorded over and controlled. Some days I don't even feel like a real person. Like I'm more of a carefully-curated brand who lives in a gilded cage than an actual human being.

They mean well, of course they do.

But my cage's bars feel extra thick today. More and

more, it occurs to me that there's a reason they keep me on such a tight rein.

I wonder what Ash is doing. It's his day off. I told him I'd go see him before we leave for our weekend away.

My brothers and my cousins would kill me if they found out I've been sneaking down to the pool house to see him. Even more, they'd kill Ash.

*They* get to choose who I hang out with, in their own minds at least.

Usually I just go with the flow. Because that's what's expected of me and also because they enforce it.

But right now, I feel restless in a way that's new. Some hidden corner of my psyche wants to break free of them all.

"Weave a few more of those jade beads into her hair," Lana orders her underlings. "And make sure the emerald gemstones are at the front." My hair is braided into an elaborate up-do with jewels woven into it that makes me look like an Egyptian princess, maybe. Or a beach bum who won the lottery. I like the effect, but I had no idea it would take so long to create. If I'd known, I could have worn my hair loose, and spent the last two hours with Ash.

*Then why didn't you?*

Because I don't have the freedom to make choices like that.

Which suddenly feels very wrong. Thinking about it now, I'm not sure I've ever made a single decision about *my own life*. It's crazy. I'm so used to being told what to do, I hardly even notice. But something about the whole scenario is hitting differently today.

*Stand up to them. You're giving them too much.*

More mascara is brushed onto my eyelashes. Someone else tugs at my hair, pinning it into place.

"Ow," I grumble.

"More eyeliner," Lana snaps from where she's swiping manically through several of the garment racks. "Her look needs to scream horny-as-hell untouched heiress on the prowl."

*It does?*

For better or worse—worse, usually—I hate offending people or causing any kind of conflict. It's one of my weaknesses, so I've been told. Ironically, it's the same people telling me it's a weakness who are the ones who make sure I walk their line.

"The shy virgin needs to get her halo dirty," Lana says. "It'll add value to her brand. This pure-as-the-driven-snow schtick has a shelf life."

I've really had just about enough of this. Even worse, I *agree* with her. I *want* to get my halo dirty. Problem is, they never let me near anyone who might do me the honors.

It's part of the reason why I've been sneaking down to visit Ash almost every day. Not that we're anything more than friends at this point but I feel like that might change.

"She's only twenty, Lana," Perri says. My sister is standing in front of the mirrors as five people pin and adjust the black dress she's wearing to the party we're going to tonight. The dress is entirely sheer, revealing what looks like a minuscule black bikini underneath, leaving almost nothing to the imagination. She's curvy and the bikini doesn't cover much. It's sexy to the extreme, and I know why she's chosen it. She's hoping to get a marriage proposal tonight. From Knox Ramsey, the buff, reclusive middle son of the Ramsey family. "Vivi's holding out for the real thing."

Am I?

Sure, true love would be the ideal. It's what everyone dreams of. But my status as an inexperienced hermit isn't exactly the one I've chosen. I'm holding out because my family doesn't allow me to go anywhere without a chaperone. For my safety, according to them.

Lana has the confident, take-control personality of an army general. And when she decides my entire wardrobe is going to revolve around whether or not I'm getting laid—which everyone knows I never have—it's more than a little humiliating.

My brothers and sisters control who I see and where I go. Lana controls what I wear. My brigade of assistants, stylists, social media curators, personal trainers, nutritionists, yoga instructors, make-up artists, beauty experts, designers, event planners and publicists control every aspect of my days and nights, down to the minute.

The only person who *doesn't* have any control over my life is me.

I'm the youngest of five and all my siblings have always been overprotective of me. My mother died when I was a baby and when I was ten, my father began his downward spiral into the kind of dementia that doesn't just take a person's memory and personality but twists it into something unrecognizable. He died around two years ago and it was a mercy.

Because I was the youngest and had no mother, from the very beginning, I became everyone else's pet project.

Silas is the oldest and he's mostly done a decent job of running our family's affairs, I guess. The one exception is his heavy-handed supervision of me. Our cousin Jett is Silas's advisor and his bodyguard. Jett is also my bodyguard, or at least when he or Silas thinks I need extra protection, which happens to be most of the time. My other brother Malachi is Silas's wingman. And Tatum too, although from a young age she always loved to travel, so she's the one who has spent the most time away from Seven Mile Beach. She got cast in her first movie when she was seventeen, became a huge hit and has spent most of the past eight years on film locations. She's now one of the most bankable stars in Hollywood.

Malachi is also a major movie star but he's only interested in blockbusters and he comes home when he's not filming. He's the king of the Waikiki party scene and he has a harem of women who give him anything he wants.

As for Perri, it was always her dream to become a model. She works to achieve this goal night and day. But to her unending despair, she's never been offered a modeling contract. Not once, even though she has a massive following and gets a huge amount of publicity for being an heiress and a socialite.

After years of no offers, partly through sheer spite, she created a bunch of her own global brands purely so she can model her products herself. She doesn't need to rely on her beauty to get herself seen. She can be the face of her lines of cosmetics, fragrance, clothing, hair products and so on because she runs the company. She even has a lifestyle blog. My sister has more followers on Instagram than anyone else in the world.

I admire her ambition. I just sometimes wish she wasn't so cut-throat about everything she does. She's competitive to the extreme. That kind of obsession can't be great for a person's mental health, I figure. She's always stressed out and irritable. She can be prickly and hard to be around, especially when she's in one of her moods.

It's always bothered her that I *do* get offered modeling contracts. She's never said so but I can tell. She works out non-stop with her team of personal trainers and she's already had a lot of fillers. Tatum keeps telling her not to overdo it, but Perri already looks a little bit … plastic. Even when money is no object, there's only so much Botox you can pump into your face before it starts to look weird.

Perri is known for her savvy and her style. *But never for my beauty*, she cries to me all the time. It breaks her heart. *They've never called me beautiful. Not once.*

I tell her *I* think she's beautiful. And she is. She's my guide and she's my closest sister, even though there's the tiniest edge behind her love, which I can feel simmering there. A jealousy and a resentment she does her best to control. We both try to ignore it.

"I said sexy, not street-corner whore," Lana barks at several of the make-up artists. Cody, Lana's senior assistant, who has the patience of a saint, blinks his long eyelashes at me in solidarity as he smooths the kohl around my eyes with a tiny sponge.

"I don't know why they're bothering," I mutter, looking out the wall of windows to the white sand of our private beach with its loungers and blue umbrellas, to the turquoise ocean waves beyond. "This is all a waste of time."

"Girl, you're outshining all of them, like you always do," Cody whispers. "Ignore her. You're going to rock someone's *world*, you gorgeous thing. You just wait, you'll find your person. And once you do, you'll be glad you waited."

I wonder if I'll ever find my person.

Sometimes I wish Ash was my person. But there are gray areas with Ash that make me wonder if Ash could ever be my person. Mainly: I don't think *Ash* thinks he's my person. The way I see it, your person should *want* to be your person.

I sigh without meaning to.

"Better," Lana says approvingly, walking over to another rack of dresses.

Lana is good at her job and most of the outfits she picks out for me are custom made and to-die-for. She has a knack for putting pieces together in a way that's original and cutting edge. The looks she creates for me and my sisters get noticed. Which, according to Lana, is a key part of putting our brands on the map.

I don't bother mentioning it also puts *her* brand very much on the map and is the reason she's now the most sought-after stylist in the world.

My sisters and I get a lot of attention. Our social media

platforms are like mini-corporations. Everything we wear gets scrutinized and copied. Every post has a business plan behind it.

Gabrielle, who's in charge of my Instagram team, comes over and holds one of my phones up to me. It's the one we use exclusively for Instagram. Her green eyes are bright with excitement. She glances over to where Perri is momentarily distracted and out of earshot.

"Check out your follower numbers," Gabrielle whispers. The screen shows my Instagram page. 775,659,308. "You've passed Perri! You're number one in the world, Vivi!"

"Wow." That's exciting, I guess. I smile, reacting the way I'm expected to react. But Perri will be seething when she finds out.

"Vivi, this is amazing!" Gabrielle gushes. "We did it!"

It *is* amazing. *Isn't it?*

But … what does it all *mean?* Why don't I *feel* anything?

At all?

Ever?

I mean, I haven't *done* anything to deserve this kind of attention.

It probably sounds like I'm ungrateful.

I'm not ungrateful. I know how lucky I am and I try to share my luck. On my eighteenth birthday, I secretly set up a foundation that donates money to charities, medical research and scholarships. No one knows about it except my cousin Jericho, our family's senior accountant. He helped me set it up and promised it would be our secret.

Silas is more focused on growing our wealth than giving

it away. I didn't want him to know about it. I wanted it to be mine.

It's the most rebellious thing I've ever done and the one thing I'm most proud of. I did it because the shallower side of this life sometimes gets to me. The staging, the likes, the followers—it always feels just a little bit empty.

I fully realize that most people would kill for the kind of attention I get, so I try to appreciate it. My sisters love it. My brothers revel in it. As for me, none of it ever feels like a perfect fit. Like I'm wearing a diamond-studded straitjacket that's just a little too heavy and a lot too tight.

I know what Ash would say. *Poor little rich girl. It's so hard. Poor Vivi.*

It's not hard. Nothing's hard. Nothing's easy and nothing's hard. I glide through my existence with a dull ache in my heart, like now, with swarms of people fussing over me, making sure my hair and makeup are photo-worthy, dressing me and undressing me like I'm a puppet on a string.

I've spent my life following orders. But I can feel it: somewhere inside me, something is shifting.

Maybe it's the full moon.

*Right. What are you, a werewolf now?*

It's why this date was chosen for the party we're going to. To see if two of us can make a love match.

"Put this on." Lana is holding the dress she's chosen for me to wear tonight.

We're taking our jet to Kauai in a few hours, to stay with the Ramsey family for the weekend. They're having a two-day party for the three families that are part of our so-called "alliance." It's an old, weird tradition I've never paid much attention to.

There's an archaic rule that's attached to it. We're all big, extended families, but once each generation, the three families are supposed to link through marriage. According to the rule, one of us Fitzpatricks has to marry a King and one of us has to marry a Ramsey.

Some generations follow the rule and some don't. People rebel against it, not surprisingly. Some people think bad things happen to those who refuse to obey its laws.

The way I see it, bad things happen anyway. All the time. To everyone. I don't really buy into all the mysticism that surrounds the rule.

But Silas and Malachi do. And so does Perri. She wants to be the one to marry a Ramsey. She's got her heart set on it and she's been badgering Silas to arrange it for months. My sister is totally obsessed with Knox, even though she's only met him a few times.

"God, I can't wait." Perri's standing close to me now, checking her look in the mirror. "I might even be married by the end of the weekend, Vivi."

"It's so exciting," I say, trying hard to infuse my tone with something resembling enthusiasm.

I can't remember ever meeting Knox Ramsey. There aren't many photos of him online. Only one or two, which Perri has saved onto her phone. One of them is her screensaver and every time I see it I wonder if that's a good idea.

It almost feels like she's jinxing it, getting ahead of herself. But I don't say anything. I just hope it works out for her.

Echo is the youngest Ramsey and she's a year older than me. Occasionally we see each other at parties. Whenever I see her, she's fun and nice. Blaise is too. She's a few years older than Echo. She's stunning and she comes across as wise beyond her years and sort of no-nonsense. Both of them have a sense of realness I always find compelling. They're the kind of people you wish you could spend more time with.

I don't know the Ramsey brothers at all. They all seem insanely intimidating. They train in martial arts or something and they're very outdoorsy. Probably because they have a sprawling hundred square acre ranch in Kauai, which is where we're going tonight. I've never been there, but Silas has and he said it lives up to its name. They call it Paradise.

Remington is the oldest Ramsey sibling. He's gruff and serious and built like a fighter, according to Silas. Silas meets with him occasionally because the alliance families co-own a bunch of companies and have for generations.

I don't know much about Knox or the other brother, whose name is Wolf. They're not on social media and they're not part of the see-and-be-seen crowd. They mainly keep to themselves.

Rumors are that they're rough and huge and sort of wild. They carry weapons and spend most of their time swimming, hunting, surfing and living off the land.

"How do I look?" Perri asks me. I can tell she's nervous about tonight. "Do you like this dress, Vivi?"

"You look sexy." Almost *too* sexy, but then again, what do I know? Maybe that's the key to getting your halo dirty.

She's checking her phone again. I hope she hasn't noticed my Instagram numbers.

"Any reply?" I ask her.

I know she's been texting and leaving messages for Knox for the past few weeks. So far, she hasn't heard back from him. "He might be out of range," she says. "Apparently there are areas on their ranch that don't get cell phone coverage. Echo said he spends a lot of time at his beach house, which is remote."

"You'll see him tonight, though."

She's eager, but there's an edge to it. "What if …"

Perri hesitates but I know what she's thinking. What if he doesn't want to marry her? What happens then? "I'm sure he does, Perri. Didn't Remington tell Silas it's a done deal and that Knox agreed to it?"

"He hasn't actually confirmed it but Silas said he's thinking about it."

"I'm sure all the arrangements will be made this weekend. Relax."

Perri smiles at me but Lana's tapping her foot, waiting for me to try on the dress she's still holding.

I stand, and Cody takes off my robe. All I'm wearing is a tiny white thong but I'm so used to being dressed and undressed I barely notice.

"We're juxtaposing the sultry siren lips and the smoky

eyes with a more demure outfit," Lana tells me. "Tonight, you're a timid waif who's on the cusp of an awakening. A fallen angel who's about to be sullied."

*What the hell?*

I stare at myself in the wall of mirrors. I look like I've time-warped to an 90s music video, and not in a good way. "No."

Lana glares at me, half-shocked and half-dismissive. "What do you mean *no*?"

"I can't wear this. It's all wrong."

"Wrong? How can it possibly be *wrong*?"

The dress is white and flowing. It looks oversized and childish, with lacy embellishments. "It's bad enough that I *am* a shy virgin and everyone knows it—thank you for pointing out the obvious, Lana. But the last thing I want to do is to *look* like one. I'm not wearing this."

They're all speechless for a few seconds. It's not like me to have outbursts or make demands. Lana sputters. "But it's perfe—"

"Give me something darker. Edgier. Something … fierce-looking." It sounds weird and I wish I could take it back as soon as it's out there.

"Fierce-looking?" Lana regains her composure.

I walk over to one of the many racks of garments that fill the room.

"Vivi." Perri watches me, like she's concerned about my behavior. "You should wear the one you have on. It looks so pretty on you."

"I've had enough of pretty."

I pull out something that catches my eye. It's a green sequined tight-fitting mini-dress with a plunging neckline. "This."

Lana stares at the outfit. Then she gives a light shrug, like she half-approves of my choice. "It's Valentino. It just arrived yesterday."

I take off the white dress and toss it over a chair. Then I put on the sequined outfit and Cody zips it. It fits me perfectly, if maybe a little on the tight side. It makes my boobs look full and bouncy. My eyes are a deep shade of amber—the exact same shade as my mother's were. The jewel-bright jade of the sequins makes my irises look almost golden. I slide my feet into a pair of gold high-heeled sandals with gem-stone detailing, checking myself out in the mirror. "This is it."

She wants me to dirty my halo? In this outfit, I might just be able to do that.

It won't happen this weekend, since Perri and Knox will end up getting engaged and so will one of my brothers.

But at least I don't *look* as insecure as I feel.

In this dress, I can feed those tiny sparks of fire that are taking hold inside me.

Timid, obedient virgin on the cusp of a fiery awakening?

Bring it on.

TWENTY MINUTES LATER, I've changed out of my heels and pulled on my old high tops that I have to hide at the back of my closet so they don't get thrown out. I'm wearing a long coat over my dress, tied at the front. I silently make my way down the back staircase, sneaking through one of the service doors, past the kitchens, which are quieter than usual, since we won't be here for meals this weekend.

My coat and my sunglasses do their job. No one expects me to be here, so I manage to escape through the back door without being noticed. My entourage—and my hawk-eyed sister—won't miss me for another hour. The limos won't arrive until five to take us to the airport.

I told them I was going to go read for a while and they didn't even blink. I *do* read sometimes, unlike my siblings. The only things they read are spreadsheets and social media feeds.

I get to the palm grove and take a right. I walk past the fountains and through the archways, to the pool area. My great great great grandfather sailed to Hawaii a hundred years ago, straight from the California gold rush. He bought as much real estate as he could get his hands on. And then he started building on it. My family now owns many of the most exclusive, high-end resorts in Waikiki. Our house is the nicest of all of them—not exactly a resort since it's a private residence, but it looks like one.

I check behind me to make sure no one's following me.

My heart is pounding because I shouldn't be doing this. If Jett catches me, he'll … react badly.

I don't care about him.

*Yes you do. Your heart is beating like a hummingbird's wing.*

I know my disobedience is risky as hell but I'm tired of being policed by my bully of a cousin.

I try to ignore my own fear at the thought of being caught by him.

I shouldn't have to be scared of my own security guards. And I shouldn't need to sneak around my own property. Things have gotten way out of hand. It's happened sort of incrementally over time. I'm now at the point where I can't do anything without worrying about his reaction to it.

And his reactions are getting worse.

Jett's vigilance has become beyond oppressive. I don't *want* him to know about everything I do. It's none of his damn business. My cousin reacts to things in a way that doesn't always fit the situation. He has a temper and he does things that seem a little … off. Which, deep down, sort of terrifies me. I do everything I can to avoid him.

I get to the narrow staircase that leads up behind the main pool house.

This is where some of the staff accommodation is, small apartments that share a roof garden.

Checking again to make sure no one is following me, I climb up to the rooftop lanai. I see him there, laying on a wide lounger in his swim shorts, reading a book under the shade of an umbrella.

Ash.

The one person on planet Earth who *gets* me.

Over the past eight months, Ash has become the closest friend I've ever had. Which is sort of pathetic when you think about it. My siblings are my family and I love them, but if we weren't related we probably wouldn't be friends. I'm too different from the rest of them. We're more bonded by blood, circumstance and a shared history than we are by things we have in common. And the friends I had at school were always held at arm's length from my life because I'm so carefully guarded.

I've started visiting Ash every few days. Sometimes every day. It's a miracle I haven't been found out yet. They would never expect me to be sneaking around like this so it hasn't occurred to them yet to have me followed 24/7.

Ash works for my family. He's a pool boy or he helps with catering when we have parties or he works with the groundskeepers. I met him the first week he started working at Seven Mile Beach. I was doing a photoshoot by the pool one day for a swimsuit brand and he was folding towels. He handed me one and we started talking. We struck up an unlikely but sort of immediate friendship. He was easy to talk to. I started going to the pool all the time just hoping I'd run into him. One day when he didn't turn up, I went looking for him.

He was up here, where he spends most of his time when he's not working or studying. Ash is taking classes at the university part-time to complete his degree with a dual major in accounting and computer science. He said he's always been good with numbers and doesn't want to be a pool boy for the rest of his life, so he takes the bus out to the campus three times a week. He's humble about it but he's one of the smartest people I've ever met. Once Ash told me he'd hacked into a government website when he was four-teen, just to see if he could do it. He did do it, and so effectively he almost got arrested.

He looks up and smiles. "Hey, glamour girl. I thought you were going to Kauai today."

"Not until five. I told you I'd come see you."

Ash moves over on the lounger to make room for me. I sit next to him and my coat has fallen open enough for him to notice the glittery green sequins on my dress. He opens my coat further and he takes in my hair and makeup. "Holy shit, girlfriend. Check out the sexy supermodel."

"Yeah, it's a little over the top."

"You look, like, *insanely* hot in this."

Which makes me laugh a little. "Yeah, right."

"I'm serious. This is such a different look for you."

"The outfit they wanted me to wear made me look like I was twelve. I wasn't feeling it."

He seems almost stunned by the change in me. "Well, honey, you don't look twelve now. The way it fits you is borderline X-rated, girl. I like it. And your hair looks amazing." Ash gently runs his fingers along the tiny braids of my hair and the jewels that have been woven in. As I lay back in the shade, he says, "Be careful you don't mess it up."

"I can't mess it up. It's been sprayed into place with an entire can of hairspray."

Ash props himself up onto his bent elbow to gaze at me. Ash has light brown eyes and dark brown hair. He has a lanky body that, if he ate more, would probably be sort of beautiful. As it is, he's too skinny.

He's not much taller than I am and it's one of the things I like about Ash. He's not physically intimidating. We're practically the same size. My brothers and cousins and all their friends are big, imposing men. I like that Ash isn't.

"You look so gorgeous, Vivi."

"Thanks." Ash is one of the nicest people I've ever met. He's always complimenting me, but not in an over the top kind of way. He's just genuinely kind-hearted.

"So, tonight's the long-awaited matchmaking party?"

"Yeah." I tell Ash everything. Because he never judges me or complicates things. Everything about his personality is unthreatening. It's such a nice change from being told what to do all the time and being constantly critiqued for every flaw in my character, like how I'm too shy, too timid or too whatever. There's always a long list.

Ash just takes me as I am. He never pushes me to try to be something I'm not. "God, I *so* wish I could tag along and see how it all plays out tonight."

"I wish you could too, Ash. I would love it if you could come."

"Do you think Knox Ramsey will propose to Perri?" His eyes are bright. People are always interested in the alliance because it's so outrageous.

"I hope so. She'll be totally devastated if he doesn't."

"Is there any chance someone might propose to … you? Instead of Perri?" Like he's almost worried about it.

Our eyes meet. I've wondered what it might be like to be with Ash—not that my brothers would ever allow it, which makes me wonder if I'd be brave enough to defy them. Ash and I are similar people. A life with Ash would be calm and safe. I crave his company because I don't know anyone else who makes me feel so understood and so unthreatened.

If you ask me, safety is underrated. That feeling of just being able to say whatever you want to say, whenever you want to say it and not have to worry that someone will react badly to it, as though you've done something unforgivable, just for being yourself.

Maybe he wonders about it too.

"Not really," I tell him. "Knox will propose to Perri and Malachi will propose to Aurora King and that will be that. Malachi told me that he and Aurora have already slept together. So I guess it makes sense for them to be the ones to secure our family tie with the Kings."

"Really?"

"I mean, they were never exclusive or anything. He told me he doesn't know if he could ever love her but he'll choose her if he's forced to. Which was always in the cards."

"Wow. This whole arranged marriage thing is so crazy."

"Tell me about it. Besides, no one would want to propose to me. They all think I'm weird and awkward."

"That can't be true."

"It is true."

"You're by far the most beautiful of all of them, Vivi. You're famous for it, girl. Trust me." This is what Ash does. He makes me feel like I'm not a freak. "You wouldn't have, like, a gazillion followers if people weren't fascinated."

"That's different. They don't *know* me. They're following an image of me that's been created by my stylists."

"They're also following you because you're beautiful and mysterious," Ash insists. "You're an enigma. People love enigmas."

"If you say so." I lay back and look up at the blue sky. The sun is lower now. "Anyway, that's Instagram. It's staged. An entire team puts those photoshoots together. They create a personality for me that's fun and glamorous. But in any *real* situation, all I'm famous for is being socially awkward and painfully shy. You're the only one I can talk to besides my sisters who doesn't make me stutter like a fool and embarrass myself. I think you might be my soulmate." I mean that last part as a joke, but something about the statement doesn't quite come out that way.

Ash is watching me. He often looks at me the way he's looking at me now. Sort of tenderly. But he's never made a move on me.

I almost wish he would. "Ash?"

"Yeah?"

"Do you have a girlfriend?"

His expression is layered. "No."

"Do you ..." I mean, it's not out of the realm of possibility and I feel like we're close enough for me to ask it: "... have a boyfriend? Sorry, that's personal. You don't have to tell me."

"If you're asking me to define myself ... I can't. I don't. I've had boyfriends and I've had girlfriends. I am who I am and I don't really fit into any category. I go with the flow of however I'm feeling, depending on who I'm with. I guess

I'm sort of ... bi-possible. I don't like to limit my opportunities."

"That's cool." It is cool. Ash is the most free-spirited, open-minded and non-judgmental person I've ever met. It doesn't surprise me that he doesn't limit himself in a conventional way. "How are you feeling right now?"

He laughs. "You mean right this very second?"

"Yes."

"I'm feeling like you're way out of my league, sweetheart. I'm feeling like your brothers and that hulking bodyguard cousin of yours would literally kill me if they ever found out you visit me."

"Jett isn't really my cousin."

"He isn't?"

"No. He and Jericho were adopted by my aunt and uncle, my father's brother, when Jett was eight years old and Jericho was ten."

"So they're not related to you at all?"

"No. They're the sons of my aunt's cousin. She and her husband died in a car crash. So the two boys were orphans. Since my aunt and uncle couldn't have kids of their own, they adopted them. So they're not really Fitzpatricks but they took the name when they came to live at Seven Mile Beach when I was still a baby."

"Well, he'd still kill me if he found out."

"Anyway, let's not talk about him. I'd rather talk about you, Ash. Let's talk about all our dreams coming true."

"I have a feeling yours are going to come true, Vivi. I think you're going to meet your true love

24

someday soon. He's going to treat you like the queen you are and you're going to be glad you waited for him."

Like it often happens, I feel my eyes sting. "How do you always know the exact right thing to say?"

"Maybe because we're tuned into the same freaky frequency," he jokes.

But he's right. Maybe because we both feel like outcasts, we can relate to that part of each other so well. "Do you want to hear something really embarrassing?"

He smiles. "Of course."

"I'm twenty years old and I've never been kissed. Not even once." Not that this isn't public knowledge. My virginity is a detail about me people seem to love discussing. I really don't understand why.

Maybe Ash is humoring me. One of his eyebrows lifts. "Really?"

"Really. I'm on a tight leash, you might have noticed. Visiting you is the most rebellious thing I've ever done."

"So the rumors are true," he muses.

"What rumors?"

"Vivi Fitzpatrick is saving herself."

I groan. "God. How embarrassing. It's bad enough my stylist and my entire team knows I'm completely inexperienced. It's even worse that the entire *world* knows it."

"There's nothing wrong with saving yourself for true love, Vivi. So what if people speculate? It's because you're famous and beautiful and they wish they were you. Who cares, anyway? There's nothing wrong with waiting until you meet someone you actually *want* to be with. That's a good thing."

"I don't know if I am waiting. I didn't *mean* to wait. It just sort of happened that way. Because I don't control my own life."

"Maybe you need to do something about that," he suggests gently.

"I do. I absolutely do. I'm just not sure how." I sigh. "There is one thing I've done though, that no one knows about."

"What thing?"

"I started a charity. The only thing I've ever done that feels like mine. My cousin manages it but I swore him to secrecy because I didn't want Silas to know about it. I'd like to take it over."

"Wow. That's amazing."

"Yeah. Once this whole alliance thing isn't hanging over our heads, I'd like to take it to the next level." Something occurs to me then. "You could help me, Ash. If you wanted to. I mean, you're an accountant, right? Jericho has his hands full enough. He'd probably be glad to hand it over."

Ash's face literally lights up. "Are you kidding me? Of course I would want to help you. But I'm not an accountant yet."

"Close enough. You're almost finished, right?"

"Another month and I will be."

I take my phone out of the pocket of my jacket. "I'm going to send you the link. Some of the information is on there. You can take a look. Then you can decide if it's something you might be interested in doing at some point."

Ash seems touched by this. "Thank you so much, Vivi."

"You're going to be a big shot one day, Ash. I can tell. I want to poach you before someone else beats me to it."

He smiles. "I'll take a look at it this weekend. While you're living it up. Who knows, maybe you'll meet someone at the party."

"Highly unlikely."

"One day you'll find true love you'll be glad you held out for something real."

"I don't even know if I believe in true love."

He pins me with a disbelieving look, like I've offended him. "Of course you do. Everyone does."

"I've never actually seen it in action."

"Didn't your parents love each other?"

"I don't know. I never knew my mother. She died young. I know my father loved her madly but I'll never know if she felt the same way. From the way she's been described, it sounds like she was more like me than like the rest of my family. I like to think so anyway."

"How?"

"She had a library built and she stocked it with all her favorite books, old vinyl records and the kind of art that was too outrageous to go in the main houses. And there's a bedroom at the top. A romantic little room with a view of the ocean. It's sunny and private. It's my favorite place on the whole estate."

"That's so cool."

"No one ever uses it except me." My brothers and sisters aren't interested in being alone. They're only happy when they're surrounded by fawning fans. They get off on being seen. They make sure their entourages of photographers are swarming around them at all times. If they don't feel like they're getting enough attention, they'll pay people to give them more. Or they'll make a scene that puts them back in the headlines. "It's too quiet for the rest of my family. They prefer the limelight."

"You live in the limelight too," Ash points out.

"Would you believe it if I told you that wasn't by choice? I'm an introvert to my bones. Which no one in my family gets. They don't understand why I sometimes crave solitude. But I think my mother must have too."

Ash asks it carefully. "How did she die?"

"Having me."

Ash weaves his fingers through mine and holds my hand. "I'm sorry, honey."

I confess something I've never really talked about to anyone. "It sucks that I never got to know her, but it's even worse that it was *me* who killed her. She died three days after I was born, from complications."

"Shit."

"My father resented me my whole life because of it."

"I'm sure that's not true."

"He never said those exact words but I could always feel that. I stole her from him. My sisters have always told me it's not my fault and there's no way anyone could blame me for it, but the reality is: if it wasn't for me, my mother would still be alive." It's weird that I'm admitting all this to Ash. Because he's waiting for it but in a way that's completely undemanding. He'll take whatever I give and he won't push me.

So I keep going.

"I look exactly like her, which also doesn't help. Like, eerily so. And then when my father was cared for by his team of dementia nurses who did their best to keep him safe from himself, I couldn't even visit him. The sight of me sent him over some deep end of sorrow and rage. At my mother, for leaving him. And at me, because he thought I was her."

Ash is taking it all in and I can feel the empathy in him. "I bet she would have loved you the most."

I have to hold back my tears.

"Hey. Don't you dare cry," he scolds me gently. "You'll smudge your makeup. Come on, it's okay. None of it is your fault."

I take a deep breath and it helps. I guess he's right. "Anyway, the whole thing is heavy and tragic. I try not to think about it too much." It feels good to have confessed some of this. My family never, ever talks about it. Not to me, at least. Maybe because the topic can't be discussed without everyone being reminded of the final detail: it was me who killed her. "Thanks for listening to me gush."

"Anytime, sweetheart."

"What about your family, Ash? Where are they?"

It's a few seconds before he answers. "They're in Kansas."

"Kansas? Wow. I thought you were from Honolulu."

"Nope. Not even close."

"I've never been to Kansas. What's it like?"

"Flat. Amber waves of grain and all that. My family lives in a small town. I have two older brothers who were football stars in high school."

"Are you close to them?"

"I haven't talked to my family in three years. Since they kicked me out."

I squeeze his hand, which is still holding mine. "Ash, I'm sorry."

"I'm over it," he says, but I can tell it's stirring up some deeper layers of emotion than he usually shows me.

"Anyone who kicks *you* out of anywhere is an idiot. You're the nicest person I know."

His smile doesn't quite reach his eyes. "My father beat me up, threw my stuff out onto the front step and slammed the door in my face."

"Ash ... why?" But I can guess.

"That was when I was starting to discover myself and my ... range. They found out and it wasn't something they were ever going to accept. So they told me to leave and never come back. I hitchhiked to California, got a job waiting tables and saved enough money to fly to Honolulu. I always knew I wanted to come to Hawaii."

"I'm very glad you did. And I'm sorry your family didn't understand you. They're missing out on the best person I've ever met."

He smiles sort of sadly. "I'm sorry your family doesn't

always understand you either, Vivi. But at least they still love you."

"I guess so." We're quiet for a minute or two. Ash's thumb absent-mindedly strokes mine.

I lean closer to him and he watches my eyes as I do this.

Very, very gently, I touch my lips to Ash's.

He doesn't move at all. His lips are soft and warm.

It's so tender. So sweet. It feels … nice.

Neither of us takes it any further than this feather-light touch, and I pull back. "Ash?"

"Yeah?"

"I wish I could stay here with you tonight," I whisper.

"You've got the hottest ticket in town, girlfriend. Go enjoy the party. Have as much fun as that dress promises. I'm not going anywhere. I'll be right here when you get back."

We lay like that for a minute or two, just soaking in the calm before the storm, maybe. At least I am.

"What time do you need to go?" he asks me.

"What time is it now?"

He reaches for his phone and shows me the screen. 4:36.

"Shit. I better go." I sit up.

"Listen, have fun, okay?" He pulls the front of my coat together, tying the belt. "Don't be a freaky introvert. I'm ordering you to enjoy yourself. For me."

I smile, trying to summon some—any—excitement. "I'll try."

"Call me if you want to talk. Any time of day or night."

"Thanks, Ash. Have a good weekend."

So I leave him and make my way back through the archways and into the topiaries of the garden. I'm shocked to my bones when someone steps out from behind one of them.

*Oh no.*

*It's Jett.* Jett is in charge of our security team. He's big and burly and I've been terrified of him my whole life. It gets worse the older I get. He watches me … in a way that someone shouldn't be watching their own cousin. He's built like an ox, stocky and strong, with dark hair and darker eyes. It has always bothered me that he and Silas are so close and that Jett has such a strong influence over my brother. He uses his size and his relationship to Silas to get away with things he shouldn't be doing. Like he is right now.

"What are you doing out here?" Jett grabs my arm, painfully. "You said you were going to your room."

"*Ow.* It's none of your business where I go! Let *go* of me." I try to yank my arm from his grasp but his grip tightens.

"Silas is looking for you."

"You're *hurting* me, you oaf. Let *go*." I manage to pull away from him, rubbing my arm where he gripped it. He'll have left bruises. Again.

Jett does this. He loves showing off his power over me. He always takes it too far when no one else is around. "Silas wouldn't want you m-manhandling me!" I hate that I can hear the panic in my own voice. And that he can terrify me so easily.

"Silas is the one who asked me to keep an eye on you."

"He didn't ask you to *hurt* me. I'm allowed to go for a walk around my own house!" *Asshole!* I want to scream it at him but I'm afraid of what he might do. He's so much bigger than me. And his motives are unpredictable. Some days he's watchful, other days he's hot-headed. There's no rhyme or reason to his reactions.

*Why would he even care this much about where I go or what I do?*

Jett steps forward and I take a step back. But I'm cornered. My back is pressed up against a wall. Jett places his hand around the front of my neck, squeezing with measured pressure.

*Would he kill me if he thought he could get away with it? Or worse? How far will he go?* "Jett. *Please.*"

"The pool boy, huh." His gaze bores into mine as his hand grips just a little tighter.

I don't want him to see me cry. "I need to get back now," I gasp. "Please let me go."

"Silas would be interested to hear that you've been sneaking around with the help."

"He's not the help. He's just a friend."

"I think we both know Silas wouldn't see it that way. Are you fucking him?"

"What? *No.*"

"I saw you kiss him."

His grip tightens even more and he leans his huge, heavy body up against mine. Something hard presses against my hipbone. *Oh my God. Is he …?*

"You were asking for it, weren't you, Vivi? Begging like a whore."

"*N-no.*" I loathe him with every fiber of my being. I wish he would disappear. I want to kick him and swear at him. But if I do that, he'll only make this so much worse for me. "I need to go back to my room. Nothing happened. *Please.*"

Tears of fear and frustration prick my eyes. How is he so easily able to reduce me to something I don't ever, ever want to be? With Jett, I always feel completely powerless. He steels the air from my lungs, the joy from my life and all the strength from my body, like he's a big black vortex of oppression.

"If you're ready to cash in your V-card, at least get a real man to do it."

"W-what?" I hope to hell he doesn't mean what it sounds like it means. An awful, bizarre threat.

"If you *are* a virgin, that is. I have my doubts." He's a fucking monster and I'm only now realizing the extent of it. "Can you prove it, Vivi?"

I stare into his black eyes and I see there my worst nightmares. I need to get away from him. "Let me go or I'll tell Silas."

"Silas wants you kept in line."

"Not like this." My voice sounds cold and flat. "Now take your filthy hands off me."

He finally relents, probably because I'm late now. He releases me and I rush away from him.

"I'll be watching you, Vivi," he calls after me. "Now hurry the fuck up. The others are waiting for you."

I'm a prisoner in my own home. I run through the side door and up the back staircase. I get to my room and take off my coat and sneakers, changing back into my heels. Looking in the mirror, I notice my makeup is smudged from my tears. I do my best to wipe away the evidence.

I feel sick. I need to talk to Silas. He'd never stand for what Jett just did—and might have just threatened me with. *Would he?* Silas and Jett have been best friends their whole lives. Would Silas listen to me? Over Jett?

And now I'm scared Silas will have me watched even more closely. Jett will either tell him about Ash, or he'll use the secret to try to blackmail me. Either way, I'm trapped.

I'm deeply shaken by the whole thing and I fight back more tears as I grab my phone from where I left it on my dresser. There's a barrage of messages from Perri, Lana and Silas, who are all waiting for me at the main entrance, where the limos are parked.

I don't want to go. I don't know why I even need to go. The others can secure the damn alliance. It has nothing to do with me.

But they'll never allow me to stay behind.

I make my way down the main staircase to the foyer. The front door is wide open and there are a dozen or more people on the front steps, loading suitcases into the limos and other vehicles. I'm led down to one of the waiting cars.

The door is opened for me and I slide in next to Perri. Silas is popping a bottle of champagne. Jett climbs in next to him from the other side of the car and I feel the weight of his presence close around me like prison walls. I try to pretend he didn't just insinuate the most disgusting, horrific scenario I could ever imagine.

At least he can't manhandle me here and now. I don't care if he tells Silas about Ash. It's not like I was doing anything wrong. It's up to *me* to decide who I spend my time with, not them.

I could tell Silas now, that Jett grabbed me. And *bruised* me. But I honestly don't know if Silas would react in a way that would help me. And if he *doesn't* react in a way that will help me, it'll only give Jett more power.

I'll wait until I'm alone with Silas, then I'll talk to him.

"Must have been a good book," Silas comments, but there's a note of impatience. He's irritated I've kept them waiting.

Silas notices my dress. It's a very different look for me.

Jett is also staring at me.

I'm wishing I'd kept my coat on. In fact, why did I insist on wearing something so damn revealing? Maybe Lana was right. At least I wouldn't feel as ... *exposed* as I suddenly am.

"W-where are the others?" I ask Silas, just to distract them. *Damn it.* I hate it when I stumble over my words. It happens whenever I feel stressed and self-conscious.

"Malachi and Tatum are already on the jet, waiting for us," Silas says, taking a long sip of his champagne.

Silas and I aren't particularly close. He's nine years older than me and he's always been more like a guardian than a brother. His eyes are hazel, like our father's were, and have a coldness behind them, also like my father. Silas's hair is dark brown. He's tall and stoically handsome—the oldest, prodigal son—and extremely comfortable in his own skin. He's never been in a long-term relationship because so many women want to be with him—for his power, his looks and most of all, for his money. Like Malachi, he has harems of women that surround him at all times.

But not now.

This weekend is all about the alliance matches.

According to the alliance rule, all three marriages have to take place before the oldest child of the three families turns thirty. The deadline is only four months away, which is why we're going to Kauai this weekend. We've been putting it off. Time is running out.

Silas should be the one to make one of the matches, but since Malachi has an on-again-off-again thing with Aurora and Perri has her heart set on Knox, he might be able to dodge a bullet. He's been banking on it.

I watch Silas pour the champagne into the flutes. Jett hands one to Perri.

"What about Vivi?" Perri asks him.

"She's not legal," Jett sneers, and I can feel myself withdrawing. The easiness I felt when I was with Ash is completely gone now.

"Let her have some," Silas tells him. "If there's a weekend to break a few rules, this is it."

Jett pours me a glass. Then he winks at me. "She's definitely looking old enough tonight."

*You sick fuck.* I take the glass from him, dropping my gaze before he does.

The champagne helps me calm down a little and it's not long before we're at the airport.

We board the jet and Malachi and Tatum are already

partying. Lana, Cody and the rest of our team are here, traveling with us.

"You're smudged," Cody exclaims, noticing my makeup. "Come sit over here and I'll fix you."

*If only it was that easy.*

"Oh my God, look at my baby sister!" gushes Tatum, giving me a long once-over. Then she hugs me. "When did you get so *gorgeous*?" I haven't seen her for a few months and she's as bubbly and excitable as always. "And when did your boobs get so freaking big?"

*Great.*

It's going to be a long weekend.

I can't wait until this whole "alliance" thing is done and settled and I can get on with my life. Then I might leave Seven Mile Beach for a while. Maybe I'll take some time out, to get away from the circus of scrutiny and over-protectiveness. *And my very creepy cousin.*

Maybe I'll travel. Take over the management of my charity and do something useful with my life.

Yes, that's what I'll do. I'll go to New York. Or Italy. Maybe Ash could come with me and we can see where things lead. Without strings or heavy commitments. We'll just go with the flow of however we're feeling, the way Ash likes to. We'll keep it easy, and light. Even if it's not true love at least it'll be ... calm. And safe. I won't have to worry that things will move too fast or scare me.

In three days, I'll have a whole new freedom. When I think about it now, the alliance has weighed heavily on all of us, like a black cloud that's always been there, obscuring the sun. It'll be nice to be rid of it.

I've spent half of my life scared, I'm realizing. Trapped and afraid. I'm tired of it. And I feel stronger knowing I'll soon be able to step out of the shadow of my family's control. Once the alliance marriages have been sealed, they'll have no reason to keep me so guarded.

We're told to take our seats and fasten our seatbelts.

I clink my glass against Tatum's and she grins at me. I don't tell her why I'm celebrating.

"It's so good to see you, honey," she says. "I hope we don't get any curveballs this weekend."

And then we're in the air and on our way to Kauai.

# 2

# WOLF

THE FIRST TIME I saw the girl who looked like an angel, I knew we were in deep trouble.

I knew *I* was in deep trouble, more specifically.

It was just so unbelievable, that she could just show up out of the goddamn blue like that, her bandaged arm bleeding, her long, white-blond hair windblown and wild. The clothes she wore were dirty and ragged. We were all in shock, because she was such an absolute dead ringer. She literally looked like she'd stepped straight out of the old superstition my family has been obsessed with for four generations.

To an outsider, the legend sounds like a mythical story that belongs in some fucked-up fantasy. To us, it's more complicated than that—and a lot closer to home. We take it seriously because we've seen first-hand the power it has to destroy us.

When your parents die in a fiery plane crash when you're two years old and then your brother loses his beautiful wife and his tiny newborn baby before she could even take her first breath, the legend becomes a lot fucking heavier than a superstition you can laugh off as a childish myth.

Hawaiians tend to learn about the legend when we're young. For us Ramseys, it wasn't just a legend but a lesson to be taken as gospel. According to folklore, our great great great grandfather, along with two of his friends, were visited by a vision, who gave them a warning. Align their families by marriage or be cursed.

Most often she gets called the angel. Or the traveler. Some people call her the goddess.

The day this girl turned up on our doorstep only a couple of weeks ago, we could all agree she fit all three of those descriptions.

That shit was instilled into us at a young age: if she shows up where and when you least expect her, you don't mess with the angel. You give her whatever the fuck she wants.

Turns out she wants Knox.

I can hardly blame her for that. Even I can see that the two of them are some kind of cosmic match, like destiny is shining its sunlit rays directly down onto them.

I know for a fact she's *his* wildest dream.

She's also my worst nightmare.

It isn't her existence that worries me. It's the fact that my brother is already obsessed with her.

Her name is Cassidy. Just Cassidy. She didn't even give a last name.

She isn't *the* angel, of course she isn't. She's just a lost, random waif who happens to eerily fit the description. She also happens to have my brother by the goddamn balls. Because of this, she's planted a big fucking problem right in the middle of my immediate future.

Our family is linked to two other entrenched Hawaiian families in this alliance that goes back a hundred years. Which means that two of us—of me and my four siblings, since we're the direct line—will have our marriages arranged.

It's fucked up and archaic. A curse that belongs in the history books instead of here and now.

For all its twisted downsides, the alliance does have one obvious advantage. The strength of our alliance protects us from the mob that formed from the remnants of a fourth family, the Archers. Over the past hundred years, they've mobilized into a crime ring that targets the rest of us. They call themselves Arrow. Their ring leader's name is Axel Archer and he's a soulless thug with no limits. We outnumber them, we're heavily armed, well-trained and fortified as fuck. But we're always aware of Arrow's die-hard thirst for revenge.

Arrow recruits were behind the attempted kidnapping of Cassidy last week. We were forced to get rid of a few of them. We buried them at sea.

This ongoing feud is the reason the alliance was formed in the first place.

There's always been a lot of backlash against the arranged marriages. Of course there has. But every single time someone defies the curse, bad shit happens. Breaking it guarantees sickness, death and total carnage. The kind of loss that cuts in the deepest possible ways.

Remy's a perfect example of that.

It's a crazy legacy with a major dark side. If you don't happen to be involved in it, the whole thing sounds ridiculous. It *is* ridiculous. Even so, here we are, trapped by it.

And right now it's pissing me off.

I'm deep in the rainforest, at the lowest point of the valley along the southeastern boundary of my family's land. I've been following the trail for a while and I know I'm getting close. He's a monster, if his footprints are any clue.

I arm my crossbow and take aim. The wire of the bow digs into my bare chest and rests against the leather of the weapons belt I wear strapped to my body at all times. I'm 6'4" and cut, mainly because I spend every waking hour training, fighting, working out and hunting. It's 85 degrees, even under the forest's canopy, where it's too sheltered for the sea breeze. I'm sweaty and dirty, and my mood is dark because I'm distracted by the decision I'm going to have to make, and soon.

Tonight, in fact.

Blaise has been planning the party for weeks. They're all coming here to Paradise, the town that was settled by my family four generations ago, by the same great great great grandfather who started the whole angel-vision fuckery.

In some ways we still live like the early pioneers. We own

almost a fifth of the island of Kauai and our ranch includes some of the richest farmland in the world. We have every resource we could ever want. Fish, game, pristine beaches, untouched tropical rainforests and craggy mountains full of rivers clean enough to drink. It doesn't mean we don't live in the modern world—we do. But at the same time, we make the most of what we have.

My phone vibrates silently in my back pocket.

*Shit.*

I pull it out, in case it's my family. The can of worms introduced by the little blond stranger's arrival has everyone agitated.

*Cheyenne,* the screen reads.

Not my family. A girl I met a few weeks ago at a party near Sunset. She'd never been tied up before. Turns out she liked it. She's been calling me non-stop ever since I left her.

I don't bother answering it.

There are fifteen other missed calls, all from women. A few others from Oahu's North Shore. Some from the Big Island. Honolulu. Three or four on Maui. These are from encounters that were months ago, or even years. I hardly remember some of them.

Every couple of weeks, I tend to roam. A different kind of hunt. I make it clear to them that I'm only in it for one night. But they always want seconds.

I don't know if I'd go so far as to call myself a player, just a voracious animal who needs what it needs.

And it's been too long. A month? More? Either way, I'm

starting to feel fucking pent-up, like a caged lion who's gone too long without a feed.

I don't need to justify it. I tell them what's what. I don't kiss them, I always make sure the beast is securely gloved up and I tell them I don't give more than one night.

They never refuse.

I leave them as soon as I'm done with them. I learned early on that if I give them more than that, they start getting attached. It happens that fast. Even after a few hours, they start talking about visiting me in Paradise. Which is partly because my beach house is a crash pad for a lot of my friends and extended family and it gets talked about. It's sort of famous. And so am I, or so I've been told.

If I give them any time at all beyond a few hours, they're already fixating on the future, begging me to stay longer, telling me they love me, asking me when they can see me again. Even though I've already told them they won't.

That always gets me. They "love" me, after knowing me for a total of four or five hours. I don't get it. I'm gruff, punishing and rude to them. I use them and they know this. But they always beg for more.

The truth is, I don't believe in love.

Maybe for other people. For my parents. For Remy. And now, maybe even for Knox. I just hope Knox has better luck with it than the rest of them did.

Love just isn't something I happen to be wired for, maybe because I've seen how it turns out for the people in my family.

My parents were in love and now they're dead. I was

only two at the time so I don't remember it happening. Certain details have stuck with me though, from other peoples' stories and memories. They were so in love they could finish each other's sentences. They were beautiful and glamorous, as these things go. They had five healthy children and the kind of storybook life people envied. And they had to be identified by the charred remains of their teeth.

Remy was in love. Absolutely besotted. His wife and baby were taken in the most brutal way imaginable. Some rare complication even modern medicine couldn't save them from. Not doctors flown in from California. Not expensive medical equipment and every attempted intervention they could think of. Not prayers or hopes or Remy offering himself to whatever force that might change the outcome—anything—if it would only save his family. Nothing worked. He lost them anyway.

After all that, I really don't want to fucking go there. I make a point of shielding myself from feeling anything at all, because who needs the doom love seems to always promise?

I wish things weren't the way they are. There are times when a part of me craves the kind of love story that's worth dying for. But the thought of it always leaves me cold.

Anyway, so far I've been spared and I'm glad. I've barely even *liked* any of the women I've been with, so I really can't imagine what falling in love would even feel like.

I'm with the women I meet for one reason and one reason only. Once it's over, I can't wait to get the hell away from them.

Cheyenne is insistent. Another text lights up the screen.

> Wolf Ramsey, please!!! Why aren't you answering me?? Come see me this weekend? You're the hottest thing everrrrr!!!!! Please, you beast!! I want to have your little alpha babies! OMG I can't believe how hot that was!!! I need more!!!!

Fucking hell.

Delete.

I get a lot of texts like this. I don't know how they all end up tracking down my number. I don't give it to them. One girl told me she got it off Stone King at a party when she asked him if he had it—something I plan on talking to him about at some point. With my fists.

I shove my phone back into my pocket.

I've lived here in Kauai my entire life aside from four hellish years of prep school in California, where the only useful thing I learned is that when women first meet me they're both fascinated and terrified. This reaction lasts for around ten seconds, at which point their fear devolves quickly into lust and from that point on they'll give me whatever I want whenever I want it. They can't help themselves. I'm big, I'm rough, I'm more than a little twisted and I'll do things to them that'll scare them and enlighten them in equal measure.

Common sense tells them to steer clear of me. Primal need overrides all that. Every single time.

As humans, we're a lot less evolved than we like to think

we are. Women can't resist me because they can sense I'll get them off in ways their carnal instincts crave like a goddamn drug.

The other reason I don't get involved has to do with the very same angel's legend that's hanging over my head. I can't commit until my family has fulfilled the two arranged marriages of the alliance. It's not up to me to do it but it holds all of us back anyway. It always has. No commitments until the marriages are in place: that's the rule.

The whole thing would be laughable if we weren't still grieving from all the tragedies that have struck us down.

Remy thought it was laughable too and look how that turned out.

Rounding a bend, I see my prey standing there, rooting in the dug-up dirt.

He's fucking huge. With long, lethal tusks. He senses me and tenses, sniffing the air.

Without hesitating, I arm my crossbow and take aim. My shot is practiced and precise. Before the boar can even react, the wide, razor-sharp arrowhead—which I designed myself, like many of my weapons—sinks deep into its neck, neatly severing its jugular. The boar stumbles heavily to the ground and lays still, blood pouring from its fatal wound in a dark flood.

I walk over to it and crouch next to the enormous animal. I grip the arrow and tug it from the boar's neck, wiping it on damp leaves before sliding it back into the leather quiver strapped across my chest.

I recite the low chant of gratitude we always offer to the hunting gods, or the universe, or whoever might be listening.

Dipping my fingers into the boar's warm blood, I draw two stripes across my cheekbones. My family happens to be superstitious. Like, insanely so. We're probably *too* spooked for our own good, but we have reason to be. And I never take a kill for granted. These are the rituals we've practiced for generations. It's more of a reflexive action at this point than something I have to think about.

Then, groaning with the effort, I hoist the fucker over and around my shoulders—which takes every ounce of strength I have. He's heavy as fuck.

I start lugging my score up the hill toward my motorcycle.

It'll be interesting to see how the scene plays out tonight.

Knox and Cassidy spent almost a week alone together at his beach shack. As soon as they got back, our walls were breached and Cassidy was almost taken. Turns out we're not the only ones intrigued by the angel.

Since then, Knox has had her locked away with him in his apartment in the castle. Security guards patrol the walls and the doors. He won't let her out of his sight.

I know Remy was hoping Knox's obsession might have cooled down by now. Remy was thinking that maybe, after letting off some steam, Knox would get tired of her and move on, with a clearer head to make his choice and secure the link between our family and the Fitzpatricks.

At this point I think we all know it's getting less and less likely that Knox will be willing to do that.

Before Cassidy showed up only a few weeks ago, Knox told me he'd been having dreams about the angel. All the time. We talked about it. He said she was appearing to him in an erotic fever dream almost every night and it was messing with his head.

And then, only a few days later, she materializes out of fucking thin air. She was trespassing inside the walls of our family's estate before dawn. Knox saw her and chased after her. She was disguised as a thief, so he didn't recognize her right away. The two of them ended up almost killing each other.

All this has taken Knox's frenzy over this girl into overdrive. They're bonded in blood, according to him. He might still be delirious from blood loss but if anything, his resolve is only gaining momentum.

I'm assuming, since they've spent the past two weeks inseparable and mostly alone together, at his absolute insistence, that blood isn't the only bodily fluid involved in their bonding at this point. And if my brother is convinced that she's the soulmate he's been dreaming about, chances are he'll want to make that connection as binding as possible.

Which means I've got a big fucking problem on my hands.

Because if Knox won't step up—or can't, because he's too goddamn whipped—then it'll be up to me to secure the alliance.

I've never seen my brother in this kind of state before. He's a fucking goner. Completely manic with it.

This is not good news.

In fact this is exceptionally bad news.

In his haze of lust and delirium, Knox seems to genuinely believe that the angel is real. He sees it as some kind of a sign that the stars have aligned and he and Cassidy are meant to be together until the end of time or some bullshit. Which means he's probably not going to follow the rule. It means he can't. He's willing to die for her, already.

Again: fucked.

If I'm forced into an arranged marriage, which is getting more likely by the hour, I have five choices.

Raven King. A bat-shit crazy drama queen with a long list of addictions and, if not a death wish, then close enough.

Aurora King. A fuck bunny who's been on the receiving end of every available bachelor on the islands. A walking petri dish of Hawaiian primordial ooze. I'm hardly a choirboy myself but I'm really not sure I could bring myself to go there.

Tatum Fitzpatrick. A movie starlet who's currently dating at least two of her female co-stars. This is according to Echo, who keeps up with shit like that. I mean, good for Tatum, but it's hardly a recipe for wedded bliss.

Perri Fitzpatrick. A calculating bitch who's hellbent on marrying Knox—and when she finds out she can't, is sure to go ballistic, possibly commit murder and/or go off some unpredictable deep end that's unlikely to end well.

There's only one of the five I'd seriously consider.

Vivi Fitzpatrick.

She gets talked about. All five of them are constantly in

the headlines. Most of the publicity is about their messy break-ups or their public meltdowns.

But not Vivi. She gets talked about for other reasons. She rarely gives interviews. She's never been in a relationship. Apparently she's still a virgin, if rumors are to be believed.

She's known for her innocence. Her shyness. She keeps to herself more than the others and avoids the spotlight as much as it's possible for an influencer heiress to do. She's famous for her fresh, stunning beauty and her so-called purity.

Poor girl.

Then again, it might be fun to dirty all that.

I've seen photos of her online. She always looks sort of aloof, like her heart really isn't in the photoshoot or event or whatever. I saw her in person once, at a party I went to with Knox at Seven Mile Beach. It might have been two years ago. Maybe longer.

She was leaning her back up against a wall, near her sister and her entourage but standing alone. Watching the scene with her spooked, golden eyes. At the time she seemed very young, even though she had to be seventeen or eighteen at the time. She looked more like a sheltered, skinny kid not yet on the cusp.

That memory of her has always clashed with the glamour-girl image of her that gets blasted across social media. Not that I follow it, but for the past month or so, Echo has been drilling and informing the rest of us on the "candidates." To prepare us for this weekend.

I'm biding my time. I'm not going to offer anything until I absolutely have to. And until I see her in person again. To gauge whether there's something—anything—I might be able to hinge a goddamn marriage on, even if it's a marriage in name only.

Then I'll make my decision.

In some ways it makes sense for me to be the one. Since I'm not capable of falling in love, like all my siblings believe they are, I might as well be the one to take the fall.

As long as she's someone I can stand to be with when the mood strikes and who can potentially produce a tribe of beach babies to carry on my part of the Ramsey line, there's not much to lose. There's no rule in the alliance document that says we have to be faithful.

Sure, it would be nice to *want* to.

The thought makes my mood even darker. Could I be faithful? It's not something I've ever had to consider before.

*Either way, my wife would have to be.*

Hypocritical as fuck, obviously. But how could I possibly allow my own *wife* to be with someone else? I'd kill him. And maybe her.

I wonder how the curse would feel about *that* plot twist. Possibly a sticky topic that will eventually need to be worked through—and one I'm hardly going to worry about right now. If Vivi Fitzpatrick is anything like her reputation, she'll be easy to control.

Another text comes through and I check my phone to make sure it's not my family panicking over a new crisis.

It's a text from Echo. Of the very person I'm thinking

about, as it turns out. Echo sends us updates, of good news or flattering pictures of the candidates as they roll out on social media, to make this whole clusterfuck seem more appetizing, maybe. Echo's trying to give our doom an optimistic spin. I admire the effort, but so far it's not quite working.

In the photos, Vivi Fitzpatrick is modeling. She's cute, I'll give her that much. Dressed in her high fashion outfits, posing for the camera like a pro. In the next photo, she's more than cute. Almost painfully beautiful, in fact.

*But is it enough?*

I don't want to marry a stranger, of course I don't. I don't want to marry anyone. Marriage without love will be fucking tedious.

But maybe it's better this way. All the marriages I've been closest to have been deep and real—and they crashed and burned with the kind of tragedy you wouldn't wish on your worst fucking enemy. At this point I'm convinced love *is* the curse. I'm relieved I won't be touched by it. Love is where the deepest pain lies.

As for Vivi Fitzpatrick, she'll have the worst of it. She'll be mine to use as I please. She'll be in my bed every night to take whatever I give, to receive my feral lust in whatever way I choose to spend it. She'll carry my babies which means she'll be under my extremely thorough protection. In other words, she won't leave my sight.

I mean, *I* wouldn't choose this for an innocent little virgin who's scared of her own shadow.

I can admit that detail sweetens the deal. She's completely untouched.

She'll be mine and *only* mine.

This thought stirs something in me. A primal sense of ownership.

I almost feel sorry for her, even now.

But it's not up to me. If I could change things, I would.

When I meet her face to face, I'll be able to tell if there's any animal chemistry. Which is probably unlikely.

If I can stand the thought of taking her as my own, I'll make my decision and in the process, I'll save my brother. And possibly my entire family.

Lugging the giant boar up the steep incline of thick underbrush gives me one hell of a fucking workout. It takes me more than an hour. I'm covered in dirt and blood and drenched in sweat by the time I reach the clearing where my DR650 is parked.

I drop the massive animal onto the trailer behind my motorcycle, then rev my bike to life.

It takes me around twenty minutes to get back to the center of town, with its views out over the sloping farmland. It's surrounded by hills that rise into steep mountains, with the long stretch of golden-sand beach down below.

Paradise has a population of around a thousand but people tend to come and go. There are usually around six to eight hundred of us living here at any given time. We're literally in paradise, but it's remote. And it's extremely limited as far as trying to hook up with the opposite sex goes, since most of us are related. So the people in my extended family tend to travel for years on end when they're young, searching for their perfect match. Once they find them, they bring them back, build a house and start breeding.

As for me and my immediate family, we stay closer to home since we're bound by the alliance.

We've been putting off the inevitable but it's time. Remy and Silas want the decisions made tonight.

And I'm late.

The Fitzpatricks and the Kings will be arriving soon. They'll stay for the weekend, to see if anyone hits it off. There will be plenty of alcohol on hand. Blaise said something about a 24-hour open bar and champagne fountains.

If no one *does* hit it off, Blaise and Knox will be forced to step up.

Blaise has been seeing an artist who lives on the North Shore of Oahu. She told us she thinks she's in love with him. But instead, she'll be marrying Enzo, Stone or Jagger King. All three are shady gangsters with more money and women than most men even dream of and it's highly unlikely any of them could make my sister, who happens to be one of the best people I know, even remotely happy. Which fucking sucks.

Jagger's the most laid back of the three and he's fun to hang out with in the right circumstances but he also gets off on his status as a player.

Enzo is smart as hell but lives by his own set of rules. Which are very unlikely to include fidelity.

As for Stone, I once saw him kill an Arrow recruit with

his bare hands. It was justified—and I've done the same thing when I was forced to—but there was something absolutely chilling about the way he did it. I've warned Blaise and told her she should avoid Stone at all costs. He's the one I would hate to see one of my sisters end up with most of all.

But unless a miracle happens, Blaise will have no choice but to take one for the team. I can't rescue her *and* Knox.

I might have an ace up my sleeve, but I'm not going to offer it if I can't follow through.

I ride along the ridge to my family's homestead, which looks like a castle. It's been added to over the generations. The main part of the house looks almost medieval, but there's a plantation-style wing, a modern wing made of wood and glass and other add-ons.

It's almost dusk and the outdoor area has been decorated with hanging lights, lanterns and torches. The fire pits are lit and the band is setting up.

Blaise and Echo are dressed in their party outfits, doling out instructions to the teams of caterers, bar people and staff.

Their eyes go wide as I pull up.

I kill the engine.

"Wolf, what the *hell?* Where have you been?" Blaise has her hands on her hips as she scolds me.

"Kind of obvious, isn't it?"

"The limos are on their way up the driveway! They'll be here any minute. You can't let them see you like this! You'll scare them off. Go get cleaned up. And get rid of that awful ... *thing.*"

Echo is staring at the bloody boar. "That is *so* disgusting."

"What, you think bacon grows on trees?" My sisters aren't into hunting.

"I'm a *vegan*, Wolf," Echo says. "That's just vile."

Zeke, our cousin, who's a pyromaniac and has been commissioned to deal with the torches, bonfires and fireworks, walks over to admire my motherlode. "Holy fuck. Where'd you find it?"

"At the bottom of Cold Water Gully." Practically every hill, creek, rock, field and tree in Paradise has a name and most of us know the detailed map of it intimately. We've grown up exploring it, farming it, hunting it, fishing it, growing crops on it and generally making every memory we've ever had on this land. We know it like we know the rhythm of our own heartbeats.

Zeke gives me a once-over and laughs. I'm absolutely filthy. "Shit, man. I'll deal with this. You'll freak out the guests."

Blaise is less amused. "Hurry *up*, Wolf."

My family is used to me but it's probably better if our weekend guests don't see me looking like I just murdered half of Hawaii. And one of the limos is pulling up now, on the other side of the fountains. There are four more sets of headlights further up the driveway.

So I go inside and take the back staircase up to my fourth-floor apartment. It's the highest, located in the oldest section of the castle. According to family history, it's the part that's haunted but I like the view from the turret.

I don't spend a lot of time here. I have a mountain hunting cabin that's more like an off-grid hut. And I have my beach house, which is usually full of my cousins and friends, who all use it as a party headquarters. There's also my boat.

I take a hot shower and wash off the blood and the grime.

Then I pull on a pair of jeans and a shirt. I put on a leather belt with several holsters hanging off of it because even though it's a party, that doesn't mean there aren't threats. Then I make my way down to our main office, to see if Remy's there.

I find him talking to Knox. It's just the two of them. Their voices are low but I can tell they're arguing. About the thing that's been on everyone's mind since the little thief showed up.

She probably doesn't even know she's messing with the alliance. I wonder how much Knox has told her.

"You can and you will," I hear Remy say to Knox. It's an order but the gleam in Knox's eyes is defiant.

All three of us are big, well over six feet, and honed from a lifetime spent running wild, preparing for danger, training, fighting and generally beefing ourselves up to the extreme. We're not only athletes, we're lethal, well-oiled fighting machines.

Remy is maybe half an inch taller than Knox, but Knox has had the edge lately, on both me and Remy. We train in MMA and we're constantly practicing. Knox has been fueled by his fever dreams and, now that his fantasy has materialized out of thin air, his rage. That he might not be able to keep her.

These past few weeks, he can take any one of us in a fight.

"Let's just see how the night plays out," I suggest, trying to diffuse the situation. "Nothing's been decided yet. We can try to get through the weekend without you two having another punch-up over it. Yeah?"

They both glare at me.

"The guests are here," I tell them. And, because I can't resist firing Knox up, "Your future wife is in the building."

"That's true, but probably not the way you mean it," Knox seethes. "Which means you can fuck off, Wolf."

I can't help smiling at him. He's ridiculously wound up. "Easy, tiger." Someone has to have a sense of humor around here and neither one of them is feeling it. "Let's do this."

We go outside to the patio area, now full of people. The fires are lit and the full moon hangs over the scene, giving the whole place a romantic glow.

Knox is tense as fuck. His gaze goes directly to Cassidy. She's over by the bar, being checked out by Malachi Fitzpatrick and Jagger King. I can feel the heat of my brother's fury from several feet away.

"Keep your cool, man," I murmur, but I can already read the writing on the wall.

Knox storms over to them. And I scan the crowd for the one I'm looking for.

That's when I see her.

Vivi Fitzpatrick.

She's standing with her sister, like a swan standing next to an ugly duckling. Which might be a cruel way of describing it but it's true. She looks a lot different than she did last time I saw her a few years ago.

In fact … hell. She's grown up since then.

*Way* the hell up.

Her green dress is tight and shows off her absurdly banging body. But it's obvious she's somehow completely unaware of how gorgeous she is.

She looks wildly uncomfortable. She's standing a few feet away from the circle she's a part of, staring out across the water of the pool, like she's wishing she could dive into it, or run.

The other sister, Perri, is five or six inches shorter than Vivi. She's dressed in a weird, see-through black outfit. She's trying too hard, no doubt hoping to entice Knox. *Good luck with that, babe.* She doesn't have the body to pull it off. With the angel as her competition, and especially in the shadow of her smoking-hot-but-doesn't-even-realize-it little sister, Perri doesn't have a snowball's chance in hell of landing anyone here tonight.

My gaze returns to Vivi.

*Holy fuck.* She's fucking gorgeous.

The short, glittery dress shows off her long legs. She's petite but curvy, with full, perfect tits that are half exposed by the low-cut outfit, giving the whole look a sultry, almost-indecent edge.

Maybe only recently, Vivi Fitzpatrick crossed some threshold, stepping over the line from pure innocence and into the realm of sexy little hellcat. Even *she* hasn't realized she's arrived yet.

But I have.

The taut, high peaks of her nipples are poking against the dress. I can almost see the darker, rosy color of them through the thin, straining fabric. At the sight, my cock thickens.

Her body is ludicrously lush. The flare of her hips, her long legs and her mind-numbing curves under that very-short skirt are getting me all worked up.

*Damn it.*

And so's her pissed-off little pout. I adjust the holster on my belt to shield my straining hard-on.

*Calm the fuck down, boy.*

It's obvious she wishes she was anywhere but here. If she had one shred of confidence, she'd be the most stunning creature on earth. But she's not owning it at all. It makes me wonder who's putting her down, trying to control her or dominating her against her will.

For some reason the thought enrages me.

*Mine.*

The flare of protective possessiveness almost surprises me.

I walk closer, circling her from a distance, like a stalking panther checking out a newborn fawn.

This is potentially my future wife I'm dealing with. I need a better look.

Her dark hair is braided, with green jewels woven into it. Her skin isn't pale. There's Spanish blood in the Fitzpatrick line and she has that exotic edge, with cat-like eyes that flicker with gold in the firelight.

The closer I get to her, the more mesmerizing she becomes. Her face has a young freshness to it. A dewy, flawless glow. It's easy to see why she's a cover model for all the top fashion magazines. The rumors and the photographs don't do her justice. In person, her beauty is a hundred times more spellbinding.

She's gorgeous but there's more to it than surface beauty. It's the sassy little attitude that's getting me harder than anything else. The wide-eyed, sheltered innocence has layers. There's fire under that petulant scowl.

*I'll make that sultry little mouth moan and beg for more. I'll cover those sweet, bouncy tits and those rosy little nipples with my hot cum. I'll rub it all over her smooth, golden skin as I claim her.*

If I want to, I can. There's nothing she can do to stop me.

She senses the heat of my awareness and she turns.

Our eyes meet. She takes in my height, my weight. My brute, tension-coiled strength.

The usual fear is there but there's a lot more of it. Her eyes get wide and her face pales. She's absolutely terrified of me.

I wait for the fear to turn to fascination. And it does, but barely. What I'm thinking is: I want it. I *want* this girl's fascination. I want *her* base urges to crave me. Her fear overwhelms any hint of this. She's too inexperienced to know that the threat of me is just as much about pleasure as it is about pain.

I'm surprised by my reaction to this girl. By how *much* I want her to want me. I want her to need things from me. I want her to cry with the kind of ecstasy she doesn't even know exists yet.

It'll be a marriage in name only. Seeing her now, I know I can live with that. One of us was always going to suffer for the rule.

And it's going to be me. Because with this little thing, it won't be *all* suffering. For either one of us. I'll make sure of that.

So I make my decision.

# 3

# Vivi

It's easy to see why they call it Paradise. There's no other word for it.

Our limo drives us through the gates of the Ramsey estate and up the winding road toward the main house. It's a giant castle with rambling add-ons and modern flair. The hills slope down to a wide bay and a golden-sand beach. Steep, dramatic mountains rise up behind the rolling farm-land, which is dotted with palm trees and winding streams. There's even a waterfall. A rainbow glitters in its mist.

It's almost dusk. Along the far-away horizon line, the ocean glows orange where the sun's final sliver sinks into the sea.

We pull up in front of the impressive main house which is an eclectic blend of architectural styles put together in a way that somehow works. Clearly no expense has been spared at any stage of its design. The main part of the castle is made of stone. Off the central structure, there's a planta-tion-style wing that gets more modern as it rambles. At the end of it, there's a huge lanai, which opens out onto the outdoor entertaining area.

Even though I'm nervous, there's something exciting about being here. The air feels clean and sparked with … I don't know how to describe it. Possibility, maybe. The feeling that something unexpected is about to happen.

But then, a cloud passes over the rising moon and the feeling takes on an edge of dread.

Before I can worry about it, we're greeted by valets and we're led through an archway. Next to a stone fountain, there's a large patio area with pools, decorated with hanging lights. Several bartenders are pouring drinks from behind an upscale tiki bar. There's a champagne fountain. Next to it, a white table has been stacked with a pyramid of full cham-pagne glasses.

Bonfires crackle festively in several fire pits. A band is setting up on a raised stage by a dance floor. Six or seven large tables are set, decorated with flower arrangements and tall glass lanterns.

"Wow," I whisper. I'm used to luxury but, showcased by the wide-open seascape, the moody sky and the rising mountains, this place takes it to another level.

We're greeted by Echo and Blaise. Echo is wearing a cute black dress that shows off her slim, perfect figure. Her dark hair is long, cut in a flattering, modern style.

"Hi, Vivi. Welcome to Paradise," Echo smiles, air kissing

me on the cheek, whispering in my ear, "Aren't we lucky we're the youngest?"

"So lucky," I whisper back. Even though we haven't spent much time together, we always sort of click when we see each other. She's nice and I consider her a friend.

Echo's presence calms me and I'm grateful. I don't know why I'm so jumpy. Everything will be fine. We'll have a fun weekend in this picturesque place, the marriage plans between our older siblings will be decided and that will be that. Then I can get on with a life that's more about getting what *I* want than taking other people's orders.

We're offered champagne. Echo and I both I take a glass as more limos pull up.

The Kings have arrived. They live in some of the extremely luxurious high rise buildings they own in Honolulu, not far from us, and we see them every now and then. Some of them occasionally come to Seven Mile Beach for meetings or for dinner.

Enzo meets with Silas regularly. Stone and Jagger, less often. Occasionally I see Raven and Aurora at parties.

Enzo has black hair and incredibly blue eyes. He practically oozes power and a dark energy I find crazily intimidating. True, I find a lot of people intimidating but Enzo more than most. Stone is even worse. They're men without boundaries, you can just tell. It makes me wonder if the Ramseys are the same.

None of the Kings look alike. Apparently their father preferred to mix it up when it came to his romances.

According to Silas, only two of them, Stone and Raven, have the same mother.

Stone has dark brown hair and a restless, almost-sinister vibe.

Raven is borderline unhinged, with distinctive, mad-looking silver eyes.

Aurora's hair is red and her pink catsuit reveals more than it covers. She prefers not to leave much to the imagination with her fashion choices, and why not? She's gorgeous and she makes the most of it.

Aurora hugs me lightly and I watch her breeze her way over to where Silas and Malachi are standing by the bar, wishing I had one ounce of her confidence.

*You can do this. It's only two days. Drink your champagne, hang out with Echo and try to act like a normal human being. Two days will fly by and before you know it you'll be home, hanging out with Ash and making plans to run your foundation together, travel and live life on your own terms.*

Jagger has dark gold hair and a surfie, more carefree look than the rest of his family. "Hey, Vivi." He kisses my cheek. But he's distracted by someone else who's joined our circle.

"This is Cassidy," Echo introduces her, not giving a last name. "Cassidy, this is Vivi Fitzpatrick. And Jagger King."

Her hair is white-blond, tied up into a braided crown. She's wearing an off-white mini-dress with fur detailing. She's very, very beautiful and almost familiar-looking, although I can't place why she would be.

It seems a little strange that she would be invited this

weekend, since the only other people here are connected to our three families. Maybe she comes from the mainland or something and is here for an extended stay.

People are laughing and mingling and I overhear Perri talking to Cassidy. "We haven't met," Perri says icily.

"I'm Cassidy. I'm a friend of Echo's."

"Are you staying the whole weekend?" Perri's tone isn't friendly. It's rude. I find myself hoping Cassidy doesn't pick up on that or take offense to it. It's just Perri's way. Her resentment about all the things in life that feel unfair to her tend to bubble over and color her entire personality.

Cassidy doesn't seem to notice, or she's tactful enough not to show it. "I'm not sure yet." But then I hear the light challenge in her reply. "Probably."

After a few seconds of tense silence, Cassidy drifts away. Perri looks up toward the house and gasps, gripping my arm for support. There's a twinge of pain and I realize Jett *did* bruise me when he threatened me in the garden. The thought makes me feel sort of nauseous again, at the memory of his low warning.

"*Oh my God,* he's here," Perri whispers. I follow her gaze to see who she's talking about. But of course I already know.

The three Ramsey brothers are standing at the top of the wide stone steps of the house.

They're big, imposing men. With their brazen size dramatically lit by the torches that surround them, they command attention. Like, *all* of it. They look like freaking Vikings.

Remington Ramsey is huge. The loss of his wife and

baby has made him hard, they say. Not surprisingly. We all know about tragedy and grief, but he wears his like a suit of armor.

Knox is known for his good looks and his reclusiveness. And he lives up to the hype. His handsomeness is sun-drenched and riveting, even in the firelit twilight. But his blue eyes are focused. Not on my sister, whose grip is locked onto my arm with desperate fascination.

On the only girl here he *shouldn't* be staring at, and there's a hell of a lot going on behind his expression.

He's staring at Cassidy.

We can all see it. His rage. His dilemma. *His love.* It's obvious. He's infatuated with her. This is gleaming out of his eyes in laser beams of worshipful obsession. Which sounds like an over the top description but it's true.

*This is not good,* some little instinct whispers.

It's the third brother—Wolf Ramsey—who holds my attention most of all. He's just as tall and muscular as his brothers but somehow more lithe and predatory in the way he holds himself, like a jungle cat on the prowl. His hair is a shade darker than Knox's, catching the dancing firelight, giving him a subtle halo and the aura of a dangerous rogue angel. He might have been blond as a child, but virile, full-blown manhood has seasoned him into … *this.* Beefed-up, athletic masculinity on overdrive, with a menacing edge.

*The killing machine,* my brothers call him. I have no idea why and I don't want to.

An arsenal of weapons is strapped to his body. In fact,

he's armed to the teeth. Firelight glints off the metal of his weapons sort of ominously.

*At a party? Inside a fortress? Is it really necessary to be so heavily armed?*

He's outrageously good-looking, like all the Ramseys, but his looks are overshadowed by his wild intensity. You can tell he'd be reckless and brutal. Even from a distance, his dangerous energy makes my heart beat faster. He'd ruin you, body and soul, this is written all over him. I don't know why I say that, but his effect is forceful.

When his gaze lands directly on me, I freeze.

*Holy shit.*

I try to look away but I can't.

The tiny hairs on my arms lift. I don't know why I'm so crazily *aware* of him, like he's emitting electric sparks and I can feel the damn zing of them from all the way over here.

I have a very bad feeling about what's happening here.

I want to leave. I'm not cut out for this. I don't even *believe* in the alliance. Why do I have to be here at all?

Wolf Ramsey and his brothers make their way down the steps and into the thick of the party. I'm wildly relieved when his attention is diverted by the people who surround him.

Perri and I stick together. She needs me as much as I need her. "Do you think I should go talk to him?" she whispers.

I try to be a good sister but it's obvious nothing's going to help her at this point. Knox hasn't even acknowledged her. Everything about him is focused on Cassidy. "Yes. He probably hasn't seen you yet."

I watch from my safe distance as Malachi shakes Wolf's hand. He slaps Wolf on the back like he's greeting an old friend, which maybe he is. They're around the same age. Malachi says something under his breath and Wolf laughs.

"Who *is* that girl?" Perri's low question is equal parts pissed off and heartbroken. Very clearly, a proposal from Knox Ramsey is unlikely to happen tonight—or any night.

The way Knox has just grabbed Malachi's wrist because he's flirting with Cassidy sort of confirms the worst. But I can't help noticing that Cassidy seems upset by all the attention she's getting. I watch as she says something to Knox, then she makes her way toward the door of the house.

She goes inside.

Perri also notices. "I'm going to go find the bathroom," she says.

I know what she's thinking. She's going to follow Cassidy inside and confront her, where no one else can overhear. I almost tell her to wait. I know my sister and whatever intentions she has probably aren't particularly kind-hearted. "Perri—"

"I'll be right back." She's determined. The marriage she's been dreaming of for months or even years is on the line here. There's no way she isn't going to find out what's going on with the beautiful stranger who's standing in her way.

She follows Cassidy inside.

And now I'm alone, like the awkward wallflower I am.

*Damn it.* Why can't I be outgoing and fun, like Aurora or Tatum? Why does anxiety feel like it's squeezing my racing heart every time I'm in a social situation? Especially this one?

Shyness is a curse.

I could say I have a headache. I could find out where we're sleeping tonight from Echo. I can leave it up to the rest of them to secure the ridiculousness of the alliance matches. I could call Ash and he could calm me down and do that thing he does where he makes me feel like I'm not an outcast or a freak.

I start making my way over to where Echo is talking to Aurora and Jagger.

But someone blocks my way.

*Holy hell.*

It's *him.*

Wolf Ramsey.

*Help me.*

He's even bigger up close. Looming over me, all fierce and gigantic.

I have to admit he's ridiculously … toned. Tall. His shoulders are squared and solid, straining at the fabric of his shirt. The whiteness of it emphasizes the deep tan of his sun-bronzed skin.

He looks every inch the savage fighter he's rumored to be. His eyes are a vivid shade of light blue. They're watching me with a cool alertness.

The sudden presence of this built Ramsey brother is ten times more daunting than it was from across the party. *This* is why I prefer the mild, soothing peacefulness of people like Ash.

There's not a single thing that's mild or soothing about Wolf Ramsey.

It's shocking to be up close and personal with so much … pumped-up muscle and broad, rock-hard chest. There's a tattoo snaking up from under the collar of his shirt. A few more are inked to his forearms, where his sleeves are rolled up, which are just as muscular as the rest of him. He's radiating testosterone and it's literally heating up the space around me. My cheeks feel flushed.

*And not only my cheeks.*

He's scaring me.

He's also doing something else to me.

I can feel my heartbeat in the tips of my nipples. And in the soft, secret place between my thighs, which feels warm and … wet.

*OMG.*

I can hardly breathe.

I'm not expecting it. I try to tone down my reactions to this big, buff stranger, but my body has a mind of its own.

What the hell is happening to me?

*He's getting you all hot and bothered with those wildman pheromones and the dark look behind those ice-blue eyes, that's what's freaking happening.*

I need to get away from him. I think about stepping around him, but the thought of him touching me, grabbing my arm or moving to block my way, stops me.

"Vivi Fitzpatrick," he drawls. His voice is deep with a

distinctive huskiness. There's a relaxed arrogance to him, spliced with a cutting, playful sense of humor. "Wolf Ramsey."

"I know." My voice sounds breathless.

"We've met, but it was a few years ago. You probably don't remember."

I don't remember. I used to hide when we had guests.

The air between us feels charged with a barely restrained warning. I can tell that Wolf Ramsey is unpredictable. He senses my unease and he almost smiles. But not quite. This humor in him annoys me a little. He *knows* he's freaking me out and this is entertaining to him. "Are you having fun?" There's a dark edge to his question.

Fun?

I could lie. I *should* lie. It's his family who's hosting this party, after all. Instead, I hear myself say, "No. Not really."

His smile is cocky. As nervous as he's making me, it's impossible not to notice how good-looking he is. There's a shadow of his beard across his square jaw. His neck is corded and strong-looking, tawny with sun.

Knox is the one who gets talked about as being handsome. I would never admit this to anyone but I find myself thinking Wolf is even more striking. He's too complicated to be conventional about it, though. His looks are dominated by reckless layers of the unknown.

Not my type at all. I prefer the company of people who are unthreatening and calm. Exactly what Wolf Ramsey is not.

His lips are perfectly shaped. You can tell by the light

sneer as he checks me out that he's as dirty and debauched as they come. I have no idea how I know this but I do. His moral compass is pointing due south and he's absolutely filthy. I can read this in his eyes by the way he's watching me. And it's only ramping up my unease.

It's a different kind of threat than the one I'm used to. It's a threat that's laced with … something you want. I don't know exactly *what* but my deepest primal feminine urges feel it.

I mean, I didn't even know I *had* primal feminine urges … until now. And I don't like what they're thinking about.

"I'll admit, you're not at all what I was expecting," he says.

He's baiting me on purpose, but I ask it anyway. "What were you expecting?"

His gaze roves lower and paints my half-exposed breasts with warmth.

*God.*

As he does this, I can feel my pulse throbbing gently in the most intimate place imaginable.

*Wow.*

He smirks, like he's fully aware of the effect he's having on me. "I was expecting a mildly pleasing, pampered little princess who always does what she's told. But I was way off."

What?

"The petulant pout is sweet as fuck, I'll give you that much. Dripping with attitude."

*What the hell?* I think he might have just insulted me. Or

maybe he just gave me a compliment. I can't quite tell either way. He's obviously trying to rile me and it's working.

"I don't know what you mean," I say—okay, *with* attitude. Because he's rude and aggressive and it's the only defense I have.

He grins wolfishly. Which is to be expected, I guess. I can't help thinking his name suits him. Even his teeth have those slightly pointed ones, like he might grow fangs at midnight under a full moon. Like tonight.

"She's feisty. I like it." Leaning a brawny shoulder against a stone column, he folds his strong arms across his chest with the easy, ultra-masculine confidence of a man who knows he's lethal in a fight.

He's doing that *thing* again as he watches me. Making me aware of the soft, secret pulse … *there*. My mouth feels weirdly thirsty. "If you don't like my attitude then maybe you should go and find someone more 'pleasing'." He's right, I do sound feisty.

"That would be impossible."

I glare at him and there's that dark glimmer of amusement in him again. He's toying with me. "What do you mean?"

"I mean you're fucking *beautiful*. But you already know that, don't you, princess." It's not a question.

I stand mutely, completely lost for words. It's pathetic, maybe, but that might be one of the nicest things anyone has ever said to me. Even so, everything about him is overwhelming me. "Don't call me that."

"Feisty women are my favorite kind." He's enjoying his game.

"Then you should go find one." But I'm reeling. His offhand comments are delivering so much *feeling*, I can't keep up. He's offending me and at the same time his wicked allure is igniting my body in ways I don't know how to control. It's hard to know how to react.

"I happen to be able to cure even the sassiest attitude into complete, willing submission almost entirely, under the right circumstances. Although I might make you work for it. It would be a shame not to."

*What … circumstances? Work for what?* I don't know exactly what he means. He knows this and he finds it darkly funny, which flusters me even more. He's implying something … dirty. Some scenario that includes us both. Considering the reason we're all here tonight, I really don't like where this conversation is going.

His lingering smile is irritatingly perceptive. "Am I making you nervous?" he asks softly.

I try to look away from him but he's too magnetic. And I don't want to give him the satisfaction of being right. "No," I say, although he clearly is.

He's actually sort of devastating me. With his blue eyes and the spark behind them, he's somehow shining a light on all my inadequacies.

Every single day of my life, I've felt like something is missing. I never *feel* much of anything. I'm never as enthusiastic as Perri about the clothes or the followers. I can never quite bring myself to luxuriate in the high life like Malachi, or embrace my own talents, like Tatum. I'm never as excited as the people around me are, about anything. The couture outfits, the gifts they want us to promote, the millions of likes. I've often wondered if something was wrong with me, if maybe my emotions are just set on a lower dial than most people's.

But right now, I'm strangely *alive*. My heart is racing. My skin is flushed. I'm craving things I can't even name. *My panties are wet.*

It's like this rough, rugged stranger holds a key to hidden recesses of my body and soul that even *I* didn't know about.

One thing I know for sure: I don't *want* him to hold that key.

"Or am I affecting you in some other way?" There's a glimmer of a challenge in his eyes. His voice has that rasped, deep edge to it. "Some unexpected, visceral reaction that has you questioning all your powers of resistance?"

I watch his mouth as he speaks, and I literally can't control how … absorbed I am. How terrified and how beguiled. Something about the way he's looking at me isn't just curious. It's focused. Like he's weighing up a decision.

"And there's more to it than that, isn't there, gorgeous little Vivi. A new hunger you can't describe. I think we both know it's a craving that will keep you up at night from now on, wondering how it's going to feel."

"How w-what's going to feel?" *Damn it.* I can't take this. I need to get away from him. He's too intense, too arrogant, too masculine, *too everything*.

I'm relieved when a commotion interrupts us.

It's Wolf's brothers. They're having a low but obviously heated argument near the pool. Remy is saying something to Knox and gripping his arm. Knox shrugs him off.

Everyone's watching them.

Knox turns down the music the band must have put on during a break. He steps onto a low stone wall that runs the length of the pool. "I've got something to tell you all," he says loudly.

I think we can all guess what he's about to say.

I look around for Cassidy but she's gone.

Wolf leaves me, storming over to his brothers. He climbs up next to Knox and grabs the front of Knox's shirt with his fist. Knox tries to shake him off but Wolf is strong and insistent. Wolf says something to him under his breath. The two of them are talking but it's too low for me to hear from here. Whatever Wolf is saying gets Knox's full attention.

Perri's arm brushes against mine. She's returned from inside the house. "What are they doing?" Breathlessly, like maybe this is a sign.

*Please, no.* "I don't know."

"False alarm, everyone," Wolf says to the crowd, laughing off Knox's behavior. "Someone crank the music back up."

Wolf pulls Knox off the low wall and the three Ramsey brothers are having an intense, murmured discussion, out of earshot. The music gets loud again.

"What are they talking about?" Perri asks, but of course I can't know.

*I really, really hope it's not what I think they might be talking about.*

In my heart, I think I already know it is.

Because Knox gives Wolf a manly almost-hug and pats him on the back. The argument is over. Remy is pleased about something. And Knox looks almost … happy. Wild with relief. He leaves them abruptly, heading toward the house like he's on a mission.

*No.*

*I won't do it.*

Remington and Wolf are talking to Silas. Silas glances over to where Perri and I are standing.

The men shake hands.

*Please. No.*

*It's not up to them. It's up to me.*

The night takes on an eerie haze, like I'm dreaming this. Or having a terrible nightmare.

Silas leaves the Ramseys where they're still talking and walks over to us. His eyes are directly on me. Not on Perri. I can read in his gaze all my worst fears. And I can tell by the waver of Perri's gasp that Silas is realizing all *her* worst fears too.

"There's been a change of plans," Silas tells us. "It's decided."

*This can't be happening.*

But it is happening.

"Vivi, it's going to be you and Wolf to lock in the Ramsey-Fitzpatrick alliance. Your wedding is on Sunday."

# 4

# Vivi

AFTER A FEW SECONDS of shocked silence, I'm finally able to react. I almost laugh, at how preposterous it is. "What? *No.* Absolutely not. I'm not doing it. I won't."

"Vivi. It's happening," Silas says gruffly. "It's for the good of all of us, you know that."

"The good of *all* of us? What about the good of *me*? You can't decide this for me. No way! I'm absolutely not doing it."

Silas runs a hand through his hair, ruffling his perfection.

His steely silence is too much for me. "If it was for the good of all of us, *you* would have done it, Silas. It should be you."

"Don't be belligerent about it. He's a Ramsey, what's not to like? They're even more loaded than we are."

"I don't care how *loaded* he is, Silas. *God.* It's not about that. It's about making my own choice about who I'm going to *marry!* I refuse to do it."

"Don't make a scene," my brother growls.

"A scene? A *scene?* This is unbelievable! You can't really expect me to go through with it, Silas. I won't."

"You need to accept that this is happening, Vivi. We can go somewhere more private to talk it through if you're going to have a fucking meltdown about it."

"A fucking *meltdown?* Because I'm being ordered to marry some crazy 'killing machine' who I've met only once and would prefer to never meet again? There's no way in hell I'm doing it, Silas. You're an over-controlling bully, that's what you are. You always have been. You don't care about me or what's best for me at all! You only care about yourself."

Silas glares at me with that impatience again. He hates when I make anything difficult for him. "You're marrying Wolf Ramsey, Vivi," he growls. "End of story."

"Wrong, Silas. It's not the end of *my* story. Because I refuse."

And I need a minute.

I'm about to either cry or scream and I don't want to do it in front of all these people. I need to be alone so I can think. I need to figure out how I'm going to get the hell out of this. This farce. This family. This *marriage.* I never asked for any of it. And I've had enough.

There *will* be a way to get out of marrying Wolf Ramsey.

*There has to be a way.*

I turn from Silas and run into the house. I don't know where I'm going. Down a wide hallway, there's a closed door. It's unlocked. I open it and let myself into a large, quiet room. No one else is here so I shut the door behind me. I feel like I'm walking a fine line between my sanity and … something else entirely. Maybe I'm having a panic attack.

I look around the dark, spacious room. There are desks with computers. Leather couches sit on either side of a long coffee table and are piled with neatly-stacked books and magazines. Walls of windows look out over an orchard. One full wall is made of stone, framing an unlit fireplace. Another wall is filled with modern art. This room is an office. It's most likely the Ramseys' headquarters.

A low lamp offers the only soft light from a corner, but the moon is so bright the room glows with its silvery cast.

I look for a back door. I need to get off this island. How am I going to escape this nightmare?

I'll walk to the airport, I don't care. I'll hide. I'll get the next plane to New York.

*But I don't have any money.*

I don't handle my own money. I never need to buy anything. Everything is done for me. The few times I've brought it up they always tell me I don't need to worry about things like that. I have managers and assistants on hand at all times, they said.

*You're an idiot! For allowing it.*

They can't expect me to throw my life away like this! I refuse and that's all there is to it. They can figure out

84

another way to honor their damn alliance. Silas can take the fall. It's *his* duty, not mine.

Maybe Tatum has a credit card I can use. I'll find her and ask her. I'll tell her everything and she'll help me. I have tonight and all day tomorrow to come up with a plan. She'll help me, I know she will.

*Will she?*

Tatum believes in the curse too. She'll want it taken care of. In fact, all my siblings are fully invested in making sure the alliance is sealed. *Even if they have to sacrifice me to do it.*

I wish the realization wasn't hitting me as hard as it is. I'm the Plan B. The back-up, in case things didn't pan out for the others. Maybe I always have been. Maybe *that's* the reason they've always kept me so closely guarded. Untouched and on offer to whoever will take me.

The door opens and I turn.

Perri has followed me.

So has Silas.

Followed closely by Jett. The last person on the planet I want to see.

"I'm not marrying him," I tell Silas again. I sound stubborn and I am. Hopefully he'll begin to see that he can't push me around or change my mind. He'll have to come up with another solution.

Perri sits heavily onto one of the couches. She's sobbing. Her makeup is smudged beyond repair. Her see-through dress looks strange now. It was the wrong choice, in hindsight. But it's not like a different dress would have changed the outcome of what's happened here tonight.

I don't feel as much sympathy for her as I usually do. She wanted to marry Knox Ramsey for her own reasons, which had nothing to do with saving me, or any of us. Her devastation is all about herself. Not a single tear is for me, for what I'm being forced to do or for how I feel about any of it.

My family doesn't really care about me or how I feel. Maybe they never really have. This revelation is hitting me hard and it's upsetting me even more.

Silas half-sits against a desk, folding his arms, making an effort to keep things calm. "Vivi, let's be reasonable. We can talk this through."

"Reasonable? You want reasonable? Well, here's reasonable: *you're* the oldest, Silas. It's up to *you* to do it, not me. Step up and do the right thing by your family." I've had obedience up to my damn eyeballs. "I don't care about the stupid alliance. Marry Blaise. Or Echo." Even as I say it, I feel bad, for Blaise, and Echo. Silas would be hard to be married to. He doesn't have a faithful bone in his body.

"Wolf Ramsey wants you," Silas says. "He's *choosing* you. It's a good option."

"It's a good option for *you*, Silas! Not for me." I'm pacing now. "You can't force me to do it."

My brother takes a deep breath. "I would ask Blaise or Echo to marry me. But I can't. It's no longer an option. Sasha Silver is expecting my baby."

"What?"

"You heard me."

"Who's Sasha Silver?"

"She's … a friend. A girlfriend. It doesn't really matter who she is. What matters is that alliance marriages can't have other children involved. When it comes to children, the marriages need to be pure."

"What? Since *when*? I've never heard of that rule."

"It's in the fine print," Silas says.

"Well, then, that's something you should have considered more fucking carefully over the past twenty-nine years, isn't it, Silas?" My brother's eyes darken. I don't know if I've ever sworn at anyone. Ever. And especially not him. But now feels like a good time to start. And I'm not finished. "You can't pass this off to me just because you don't want to do it! It doesn't work that way."

What I'm realizing is that maybe it *does* work that way.

I've never been so angry in my life. Silas might have even knocked up Sasha Silver—whoever she is—on purpose. Just to get out of it. I bet he did.

I notice then that Jett is blocking my way out. Silas might even be aware of this. Could Silas have *told* Jett to make sure I comply?

My brother is using me as a pawn. He's always been in control of every aspect of my life. He's offering me up like a sacrificial lamb so he can be free to make his own choices. I wonder if Silas would even stop Jett if he tried manhandling me again.

I have the terrible feeling they'll be watching me. Tonight. This weekend. To make sure I don't try to run.

"Silas." I try to appeal to his sense of … family. Of being my brother. "Please. I'm not marrying Wolf Ramsey. I don't even know him. We're not well-matched at all. It would never work."

"It's a marriage in name only, Vivi. You'll be free to do whatever you want … on the side."

"I don't *want* a marriage in name only, Silas! That's something you'd be better at than me." It's true. Maybe he can see that. "*Please*, Silas. This is my *life* we're talking about! I don't want to be Wolf Ramsey's wife." I don't say it, but I'm also thinking: and I don't want to have to share his bed. To be bound forever to that dark, volatile energy. It doesn't matter that his presence and the heat of his body infused me with … something. Awareness. Fear. Even if there was a spark to him—and I can admit it was insanely intense—he's obviously dangerous. Strong as hell. If Jett can bruise me with his grip, I can only imagine the kind of damage Wolf Ramsey could do to me. "You call him *the killing machine,* Silas. You can't expect me to be shackled to him for the rest of eternity!"

*I think we both know that craving will keep you up at night from now on, wondering how it's going to feel.*

The flashback upsets me even more.

"He's a good fighter, that's all, Vivi. Outside the fighting ring, he's no worse than any of the rest of us."

The comment does nothing to comfort me.

Silas stands, walking over to the window, where the light of the night outlines his tall, well-formed silhouette. My brother is a beautiful man. On the outside. What I'm learning is that I don't know if I can trust him. In fact, it's clear I *can't* trust him to think of me and my best interests. I thought I could, but how could he really expect me to do this? To take the fall for something he's unwilling to do?

"And if I refuse?"

"You won't." Silas's anger takes me off-guard. "The alliance will be honored. You'll do what needs to be done and that's that. The matter is settled, Vivi. Don't push your luck."

"Push my *luck*? What does that even *mean*, Silas? What luck? What are you going to do, lock me up? I'm *already* locked up. Or get your goon over here to police me and constrain me whenever I do something wrong? He already does that. He threatens me, Silas. He *hurts* me."

Silas spears Jett with a look. He's quiet for a long moment.

"I don't want him following me anymore, Silas. Call off your dog."

"She's been visiting the pool boy," Jett tells him.

*You asshole.*

But it doesn't surprise me that he's loyal to Silas and will use every weapon available to him to control me. "She's been sneaking around."

Silas's eyes smolder.

"He's a friend," I tell Silas. "And I'm allowed to walk around the grounds of my own house and my own garden and talk to whoever I want to talk to, whenever I want to talk to them. That's why we have walls, isn't it? To protect us? I'm not a prisoner, Silas."

"A friend?" My crime is clearly much worse than Jett's.

"A *friend*. Not that it's any of your business."

"I can assure you," Silas says, "that it's very much my business." So now he's going to use this as another reason I need to marry. "If you'd stop to think about it rationally, you'd realize that Wolf Ramsey is not a terrible option. You'll spend time here in Paradise. You'll have more wealth than you could ever spend. Your children will be well taken care of. It's more than most people can ever hope for, Vivi. You'll walk down that aisle on Sunday and you'll marry Wolf Ramsey and that's the end of it. As the oldest, the final decision is mine. You know that."

I don't care anymore, about pleasing him, or any of them. If my family is so willing to throw me under the bus, then to hell with them. "Actually, the final decision is mine. Marriage vows have to be agreed to," I remind him. "You can't force me to say the words. Unlike the rest of you, I don't actually care if the alliance is broken or not. My mother died giving birth to me. To me, it never felt like it could get much worse than that. I'm not afraid of the curse, Silas. If you're so afraid of it, *you* do it. If you were *that* worried about the curse, you wouldn't have knocked up Sasha Silver in the first place. Or was that all just part of the plan?"

With that, I walk toward the door, past Jett.

"Don't touch me," I seethe.

I don't know if they'll even let me get as far as the door. I don't get to find out. Because just then, the door opens.

It's Echo, Blaise and Remington. Everyone's invested in getting these marriages over the line, obviously.

Wolf isn't with them.

Echo notices the look on my face. The tears. The smudged makeup.

Perri is still sobbing on the couch.

The Ramseys walk into the room and Remy closes the door behind him.

"I'm sure this has come as a shock to you both," Remy says. There's actual empathy in him. Unlike Silas. He's a better person, is what I'm realizing. He has integrity. *He* wouldn't expect this of his sisters. For the right reasons, maybe, but not the wrong ones.

I once heard Silas and Malachi talking about Remy's choice to marry the love of his life, a few years ago, which meant he would pass the alliance duty on to one of his siblings.

At the time, they mentioned that the other Ramseys had been willing to do that for him. Because they loved him. They all believed it was the right thing to do, to give him that chance at happiness even if it meant one of them might go without it.

It occurs to me now that my siblings wouldn't have done that for me. None of them would. Silas and Malachi are having too much fun being playboys. Perri always thinks of herself before anyone else, even me, the person she probably cares about most. Even Tatum is too distracted by her glitzy lifestyle and her own freedom—and I can hardly blame her for that.

I wish my family wasn't so broken.

Maybe losing our parents the way we did had that effect. Maybe it made my siblings hard while it made me retreat into myself more than I might have if my mother had lived, who knows. Or maybe they really do resent me, for killing her, even though they've always assured me that it wasn't my fault. Or maybe they're just incapable of anything but decadence and hedonism.

Whatever the reasons, something about the decency and empathy of Remington Ramsey hits me hard. Because it's different to what I'm used to.

*If he's a good person, maybe his brother is too.*

Blaise does something I'm not expecting. She gently wipes some smudged mascara from my cheekbone. It's a kindness with strength behind it. It would be empowering to have a sister like Blaise. No wonder Echo is so grounded and secure in herself.

"He's wild, there's no doubt about that," Blaise says, "but you could do a lot worse, Vivi." She's talking about Wolf, of course. "We thought you might like Echo to show you and Perri to where you'll be staying tonight."

"Thank you." Exhaustion and despair overwhelm me. I can see in the Ramseys' intensity that they believe in the curse. Deeply. They're worried about it. They're afraid of its power.

I've always brushed it off as something foolish. Some weird superstition that belonged in a different time. Something that would never affect me directly.

Here, with them, it feels a lot heavier.

Echo leads us from the room, but not before I glance over to where Jett is standing next to Silas. He gives me an I'll-be-watching-you glare.

Echo shows us to one of the elevators, which takes us up to a foyer area with seven or eight doors leading off of it. She opens one of them into a large living area.

There's a wall of windows, a table and two leather chairs looking out over the view of the pool area and the landscape surrounding it. There's also a small kitchen and three bedrooms, each with its own bathroom.

Perri, who can't stop crying, murmurs a goodnight and disappears into one of the bedrooms, closing the door.

"The way things have happened with Knox and Cassidy took all of us by surprise," Echo says quietly. "Are you okay, Vivi?"

How to answer that? "What if I can't go through with it, Echo? I don't think I can do it. What happens then?"

"I know it's a shock. I'd be shocked too." She hugs me and my eyes fill with fresh tears because it's exactly what I needed. A real hug. "See how you feel tomorrow. We're having a games day."

"Games?"

"Yes. It was supposed to, you know, break the ice. Which might not even be necessary at this point but we'll hang out and people can get to know each other a little better. Then tomorrow night there's a party at Wolf's beach house."

The last thing in the world I feel like doing is playing games or partying.

"Breakfast will be delivered at eight, or you can come downstairs to the breakfast buffet on the lanai if you want to. If I don't see you down there I'll knock on your door at nine and we'll go to my studio. How does that sound? I have some …" Echo pauses, watching my eyes sort of soulfully. "I have a few wedding dresses I've made. I design clothes. I don't know if you knew that."

"I … no, I didn't." Echo, like all the rest of them, considers my marriage as good as a done deal. "But I'm—"

"I can show you my favorite ones."

She's so genuinely kind about how she's handling the topic I don't bother having a tantrum and explaining to her that there's no way in hell I'm marrying her brother.

I don't tell her, either, that I won't be here tomorrow at nine because, between now and then, I will have figured out a way to escape even if it means running off into the night.

I have options.

*Like what?*

There are people I can call on.

*Like who?*

There are places I can run to and hide until this all blows over and they come to their senses.

*Like where?*

I'll figure it out. I have to.

Either way, Wolf Ramsey's sister is a point in his favor.

But it's not his sister who will be in my bed every night.

*I happen to be able to cure even the sassiest attitude into complete, willing submission almost entirely, under the right circumstances.*

Even now, the soft threat affects me in that *way* he has. That fear-infused awareness.

I'm trapped and terrified. If my family—and his—get their way, I'll be married to Wolf Ramsey and completely at the mercy of his brute strength by the end of this weekend.

No one cares if I want any of this to happen or not. None of this is even remotely fair.

I need to figure out a way to reason with them.

There *has* to be a way.

After Echo leaves, I pace for a while.

Who can I call?

I don't want to call Ash. He doesn't have any money. He wouldn't be able to shield me from my family. I would only be putting him in danger.

Would Lana help me? Very unlikely.

Cody? Maybe. But then he'd lose his job.

I'll find Tatum. I'll explain to her that I want to buy some things for the wedding. Yes. She might believe that. She'll lend me her credit card and I'll sneak out of the castle and find a way to escape.

But when I check the door of the apartment we're staying in, it's locked.

*Damn it.*

I try calling Tatum's number. It rings ten times before going to voicemail.

I really am trapped.

I go to the sliding glass doors that lead out to the balcony. They're unlocked.

Quietly, I slide the door open enough to squeeze through. Glancing down, I see that I'm three stories up. Down below, Jett is standing there, leaning against a wall, looking up at me.

# 5

# WOLF

It's late and the party is starting to wind down. Malachi Fitzpatrick and Aurora King haven't officially announced it yet but they're practically having sex on one of the loungers so it seems like the second marriage is as good as locked in.

I wonder how Blaise is feeling. If any of the Kings would be bearable for her. It's unlikely.

Vivi disappeared a while ago. As soon as she was told the news by Silas, in fact.

I would have told her myself but Silas beat me to it, not that it would have made a difference either way. It's not like she would have preferred to hear it from me.

She ran off, no doubt in a state of terror and devastation. If I thought it would help to go after her, maybe I would. Poor little princess. She knows what's coming. Or at least some of what's coming.

My future wife might have a buried feistiness somewhere

behind all that innocence but she's also broken. Spooked and subjugated into a shadow of who she could be. She's trapped under the weight of her family's control, that's obvious.

This bothers me. More than that. It fucking infuriates me.

I've never fully trusted Silas Fitzpatrick and even less now. He's a bully. Malachi's more laid-back but I've never met anyone so dedicated to his own immediate self-gratification.

And I'm suddenly invested in whatever effect their behavior is having on their youngest sister.

I've stepped up to protect my family, that's the only reason. I can take what I want from my nubile little wife and live my life exactly as I always have.

But now that I've offered myself to the alliance—and to Vivi—some protective instinct has taken hold inside me. I've always been fiercely protective of my family.

*She'll* be my family. In a matter of days.

She'll be my *wife*.

And I don't fucking like how scared she is, of everyone and everything.

It's true I sometimes get off on women's fear. Mainly because they don't *stay* afraid. On some level they know their fear is about to be overridden by so much pleasure they'll forget all about the fear.

Vivi's fear was different. Layered. Compounded by years of oppression and control.

I don't know if I'm capable of love. But if there's one

thing I know I *am* capable of, it's protection. The flare of it I suddenly feel for Vivi Fitzpatrick is an unfamiliar one, only because it's surprisingly ferocious.

*My wife.*

The thought is jarring.

And not completely unappealing.

Those full, pouting lips and those wide, golden eyes. Those taut little nipples high on her creamy breasts. The lush curves of her body that are too sultry for the way she feels about herself.

Her insolent little question. *What were you expecting?*

Not *that*. Not the kind of sassy-innocent, dazzling, straight-to-gut beauty that could bring you to your goddamn knees.

Those fuckers are going to leave her alone. Even if I can't give her a marriage of love, at least I can free her. I can make sure her light is allowed to shine brighter, without getting eclipsed by her self-centered family's over-fed egos.

The temptation of her feels like a new, addictive craving.

She's somewhere inside the castle.

*I could find her. I could break into her room.*

The ugly sister is probably with her.

My little virgin would be terrified to find me in her bed, but she'll get over it as soon as I start to enlighten her.

Would she scream before I could?

Probably. Anyway, she'll be mine to do what I please with, by the end of the weekend.

Patience isn't something I'm good at. I force myself to

make my way up to my apartment to sleep for a few hours, climbing up the circular staircase of the turret.

The small space is made almost entirely of windows. It holds my bed, an old leather chair that looks out over the view, a wooden wardrobe and a weapons rack.

I don't bother turning on the light. I strip down and lay on my bed but I can't sleep.

The moon is low and the night sky is tinted with the faintest lavender glow along the horizon line where it meets the night-black ocean water, flickering with moonlight. I check my phone. It's 3:27 a.m.

I can't sleep.

*Somewhere here in the castle, she's asleep. What does she wear to bed? A tight little top and panties? Those full, perfect tits will be filling it, straining against it. Her soft nipples will be poking against the fabric. Her pink, untouched pussy will be warm and damp and sugar-sweet. I want to taste her. I want to lick her clit and suck on her until she's coming in my mouth.*

My cock is hard and hot, thick with throbbing agony. I've gone too long without and the thought of Vivi Fitzpatrick's luscious innocence is too much to bear.

*I'll make her come first so she's soft and so wet I'll be able to slide deep into her slick, clenching tightness.*

It takes only a few strokes and I'm coming hard. Hot cum spurts all over my stomach. An absolute flood of it.

*Fuck.*

I lay in the dark for a while, breathing heavily as I come down from all that.

*Goddamn it.* I don't know if I've ever come so hard in my life.

My new wife-to-be is having an effect on me I'm not sure I want.

*If you don't like my attitude then maybe you should go and find someone more 'pleasing.'*

I'd told her that would be impossible, half joking at the time. But now, at the memory of her, what I'm realizing is that it's true. I've never had such a visceral reaction to a woman. Even now, the memory of her petulant mouth, her seraphic face and her absurdly sweet body is having its way with me.

Knowing she's close by is so tempting. Those pouting lips with too much red lipstick, just begging to be kissed— and I don't kiss. It's giving too much. It always felt more inti-mate than I ever wanted to get.

*Not this time. I want to slide my tongue deep into her mouth. I want to devour her.*

Those curves, of a girl who's just recently bloomed into full-blown, lush, fertile-as-fuck womanhood.

*My wife.*

*I'm going to fucking pump her full of my gushing cum. I want to breed her until she's full with my baby.*

Fuck.

What the hell is happening here?

I almost do it.

I could seduce her while she's asleep. I have a master key to all the rooms. I can be stealthy. She'll think she's dreaming me. By the time she realizes I'm real, she'll already be coming. I'll make it so good she'll be moaning and begging for it.

*I could steal her. Bring her up here. Tie her up so she can't run. Eat her pussy like the starving beast I am until she's moaning and coming hard. Then I'll slide my big cock into that tight, juicy—*

Goddamn it.

I need to get a grip.

Even though I just came ridiculously hard, my cock stirs again, thickening hotly. I need relief. It comes, in another rush, until my stomach is literally covered in my own cum.

But the relief doesn't last. Somehow, it barely touches the edges.

I need more.

*I want to taste her. I want to slake my raging lust all over her. I need her.*

This is crazy. I feel like a fully loaded weapon of mass destruction, pointed at one sassy little virgin target.

It's sudden and unexpected.

Something about her is getting under my skin.

*She's more than under your skin, you lunatic. You're already fucking obsessed with her.*

My phone vibrates from the pocket of my jeans, which are on the chair, out of reach. I groan and get up. Fuck, I'm a mess.

I don't know why I'm bothering to answer it. It's probably some chick who somehow got a hold of my number. It occurs to me that I could meet up with one of them, before the wedding. Take the edge off whatever's happening to me.

*Fuck no.* The thought of it makes me feel like punching a fucking wall. I have no idea why.

Okay, I do know why. Everything about me has already made a decision about who it wants. My craving to find her again and feast on her sassy perfection is burning me up.

Pulling the phone out of my jeans pocket, the screen is lit with Remy's name. A surge of adrenaline hits my bloodstream. He'd never call at 5 a.m. unless something was wrong. "Remy. What's up?"

"Wolf, get down here. Meet me at the helicopter."

"Why? What's happening?"

"It's Knox. Cassidy ran up to the caves last night and he followed her. They were attacked by Axel Archer and his recruits."

"What? Are they hurt?"

"They killed Axel."

"Holy fuck."

"Yeah. And two other Arrow recruits. Knox got tasered a couple times but he's okay. Cassidy wasn't hurt but she's badly shaken. Knox said he's got something to show us that changes everything."

"What is it?"

"I don't know. Come now. We're leaving as soon as you can get down here."

He ends the call and I grab a towel and do my best to clean myself up before pulling on some clothes and strapping two different fully-loaded weapons belts across my chest.

By the time I get down to the helicopter pad, the propellors are already starting up and Remy's got a posse assembled. Blaise. Malachi. Stone. Jagger. Hana, our cousin's wife who's a doctor.

We take off and fly over the hills of our ranch, over the boundary wall, where the landscape rises up to steep, craggy mountains. There are a series of caves etched into the northeastern cliff face that have a view out over the ranch and the beach. A couple of natural pools sit next to them and there's a clearing nearby, which is where we land.

We all jump out and it's a crazy scene. Axel Archer is dead, shot through the heart and lying in a pool of his own blood. Our nemesis was also, as it turned out, Cassidy's landlord in Honolulu. He tried to force himself on her. She told us that when she first arrived here. She retaliated and escaped, which is why she ended up here in Kauai the first place. It's also why he came after her.

Knox and Cassidy are sitting together near the larger of the two pools. Knox is holding her on his lap. They both look dazed. Knox is still gripping our old Remington, the one that once belonged to our great great great grandfather, whose name was Nathaniel.

There's some poetic justice in this, I guess. Our grandfather killed Axel's grandfather exactly the same way, which is partly how the whole fucking feud first started.

Two other Arrow recruits have also been fatally shot.

A priest is standing nearby, clutching a bible and mumbling prayers in a low mumble. He seems almost out of his mind with the residual terror. He's in his own little world.

A third Arrow recruit has been shot in the leg. He's

bleeding badly but he's still alive, sitting up, leaning against a tree. I walk over to him, click off the safety and point my Glock at his face.

"Wolf!" Cassidy cries. "No! *Please!* Stop!"

"Don't do it, Wolf," Knox growls. "He saved our lives. Cassidy knows him."

I turn to stare at my brother and his ... whatever she is. His lover. His chosen one. The way his arms are wrapped around her protectively and the look on his face make it clear that he would do anything to keep her safe. And to keep her. His eyes are bloodshot but determined. He's as resolute as I've ever seen him.

"Crew is a friend," Cassidy says. "Hana, please help him."

Hana rushes past me with her medical bag and kneels next to the guy.

The others are gathering around Knox and Cassidy. My brother looks strung out as fuck, not surprisingly.

"You all right, man?" I ask him.

"Come here, Wolf," he says. "Remy. Blaise. Jagger. All of you." To Cassidy he says, "I'm going to show them now, sweetheart. All right? They need to see this."

She stares up into his eyes like he's the answer to all her prayers and maybe he is. It's obvious the feeling is mutual.

Then she leans against him wearily and Knox pulls her long, white-blond hair aside and lowers the back of the blood-stained dress she's wearing. Inked between her shoulder blades is a small circular tattoo.

We all take a closer look.

Stone King reaches out to touch it. Knox tenses but he allows this.

I recognize it. We all do. We've seen it on the wax seal that was on every piece of correspondence sent by Jethro King over the years. We used to comment on it, on how old-fashioned his style was, to send letters with a seal of wax on them. No one else we knew did that kind of thing. It felt like something out of movie or a history book. We used to study the pattern of it. The pictures etched into it. A sun. A turtle. A fish hook. They're all there, on this intricate tattoo.

"It's our father's seal," Stone says.

Jagger steps closer too and the realization clicks into place for all of us.

"Holy shit," Jagger gasps. "This means …"

Knox's voice is rasped. "It means she's your sister, Jagger. Your mother was Cassidy's mother. And Jethro is her father. It means she's a King. It means we're getting married. And it means Cassidy and I will be the ones to secure the King-Ramsey alliance."

Blaise looks stunned. Wide-eyed and wildly relieved.

Malachi is grinning. "Well, fuck me."

I'm staggered by the flare of my own possessiveness. "I'm still marrying Vivi," I hear myself say. "Tomorrow."

*You can't stop me,* is what I'm thinking. *She's mine.*

Malachi adds, "And I already proposed to Aurora, last night. So that's all three marriages decided."

This is a crazy twist. I'm happy for Knox, and for Blaise. And weirdly, for myself. One thing's clear in my mind: *no one's going to stop me from making Vivi Fitzpatrick my wife.*

I don't know where the fuck my new obsession is coming from, but I'm feeling it.

From the shock, probably, of what just happened here, Cassidy swoons against Knox and loses consciousness. He lifts her and carries her to the helicopter with more care than I've ever seen my brother give anything or anyone.

The gravity of his devotion hits me in an unfamiliar way. I watch him as everyone climbs on board the helicopter. We take off. He smooths her hair and murmurs low words to her until she wakes. The two of them spend the whole ride back to the castle staring into each other's eyes.

Something about the whole thing makes my chest sort of ache.

And even though I've spent a lifetime knowing for a fact that I'm not the kind of person who's ever going to fall in love, it almost makes me wonder what that level of awe would *feel* like.

# 6

# Vivi

TAP TAP TAP.

*I'm near the pool and the moon is huge and bright. I'm being hunted, I can feel this. I start to run but the night is so murky and thick, it's like trying to run through a veil of invisible gauze. He's gaining on me. I can't see his face but the blue of his eyes glows in the moonlight. I trip and fall and my heart is beating fast. He's behind me and I don't want him to catch me. Except that some fiery flare inside me does. There's a visceral excitement to his danger. He's all around me. His presence consumes me like a cloud of heavy warmth. This warmth feels … good. More than good. It's touching me in the most intimate place imaginable and … something's happening. The feeling is indescribable. I'm on the verge of … I don't know what. Oh my God, I'm going to—*

Tap tap tap.

*The noise causes him to slow his chase. The darkness begins to swallow him but I can feel his promise: he'll be back. His eyes are bright with this warning. Then he's gone. He's taken his pleasure-warmth with him and I want to cry. Give it back. Don't go.*

"Vivi?"

My eyes blink open.

It takes me a few seconds to remember where I am. I'm breathing heavily and my skin is dewy with a light sweat.

The Ramseys.

Paradise.

I'm on Kauai.

It's Echo. She's in my room and she's opening the curtains a crack. A gentle, golden beam of sunlight streams into the plush bedroom. It's simply decorated but everything is tasteful and calming. If I was capable of being calmed. Which I'm not.

I cried myself to sleep last night. I'm still fully clothed, laying on top of the tangled covers.

Even so, I'm very aware of a lingering sweet, wet pulse. *There.*

God.

"Hi," Echo says. She's brought a tray with a coffee plunger and some fruit and bread. She's wearing a pair of cut-off jean shorts and a cute white lacy halter top that shows off her olive skin and her slender figure.

"Hi."

She sits on the far side of the huge bed. "I'm sorry. I let myself in and I had to wake you. It's nine o'clock and I couldn't wait a second longer. I have huge news. That must have been some dream, by the way. What were you dreaming about?"

"Oh. It was nothing. A nightmare."

Her smile is mischievous. "It didn't sound like a nightmare."

I'm still dazed from the intensity of my dream. And I'm hardly going to tell her who I was dreaming about. *Or what he was about to do.* So I try to change the subject. "What's the news?"

"You're not going to believe what happened." Echo notices that I'm still in my sequined dress, my make-up no doubt smudged and smeared, my suitcases standing untouched and unopened in the corner of the room, but she doesn't comment.

"What happened?" I sit up a little and lean against the padded headboard.

*I was so close to … whatever that was. It would have happened. The dream man—him—would have made it happen …*

Echo is bursting with whatever news she's dying to share. "Last night, after Cassidy left the party, she ran up to these caves that are on the other side of our boundary wall, up the cliff that looks out over the castle. And Knox knew where she'd run to so he went after her—"

"Why did she leave?" But I can guess. Perri might have said something to her. She would have told Cassidy about the curse, I'm sure of it. She would have tried to convince Cassidy that Perri should be the one to marry Knox. For his family's sake.

Echo doesn't know Perri as well as I do. "We don't know," she says. "But when they got to the caves, they got ambushed. By Arrow. By Axel Archer himself and a few of his Arrow thugs."

My stomach swoops with horror at the shocking thought. "What?" Arrow has always been our biggest threat. Axel is the mastermind and the ringleader of the crime ring that targets my family—and Echo's family—and has for as long as I can remember. According to Silas and Malachi, they're always looking for opportunities to kidnap me or my sisters, so Axel can marry back into the alliance. He and his recruits are the reason I have so much security whenever I go anywhere. The same would be true for Echo. "Are Knox and Cassidy okay? Where are they?"

"They're okay. They're back here now. You're not going to believe this, but they *killed* Axel. And two of his men."

I stare at her in mute shock. "They did?"

"Yeah. Knox shot him in the chest. It was a direct hit to his heart."

"Echo. Oh my God."

"I know. The reason Axel was hunting for Cassidy is because he used to be her landlord, in Honolulu. One night, just a few weeks ago, he broke into her apartment and tried to … well, to force himself on her. So she stabbed him and ran. But not before he saw the tattoo on her back."

"*Force* her? But she got away?"

"She did. She stabbed him in the stomach and got away from him. It wasn't deep enough to cause any major damage but it gave her enough time to escape. That was when she came to Kauai. To hide. She found the caves and she climbed over the wall looking for food. That's when Knox saw her and he chased after her."

"Wow. Is that how they met?"

"Yes. She was disguised. They almost killed each other in the process. And they also fell in love. Like, instantly, as soon as he saw her face, he said. But she has this tattoo she kept hidden from him the whole time because she never knew what it was and she was afraid of what it might mean. She was an orphan and she was in foster care for most of her life and she never knew who her parents were. And she thought the tattoo might be something bad. Like she might be part of Arrow or some other secret society or cult. So she never showed it to anyone. But Axel saw it when he attacked her and he knew what it was. That's another reason he was so determined to find Cassidy."

"What is it? What does it mean?"

"You're not going to believe this, Vivi. It's Jethro King's seal. *Jethro King* is Cassidy's father. She's a King. And her mother is Jagger's mother."

I stare at her, in disbelief. "She's a *King*?"

"Yes."

"So that means—"

"It means Blaise won't have to marry one of them. Knox and Cassidy can make the link."

It's a lot to absorb. This is huge news. I think about how devastated Perri will be. But I can't feel too sad about that. Perri and Knox's marriage wouldn't ever have turned out to be a happy one. You could see by the way he looked at her that he *really* didn't want to marry her.

And I have my own life to worry about. Because one thing remains crystal clear: Cassidy's revelation is good for Knox and Cassidy—but it doesn't get me out of marrying Wolf Ramsey. "So all three marriages are arranged now."

"Yes." She's careful about it, but I can also detect that she's happy. For Blaise. For Knox. And maybe, for Wolf. She knows I'm being forced into something I don't want to do. She also believes in the curse. She thinks my sacrifice will save our families from whatever might happen to us if we don't honor it. She respects me for what I'm about to do.

And there's more to it than that. *She's* not scared of Wolf. He's her brother. She loves him and she trusts him. As wild and fierce as he might be, she thinks I could do a lot worse.

She's also offering herself as my friend. My sister-to-be. My support.

This means something.

I'm glad she's here but I don't know how to feel.

Dread.

Fury, at my family for putting me in this position in the first place.

Terror, because tomorrow night is going to be my *wedding night*.

Ruffled, *because I can still feel the effects of my dream. Of him.*

And something else: a tiny but still detectable sense of empowerment. I don't know why. Because my "killing machine" husband might protect me from the people I'm starting to realize I've been intimidated by my whole life. My oldest brother, who controls me. And his bodyguard, who's too rough and whose threats are lewd and disturbing. The bullying is nothing new, it's just gotten worse lately.

I'll have someone new to be scared of.

And I'm still trying to process everything Echo just told me. "I can't believe they *killed* Axel. I can't believe Cassidy's a *King*."

"I know. It's crazy."

"Does Jethro know?"

"They were getting ready to call him."

Echo pours us both mugs of steaming black coffee and hands me one. "Vivi?"

"Yeah?"

"Wolf won't be back until later this afternoon. He and a few of our cousins are … taking care of the evidence."

"Oh." I guess that means they're doing something about Axel and the two other men.

"At sea," she says softly.

Our eyes meet and this bonds us a little more. Neither one of us is new to this kind of thing, unfortunately. Our families are wealthy, powerful and very visible. An organized mob has spent four generations trying to steal our money and kidnap us in order to do things to us that are too terrifying to think about—but we do anyway, every time we leave our houses.

Sometimes, when the threats get too close, extreme measures have to be taken. Unpleasant matters need to be dealt with. Even I know that, and I'm protected from the worst of it.

"There's a party at his beach house later," she tells me.

"Until then, I want to take you down to my studio, like we talked about. Do you want to?"

*To try on wedding dresses.* I sigh, without meaning to.

"It doesn't mean you still can't change your mind," she offers.

Despite everything, Echo is easy to be with. We finish our coffee and eat some of the food she brought. I take a quick shower. A short time later, she's leading me down a curving staircase and through the lower levels of the castle, to one of the more modern wings.

Her studio is a small but enchanting space. Three of the walls are exposed brick and the ceiling is painted a dark charcoal gray. Two long wooden tables are covered in sewing machines and garments in various stages of creation. Above them are rows of pendant lights. She flicks a switch and the room fills with warm light.

Racks of clothing line the walls and cloth mannequins are wearing more half-completed garments. There's so much going on, you get the feeling Echo's head is exploding with ideas. She's got at least twenty projects on the go.

The fourth wall is a single pane of thick glass that looks out over an orchard. Beyond it, I can see the Ramsey's high stone border wall and a steep hill beyond it.

I wonder if that's the route Cassidy took last night. She's brave, to take off like that without any protection. But then, by what Echo described, Cassidy has had to be brave her whole life. It's hard to imagine how hard her life must have been. Not knowing who your family is. Being completely alone. I'm glad for her, that she's discovered such a huge piece of who she is. And that she's found Knox, who's clearly besotted with her to the extreme. You can't help feeling like she deserves her happily ever after.

The thought gives me a small pang of … sadness, I guess. That I'll probably never get mine. I don't care how much Echo loves her brother—*or* what I dreamed about. I'm still being forced into a marriage with a man who scares the hell out of me, because everyone else in my family is too selfish to step up.

More than likely, I'm doomed to a loveless marriage that'll be nothing more than a piece of paper, and one that's somehow supposed to shield us from whatever tragedy they're all so afraid of.

Silas mentioned that I can … stray, if I want to.

*You'll be free to do whatever you want … on the side.*

Which means that Wolf Ramsey will be too.

More than likely he's a player. I mean, he's clearly the kind of man who could get any woman he wanted. He's a bad-boy fighter, built like a specimen of pumped-up manhood, who also happens to have more land and money than God. Crack to women who happen to *like* bullies.

If I can't figure out a way to disappear before tomorrow afternoon, I could still run away with Ash, marriage or no marriage. And do all the things I was planning to do.

Some sixth sense tells me that my new husband-to-be would track me down.

For now, I let Echo show me the dresses she's made and I have to admit, she's amazingly talented.

"This is the one I was thinking of," she says, taking a

dress from a rack. "It's actually the design of the dress I'd like to get married in, one day, if it ever happens. But I think you should have it, Vivi, if you want it. Maybe it'll bring you good luck."

Something I'm going to need a lot of.

The dress is made almost entirely of white satin, with an embroidered fitted bodice and delicate straps. The dress is floor length, with a long satin train. It's classic but has a modern, stylish twist. She's even made a matching veil of white lace.

"It's beautiful, Echo. But I don't want to take your dress." I stop myself from continuing, *Or get married. Or have anything to do with your brother.*

"It's your dress now, if you want it. It feels like it was meant for you. We're probably the same size. I'll have to adjust the fit of the bodice, but I can do that tonight. Do you like it, Vivi?"

It's sort of perfect—*if* I wanted to get married. Which I very definitely don't.

*Would Echo help me if I was honest with her? If I got down on my knees and begged?*

But I stop myself from asking her for that. It would be asking her to curse her family. "It's a beautiful dress," I manage.

"Here. Try it on. That way I can measure it and make the adjustments." The bodice is made for Echo and my boobs are bigger than hers.

As I stand in front of the mirror in a wedding dress, Echo measures and adjusts. And the gravity of this whole situation hits me hard. Another panicky urge hits me. *Run,* my instincts are screaming.

*They're going to force me to do it.*

*I'm getting married.*

Tomorrow.

To Wolf Ramsey.

I feel numb. Like a bird trapped in my gilded cage. As I always have been. The cage has taken on a slightly different shape but it's still a cage. It's still a trap I can't escape from.

But I'm not married *yet*, I remind myself. I still have time. I'll figure out a way to leave. I'll hide. I don't have money on me but I'll figure something out. I could disguise myself. Cassidy did, why can't I? She stabbed a crime lord, caught a flight to a different island and hid out in some caves on top of a cliff. There's no reason I can't at least try to take my own path.

Everyone is only one choice away from a completely different life and here's mine. Here's my choice.

*I'm going to do it.*

"I know this is easy for me to say because it's not me," Echo says, reading my anxiety, "and I know he seems crazily intimidating. But he's the most loyal person I know. And he wouldn't have agreed to marry you if he didn't want to do it. He might surprise you."

"Maybe he will."

I remember thinking it, just yesterday, and the feeling has been taking hold more and more insistently lately: I'm going to rebel against the people who control me. I just don't when yet, or how.

*Tonight.*

But what I'm also realizing is that some little kernel has lodged itself inside me. Wolf Ramsey might be a rough, lethal fighting machine. But he'll also protect me. From my own family. Including my creepy thug of a cousin.

And Echo and Blaise would become my sisters. The thought comforts me, despite the glaring reality that tomorrow night—if I can't somehow figure out a way to get out of it—I'll definitely be well and truly getting my halo about as dirty as it can get.

ECHO and I spend most of the day hanging out. She makes adjustments to my dress and I try on some of her other designs. She's amazingly good. "You could start your own line," I tell her. "I could help you promote it if you wanted to."

"Thanks, Vivi. Maybe in a year or two. For now, I like doing it for myself and Blaise and a few friends. And now I can do it for you. Blaise keeps telling me I should take it to the next level. And I will soon. I feel like I'm still finding my style, as a designer."

We spend the next few hours opening up to each other about our lives, in ways that come surprisingly easily. The pressures of social media. Friends we have in common. The crazy plot twist surrounding Cassidy and Knox.

We click, and I think about how I really would like to have her as a sister. I haven't had a conversation like this with one of my own sisters since we were children. Now, they're too absorbed with their own careers to take the time to open up.

The only topic we avoid is my looming wedding.

"Do you ..." Echo hesitates before asking it. "... have a boyfriend, Vivi?"

No one in my family bothered to ask me a question like that because they know I don't. They actively enforce it. I guess it makes sense now. If I was involved with someone else, that would complicate things.

Which makes me think about Ash. I don't mention him to Echo because there's no reason to. "No."

This is clearly good news to her. She smiles and continues working on the dress.

*Would Ash run away with me?*

*Would I want him to?*

*Would Wolf chase after me?*

There are so many unknowns. I have no idea what's going to happen or what I even *want* to happen—maybe because every decision about my life has always been made for me.

Will my new husband, if I go through with this, demand the same control? I almost ask Echo. But she can't really know how he'd be as a husband. She can't know whether or not he'll force me into total submission—which he's basically already promised to do.

*I happen to be able to cure even the sassiest attitude into complete, willing submission almost entirely, under the right circumstances.*

*Willing.* It's a word that stands out in the memory of his darkly playful warning.

Would I ever be willing?

*According to your dream, yes. Very.*

God. If only I could have some more time, to work through all this. It's too fast and too much to think about.

"There was a brigade of stylists making a bee-line for your room early this morning," Echo tells me. "They were incredibly pushy. I don't know how you stand that. But I told them—emphatically—to take the day off. I figured you could use a break from all that."

This almost makes me feel emotional. One of my own siblings would never have done that for me. They always see my staging as an opportunity for more publicity, more visibility, more of a chance to get ourselves seen. "Thank you, Echo. I can definitely use a break from all that."

"Why do you put up with it?" she asks me gently.

This question is difficult to answer. "I don't know." But it shines a light on some of the reasons I *do* put up with it— and they're reasons that didn't even occur to me until now. From here, in the safety of Echo's studio, inside a castle where my family *isn't* in control, I can see my whole life from a different vantage point.

*I put up with it because I'm scared to stand up to them. Because now that I look back on it, my brother's thug bruises me all the time. He has since we were children, whenever I acted out and Silas wanted to keep me in line. They bully me into submission with violence and they always have.*

A memory resurfaces. Of a day at the beach with my

sisters. I was around eight years old and our bodyguards were nearby but they weren't as attentive as usual. I was playing with some other children, a group of boys. They were staying at the resort next door, one of them told me. We were building sandcastles.

*They punished me for that. Jett slapped me hard and made me cry. They locked me in my room. They told me I wasn't ever allowed to play with boys.*

Wow.

I'd forgotten about that.

I must have buried it in some protective psychological cage.

*They've hurt me. They've beaten me down. It's the reason I often feel so sad and scared. Jett is abusive and Silas allows it because it keeps me quiet and subdued. For the exact reason of keeping me available. I've always been the sacrifice.*

I can feel other memories trying to resurface. Pleading with Silas to let me visit friends and go on dates in high school, like my friends did. He never allowed it. He said it was too dangerous. There were too many threats.

*He wanted to keep me "pure" so he could offer me to the curse. It was his plan all along.*

"Here," Echo says, holding up another dress, maybe reading something in my silence. "Try this one on. If you like it you can wear it to the party tonight." Her phone chirps and she checks her messages. "It's Blaise. They couldn't do the games day because of what happened with Knox and Cassidy. But they've got a bonfire on the beach starting up and they have some food trucks parked down there. The party has already started. Some of the men are showing off their MMA skills on the beach."

"They're fighting?" My stomach curls uneasily.

"They can't help themselves. My brothers spend a lot of time training. But Wolf isn't back yet, Blaise said. And Knox and Cassidy are still in his apartment. We probably won't see them tonight. Your brothers train in MMA too, right?"

"Sometimes. But I'm sure they're nowhere near as good as your brothers."

"My brothers are obsessed," she admits. "That's basically all they do." Not, as it happens, something I want to think about too carefully. *He'll be freakishly strong. It was obvious by the way his shirt was straining against his big, toned muscles.* "Wolf's beach house is, like, the party central of Paradise. He lets everyone just come and go as they please and there are always a lot of people hanging out there. We should go down there soon."

The dress she's given me to try on is white with pink flowers embroidered into the fabric. It's a sleeveless halter top with built in support that sort of lifts and plumps my boobs, accentuating them even more than last night's dress.

"Maybe this is a little over the top." I really have filled out over the last year or so.

"It's totally *not* over the top. It's *so* flattering, Vivi. It fits you like an absolute dream."

I guess it does, but I feel self-conscious. The dress doesn't leave much to the imagination.

"You *have* to wear that one. I'd put a flower behind your ear but since you're not married yet … let's wait."

In Hawaii, the tradition is for girls to wear flowers behind their right ear if they're available and behind their left if they're spoken for. But it's true, it would be sort of awkward either way. Does a forced engagement count as being "spoken for"?

Echo's dress is green and summery. She's petite and gorgeous.

When we leave her studio, closing the door behind us, I notice someone standing outside the door, leaning up against the wall and scrolling on his phone.

*Jett.*

I get that sick, scared lurch in my stomach I always get when I see him.

"W-what are you doing here?" *Damn it.* My voice sounds shaky. I hate how he's able to unsettle me so easily and reduce me to a pathetic, stuttering mess—every time. And of course I already know the answer to my own stupid question. He's following me, making sure I don't try to escape.

"Ensuring your safety," he says. After hanging out with Echo all day, my cousin looks huge and ominous.

The peacefulness of our time together is suddenly, jarringly gone. I also notice that fear isn't the only emotion I'm feeling. I'm *angry*, and it's not something I had the luxury of, before now. Before, I had no one on my side. Now, it almost feels like I do. And it makes me feel stronger.

"Who's this?" asks Echo, noticing my reaction to him. Her gaze slides from him, to me, and back to Jett again.

"No one we need to worry about." It's rude and this gets Echo's attention, but she's picked up on my anxiety. As we walk past Jett, I tell him, "I told Silas I didn't want you following me."

"I'm just looking after Silas's best interests. And yours. You know that." Jett has a distinctive voice. It's not as deep as you might expect from a man of his size. It doesn't quite match his stocky burliness. "Which means I'll be watching you like a hawk until it's signed on the dotted line, sweetheart."

Sweetheart?

*Asshole!* "Don't call me that." He's always crossing a line, the one that has all my internal red flags waving. "Fuck off, Jett."

Wow.

I would never have been bold enough to say that to him, even yesterday. My fury feels *good*.

Echo weaves her arm through mine. "Come on, Vivi, we'll take my dune buggy." To Jett, off-handedly, "Sorry, there are only two seats."

I kind of love that she's picked up on at least some of what's going on here and she's not intimidated by him in the slightest. Maybe that comes from never having to fear any of the people in your life. I wish I could be as brave as she is.

Echo leads me through an archway to a buggy parked under a palm tree. Once we're out of earshot, she asks, "Who *is* that guy?"

"My cousin. Well, not actually my cousin. He's Silas's bodyguard. And mine, sort of, even though I don't want him to be. He's making sure I don't bolt before the alliance can be sealed."

Echo gives me a soulful look as she starts up the buggy. "Would you if you could, Vivi?"

I don't know how to answer that. *Yes.* "I don't know."

"It's so crazy and unfair," she says. "I hate the alliance."

"You and me both."

She drives us down a sandy path toward the beach and I marvel again at the beauty of the view. The rolling green landscape. The turquoise water and the wispy white clouds. It really is a view a person could get used to.

Maybe I'll be okay. Maybe I'll be able to avoid my new husband and just hang out with his sister all the time.

*During the day, maybe. But what about the nights?*

The sun hangs low over the ocean, painting it a silver-edged, shimmery orange.

We're getting close to the beach and my heart starts beating faster. He might be here by now.

*My big, buff "killing machine" of a fiancé.*

I try to identify the emotions coursing through my veins. Terror. A fluttery restlessness. A layered kind of anticipation. My dream is replaying itself through my mind and it skews my fear of him into something closer to … curiosity, maybe.

*It was a dream, Vivi. The reality is going to be far different and most likely a lot more brutal. Don't delude yourself. Run while you still can.*

An enormous lone house comes into view. It's right on the beach, standing on sturdy stilts. It's high tide and waves lick the sand underneath it, where the stilts prop it high enough to be safe from surges. A expansive lanai runs the length of the house with steps leading down onto the sand.

The huge first story of the house is plantation style but there's a second story that's much more modern in design, made of glass, stone and salt-weathered wood. The top story is as big as the lower story and there's a second lanai off the front of it with chairs and a blue umbrella that are the exact same color as the ocean water.

The Ramseys seem to have a thing for buildings with more than one architectural style, I've noticed. Our whole estate is basically uniform in its design, so this detail stands out to me.

Paradise is eccentric, in the best kind of way. I love this about it. The buildings and the way they're decorated are stylish and unique—and clearly no expense has been spared. The riot of tropical orchards and gardens are creatively put together. The horses graze in herds like wild mustangs. The cute town center and the winding roads are charming and well thought-out. Even the way the Ramseys dress shows off their confidence. They seem to run with their inspiration, in whatever direction it takes them.

Their lives have a sense of freedom to them that ours lack.

Or at least that *mine* lacks.

Weirdly, this reminds me of my mother. Whenever people describe her to me from their memories, they so often used the word "eccentric."

She had to have her own haven built so she could express herself inside its private walls, with her library full of romantic books and the art that was too whimsical and expressive to be exhibited in public areas of the estate. She had a fun, quirky style that didn't match the über-luxurious vision of the decorators.

So that's the way I think of her: as someone who looked almost exactly like me, who was eccentric. *I'm* eccentric too, much more than anyone else in my family. I haven't had much of a chance to run with that side of myself, but it's there.

My mother was a caged bird, like me. It makes me sad that she never got to fly.

And I suddenly want to make sure I *do* fly. As a tribute to her, if nothing else.

*Fuck all of them and their control over me. I can fight back.*

The flare of my own rebellion almost shocks me.

*I will. Tonight.*

*I just have to figure out how. And when. And what to do.*

As my emotions and my resolve sort of churn inside my brain, I can't help but be spellbound by this house. The plantation-style first floor is perfect. And the modern second floor is beautifully sleek. The way the two fit together shouldn't work at all, but it totally does.

I *love* this house.

It's surrounded by a scenic cove with a high waterfall that splashes into a raised, naturally-formed freshwater pool. There are three giant palm trees that are perfectly placed, offering their shade.

I can see why all of Paradise wants to hang out here.

*Okay, another damn point in his favor. His house is freaking awesome.*

The music is loud and the party is already pumping.

It's crowded. Close to around a hundred people are here. The dance music gives the place a party vibe. Some people are hanging out on the lanai with drinks in their hand. Some are swimming. A few surfers are catching waves.

There are a lot of people I don't recognize. Extended family and friends of the Ramseys, no doubt. Maybe they're allowing us to mix more widely because the alliance marriages have now been decided. As we get closer I can spot all the siblings from the three alliance families except for three.

Knox and Cassidy.

And Wolf. He's not here yet.

I'm relieved.

A makeshift sparring ring has been marked out on the sand with a roughly-drawn line. Remy and Malachi are locked in a clinch and a circle of people is gathered around them.

Three food trucks are parked nearby. The scent of grilling meat reminds me that I haven't eaten since breakfast.

We pull up near the house. We climb out of the buggy and I follow Echo to where the crowd is watching the fighters, cheering them on.

"I really don't get why they need to do this all the time," Echo muses.

It's daunting to watch them fight. Malachi is 6'2" and strong. He's probably the most athletic of all of us. He's always working out, mostly so he can show off his muscles on Instagram.

Remy is a different animal altogether. He's built in a way that's less gym junkie and more rugged mountain man. He's so skilled it's mesmerizing to watch. It seems like he's playing with Malachi, just to keep the audience entertained. He gets Malachi into some kind of complicated-looking hold that looks painful.

"*Fuck*," Malachi howls. "Okay, *okay*. Mercy, man. You win. Jesus."

Remy releases his hold and climbs to his feet, barely winded. They're both covered in sand and Malachi's lip is bleeding.

Someone hands Remy a beer and he takes a long swig. There's not a thing about Remy Ramsey that's pretentious or false. A staunch realness sort of clings to him. He doesn't smile, even though the people talking to him and congratulating him are making jokes and slapping him on the back. He's strong and he's honorable, you can just see this.

I can't help thinking that this oldest brother is another point in my new fiancé's favor. You know for a fact Remy Ramsey would be a good person to have on your side in life.

"Hey, Echo." It's Jagger, holding two glasses of champagne. The white-blond tips of his hair are disheveled in sexy disarray. "Hey, Vivi." He hands me a flute. "Here. I managed to snag a full bottle." It's wedged under his arm.

"Hi, Jagger. Thanks."

"How's the planning going?" Jagger asks, more to Echo than to me.

"She's chosen her wedding dress," Echo tells him, taking a sip from her drink.

"Wow." Jagger clinks the full bottle gently against my flute. "So you're really going through with it."

"What choice does she have?" Echo says.

"For the record," Jagger grins at me, "I would've married you, Vivi."

Echo glares at him sort of warily. "The King-Fitzpatrick link has already been made, Jagger. You're too late."

I'm almost glad when a commotion interrupts us. People are calling out and we all look to see who they're calling to.

A boat has been pulled up onto the sand and four men are walking up the beach.

My husband-to-be is one of them.

*Holy shit.*

Wolf Ramsey is built and suntanned. He stands out from the others for more than one reason. He's bigger. He's dressed only in a pair of black, wet shorts that show off —*well, everyfreakingthing.* His muscular thighs are inked with tribal-style designs. He has tattoos across his sculpted chest and shoulders. There's a sun. Waves. Around one of his thick, vein-ridged biceps is a spiral-patterned band that adds to his savage vibe.

His hair is salty and windblown, still wet from swimming. The coiled muscles of his abs tighten when he moves and the sharply-defined V at his hips is visible above the waistband of his low-slung shorts. His crazy energy charges the air in a way I can feel from here.

It's impossible not to appreciate the hard, masculine beauty of him. It hits you like an ion-charged sea breeze.

*Okay, so his sister is kind, his brother is honorable, his house is amazing, his body is … ridiculous. And very big. And rock-hard.*

None of those things guarantee marital bliss, of course, or any kind of happiness at all. In fact it's more than likely he's going to use all that brute strength to dominate me and control me in ways I can't even imagine yet.

It's then that Wolf Ramsey sees me. He walks over to where we're standing, pausing to glare briefly at Jagger. Then his gaze rakes over me, taking in the tight fit of my dress. My bare legs. My painted toes.

His blue-eyed intensity kicks up all my heart-thumping fear, my anxious anticipation, my *anger* and that new craving I can't control. You name it and I freaking feel it. I feel *everything*.

His eyes don't leave me. "Hey, princess," he drawls in his deep, rasped voice.

It's his joke. His put-down. *I was expecting a mildly pleasing, pampered little princess who always does what she's told. But I was way off.*

I still don't even know what he meant by that. I don't reply to him. I *can't*, more accurately.

The crowd is calling for him. Stone wants to fight him. Wolf's the best fighter, apparently, and Stone wants to challenge the champion.

"You really think you're up for that, man?" Jagger calls out, laughing. He's a lot less intimidating than either of his brothers. I notice Enzo is up on the lanai talking to some of the Ramsey cousins. Aurora and Raven are with him.

Stone is *not* someone I would ever want to fight, if it were me. He's mean-looking.

There's a bonfire already blazing on the beach and the sun hangs low over the horizon line of the glinting ocean. Tiki torches have been lit, placed in a wide circle around the bonfire and along the beach. A bar has been set up nearby.

Wolf is still watching me and his expression is hot, but there's more to it than that. He's intrigued by me. He's … interested, in how I'm feeling. I'm not sure how I know this but I do. I'm still sort of half glaring at him and half checking him out because it's hard not to.

"I'm glad to see you haven't lost the attitude." He almost smiles. "It's one of my favorite things." This crack in his staunch ferocity makes my stomach do a funny little flip.

"I don't know why it would be."

At this he does smile, but he's interrupted. They're calling to him.

"All right, all right," he relents. To me, he says, "Don't go anywhere. I'll make this quick."

Wolf walks down to the sand and the crowd parts for him like he's some kind of god. Against the backdrop of the fire and the sun, he looks like one.

A murmur ripples through the circle of people as he takes his place in the ring.

Perri comes up next to me and lightly touches her shoulder to mine. "Hi, Vivi."

"Hi, Perri. Are you okay?"

My sister is used to disappointment, unfortunately. She's been dealing with it for most of her life. "What can I say? No, I'm not okay. I'm heartbroken. Devastated. Pissed off. But not totally surprised. And I can't compete with that … that *girl*. The fucking 'angel.' And now she's a *King*? Give me a break. I mean, what are the odds? They're already engaged, apparently."

"I'm so sorry, Perri. I'm sorry it didn't work out."

She shrugs and swipes a tear away.

"You'll find someone else."

But it's hard to be comforting when the person I'm supposed to marry—*tomorrow*—and share a wedding bed with—*tomorrow night*—is getting ready to face off against his opponent and is by far the most threatening-looking thing I've ever seen in my life. Which is not helping me right now.

The two of them crouch and begin to circle each other.

Stone is strong-looking but compared to Wolf he looks unprepared and practically frail.

Wolf lunges with such skill and force, Perri takes a step back. "Oh my *God*."

Wolf knocks Stone to the ground. Stone tries to punch Wolf but Wolf deflects easily, his movements so deft, so cuttingly concise that Stone is pinned and groaning in a matter of seconds.

Perri's gasp sounds more like a light laugh. "*Jesus*. He's *brutally* strong."

I can only agree as I watch Wolf Ramsey with a mixture of mild horror and accumulating awe. There's no denying the raw, animal power of him as he takes total control. It's terrifying to watch.

Wolf releases Stone, like he's finding the challenge too easy. He's giving Stone a chance to retaliate. Stone does his best. But he only has one move and it's predictable, even I can see that. Wolf uses this to his full advantage and pins Stone again, getting him into an unbreakable headlock type thing. Stone's nose is bleeding and his face is covered in sand.

"This is barbaric." Perri grimaces. "I can't watch this. I'm going to go get a drink up at the house. I'll see you up there, Vivi."

"Okay."

*Maybe.*

*Do I really want to be at this Ramsey berserker's mercy for the rest of freaking eternity?*

No, is the answer to that question.

So I make my decision. And if I'm going to act on it, I need to do it now.

I start to make my way through the small crowd. A dark figure steps into my path and grabs my arm with his rough hand. I know the feel of that rough grip too well. "Where are you going?" my nemesis growls.

I was almost expecting it. Reflexively, I yank my arm away and I keep going. "None of your goddamn business." This whole weekend is too much. I feel like I'm losing my mind. And I'm no longer willing to let this jerk manhandle me. Not that I ever really have been—but I never felt like I could have won against his bullying before; now, maybe I do.

Before I can get away from him, I hear his low warning. "You're really starting to piss me off, Vivi. Don't test me. You have no idea what I'm capable of."

"I don't care what you're capable of. Leave me alone."

"Once you're married, you know, you'll be fair game. You might want to remember that before you make it worse for yourself."

This stops me in my tracks and I turn to face him. His irises are as black as his pupils and it's unnerving. His face is so familiar to me because I've been doing my best to avoid it my entire life. I wish I could punch it. I wish I could make him disappear forever. "What's *that* supposed to mean?"

"You don't expect him to be faithful, do you? There's no way in hell. So there's no reason you have to be faithful either. And I'm not really your cousin. So don't fucking cross me."

I stare up at him for a second in mute shock that he would say the horrible, quiet suspicion out loud like that. "Go to hell, Jett."

I push away from him. I'm wildly unsettled. I'm trapped from all sides. I can vaguely hear the cheers of the crowd as Wolf clinches the win. I find Tatum, standing near the water, talking to Blaise.

Jett wanders off to the bar, for now.

"Vivi," says Blaise, "Wolf is having some people clean the upstairs of his beach house for you. He wants you to have it, so you can sleep there tonight. He's going to sleep on the beach, he said."

"Oh." It's a nice offer. *But that won't be necessary.*

Blaise is completely unfazed by the bloodbath taking place nearby. She must be used to it. "I'm just going to see if the caterers have delivered the rest of the platters yet," she says. "They were supposed to be here by now. I'll be right back."

She leaves us and as soon as Blaise is out of earshot, I ask my sister, "Can I have one of your credit cards? I want to … buy some things."

Tatum smiles, but there's a glimmer of a question behind her eyes, like she's wary of my intentions. "I don't have any on me, honey. My bag is up at the house. Are you okay? How are you feeling about everything?"

"Do you have any cash?"

My sister laughs. "No. Why would I bring cash to the beach?"

I am such a fool. My family is one of the wealthiest in Hawaii. I have more clothes, shoes, bags, phones, and luxury than most people will ever see in their lifetimes. *Yet I don't have direct, personal access to any of it. Because that would have given me the kind of power and independence they never wanted me to have. It would have given me an out. It would have meant they couldn't use me to take the fall.*

How could have I been so blind?

In the distance, people are helping a dazed Stone to his feet and Wolf is being congratulated and fawned over. He's distracted.

I can't see Jett.

And I take my opportunity.

It's dark now, except for the fires and the moonlight reflecting off the water.

I try to be as inconspicuous about it as I can. I walk along the sand, up the beach. Silently, I duck behind the row of food trucks, glancing behind me to see if anyone is following me.

No one is.

I sneak up a dune and into a grove of palm trees that stretches all the way down the beach.

*God.* My heart is racing. It's darker under the trees and away from the light of the flames but there's enough moonlight to follow the trail.

I don't know where I'm going.

I'm not wearing shoes. I left them in Echo's dune buggy, along with my phone. *You idiot.*

I don't have any money.

How many miles away is the nearest town? How am I going to hide from Silas? And Jett? And Wolf? *And Arrow?*

I have no idea.

Maybe I can find a hidden cove somewhere and learn how to fish.

*Yeah, right.*

Or those caves that Cassidy lived in for a while.

*Sure thing. They're over the wall and so high up the cliff that they needed a helicopter to reach it.*

I'll find a phone and figure out how to call Ash and he

can help me. We can go to New York together and disappear.

*Sure you will.*

Ash told me the other day he had twenty-seven dollars in his bank account. He laughed about it.

I'm stumbling through the sea grass that grows thick on the dunes and it's surprisingly sharp.

That's the least of my worries.

I'm running now. As fast as I can.

Because I can feel it.

Someone's following me.

# 7

# WOLF

**_Two hours earlier_**

"Heavenly father, we ask that you lead these men to a—"

"Nero, would you cut that shit out?" Hunter yells. "This is _Axel Archer_ we're talking about. He doesn't deserve a prayer, or whatever it is you think you're doing. What are you, a priest now?"

Leo chuckles darkly. "The only place the heavenly father is leading these men is straight into the fiery depths of hell."

My cousins Nero, Hunter, Leo and I are doing what needs to be done. None of us are happy to be here, but we're prepared to do whatever's necessary to keep our family safe. Which, today, happens to be burying three bodies at sea and getting rid of all the evidence before anyone else gets a whiff of what went down in Paradise last night.

"I just think it sucks that his recruits had to die like that," Nero grumbles. Nero's young, only twenty, and it still affects him when we hunt animals or kill one of our cattle for meat. This is the first time he's had to do anything like this. "They looked like they were around my age. Seems like a waste."

"That's what they signed up for when they joined up with Arrow." Leo is twenty-eight and married. He and his wife Hana just found out they have a baby on the way. He's less sympathetic, which I guess is bound to happen when you've got more to lose. "They would've known what they were getting into."

Hunter's a loose cannon who practically enjoys himself at times like these. "If you play with the devil, you're going to get burned."

This almost makes me laugh. "I guess you would know."

"That's deep stuff, Hunter." Leo secures the final knot. "Have you been studying philosophy or something?"

Hunter grins at us both. "As a matter of fact, yes. And if you're referring to my drunken arrest in Waikiki last month, that wasn't my fault. Two strippers insisted I do tequila shots with them all night. Things got a little out of hand."

"I'm sure they did." Things are always getting out of hand when it comes to Hunter.

We're on one of our fishing boats, around half a mile out to sea. Axel and two of his recruits have been wrapped in sheets. One by one, we throw them overboard.

We all watch them sink until they disappear into the murky depths. Nero makes the sign of the cross.

"We're done here," I say. "Let's get back to shore."

I don't mind cleaning up the messes that get made when the situation calls for it, but we've taken enough time for this. I'm on edge and restless to get back. I want to see how my new wife-to-be is handling everything. I feel weirdly anxious about … I don't know. Making sure she doesn't bolt.

I'm not sure why I even care. Aside from the curse, I shouldn't care.

But I spent two hours of not-quite-sleep last night getting myself off like a maniac to my feral fantasies of her and I can't get the little minx out of my head. Her crazy-as-fuck body. Her gorgeous, no-clue-about-how-cute-I-am pout. Those soft, pink lips and her sultry innocence. She's basically like a drug to my starving, lust-crazed soul—which happens to be stuck in overdrive, since the minute I saw her.

It's not just my lust that's messing with me. This lust feels tangled and downright obsessive. I feel out of control with it.

I never lose my cool over women. *Why her? Why am I craving her like I've never craved anything in my life?*

I hate the thought of anyone else even *looking* at her. Noticing how fucking beautiful she is. Do they?

Of course they do.

*She's mine.*

I have a weirdly savage urge to claim her as my own.

I *have* claimed her, at least logistically. If she'll go through with it.

It's not enough.

*I need more. I want to slide her down onto my thick cock until she's riding me as I grab fistfuls of those creamy, bouncy, gravity-defying tits. I want to hear her cries of ecstasy as she comes hard around my—*

Fuck.

*Stop.*

The last thing I need is a hard-on in front of my cousins.

We get closer to shore and the fires have been lit on the beach and around the lanai. The thumping bass of the music drifts out over the water as we anchor the boat. Leo lowers the dinghy and the others climb into it. I hand my weapons belt to Nero and dive into the water.

I'll swim.

I need to cool the fuck off.

They're waiting for me when I get to shore. Zeke is pouring more lighter fluid onto the already-raging bonfire, which is roaring and sending sparks high into the sky. "You're up next, Wolf. Remy just kicked Malachi's ass. Now Stone wants a beating."

I scan the crowd for her and I see her on the far side of the beach, with Echo and fucking Jagger, who's practically drooling. I control my urge to storm over there and kill him. I can't help thinking that, if everyone was really so concerned about the alliance marriages, all the Fitzpatricks really needed to do was to make Vivi more visible to the rest of us. They could have trotted her out like a show pony and had every red-blooded male within a ten-mile radius salivating like a junkyard dog.

She's standing there now like a little siren supernova, eclipsing everyone around her in that blasé, unaware way she has. She doesn't have any idea of the effect she's having. She's absolutely fucking gorgeous and if any one of us had known the extent of it, Silas could have had a ring on her finger a long time ago.

I'm relieved he didn't. One of the others might have seen her first.

"Who the hell is *that?*" asks Hunter.

Of course I know who he's talking about before I even glance over at him. My fists are already clenched.

"It's Wolf's new fiancée, you asshole." Leo is highly entertained by the look on my face.

Even Nero joins in. "*That's* Vivi Fitzpatrick? When did she get so—"

"Shut the fuck up. All of you."

They're all watching my reaction, which causes them to howl with laughter. Hunter holds his palms up, like he's protecting himself. "Whoa. *Someone's* wound up."

Leo finds my agony hilarious. "How long has it been since you've been away from Paradise, man? You need to hunt." I know only too well what he means. It's how we talk about our conquests on the other islands.

"He can hunt on his wedding night." Nero elbows me. "Tomorrow. And not a moment too soon, by the looks of you."

Hunter pats me on the back. "Wolf, you lucky mother-fucker. Hell. *Look* at her."

"I am," I growl as my rage kicks up several notches. It's hard to handle, not lunging at each one of them. *She's mine*, I feel like yelling. They'd have to be dead not to notice her but that doesn't mean I have to put up with it. "And you can keep your eyes off her unless you enjoy bone-splintering pain."

More laughter.

I hardly hear them.

I'm staring at my almost-wife.

*Damn, she's beautiful.*

As I get closer to her, everyone else fades out. All I can see is her. She's wearing a short white dress with flowers on it that shows off her long legs. She's barefoot. I don't know why, but this feels almost indecent, her delicate, painted toes all exposed like that, gently drawing a line in the sand as she sips her champagne. I have this urge to cover her up and protect her from everyone around her. Her bare arms and shoulders are lightly tanned. Her skin is so flawless it's almost painful to look at. She's so … *clean.* And pure-looking.

*Mine. I'm going to be the one to dirty her.*

She watches me approach and her fire-gold eyes get round. Her lips are going to be my downfall, I can already tell. They're wet and slightly parted. Her breasts are going to be even more of my downfall. *Holy fuck.* The dress is pulled tight over the soft fullness of them. Her plump little nipples are pushing against the fabric and I'm about to lose my mind.

"Hey, princess." I mean it. She's so pretty it hurts. And that sassy little pout is still firmly in place. "I'm glad to see you haven't lost the attitude." I need to tease her just to take the edge off. Otherwise I'm going to have to sling her over my shoulder and carry her upstairs. "It's one of my new favorite things."

"I don't know why it would be." She doesn't smile, but I do. Because I love how fucking feisty she is under her who-me?-I'm-just-a-clueless-little-virgin façade. A potent sexual aura oozes out of her like a stealth weapon, basically slaying me. Branding me with her ownership.

If she can do this without trying or even being aware of it, I can only imagine what she'll be like when she discovers her powers.

I'm starting to wish our wedding was tonight. Now. So I can start enlightening her. *And eating her pussy like there's no tomorrow.* I have to force myself not to wonder if she's wearing panties. *Are they damp yet? Is her little pink clit all sweet and slippery from the effects of being near me?*

"Come on, Wolf!" Zeke yells.

"Stone wants his beating now," Hunter calls out.

"You're not scared of a King, are you, Wolf?" Leo jokes.

"Let's do this, Ramsey," Stone taunts me.

I don't want to leave her, but a part of me needs to take out all the rage that's pumping through my veins on someone. Stone King will do just fine. "All right, all right." To her, I say, "Don't go anywhere. I'll make this quick."

She blinks long lashes. I seriously have never been so close to losing my control. I have to force myself not to fall to my knees and lift that scrap of cotton that barely skims her thighs …

"Hurry up, Wolf!"

I go down to the ring where Stone is waiting.

And I lunge at him.

It's too easy. It feels good to unload some of my fury on this much weaker opponent. He's strong enough but he's slow and has no idea how to defend himself against someone like me. I try to go easy on him but it's not possible. All the comments my cousins made, the stupid look on Jagger's face as he checked her out, the fact that I have to wait until tomorrow to taste her—I take all of it out on Stone King and he's a bloody mess by the time I'm finished with him.

I lose track of time. Maybe five minutes passes. Maybe ten.

I'm playing with his weaknesses, giving him false hope before crushing it again. I get him into the final clinch and I could literally pull him limb from limb if I wanted to. Part of me does.

Remy's voice interrupts. "All right, Wolf. You've made your point. These matches are supposed to be friendly."

"That was friendly." I release Stone almost reluctantly and climb to my feet.

I can hear Leo's amusement. "*He* didn't offer to marry her, Wolf. No need to go psycho on the poor dude."

Stone is moaning on the ground, covered in sand. Blood is pouring from his nose and he'll have two decent shiners by morning.

Remy and I pull him up.

"*Fuck*," Stone groans, swaying.

I turn to look for her but she's gone.

Shit. Did I scare her? Maybe I shouldn't have been so rough with Stone.

Ignoring everyone else, I walk up to the lanai to see if she's there. Echo's there, and Blaise. Silas. Enzo. Aurora.

But not Vivi.

The little nymph is having second thoughts, maybe.

As a practiced hunter I'm used to scanning the distance for the movement I'm looking for. I see a flash of white. Her dress. She ducks behind one of the food trucks parked at the end of the lane.

She's running?

She's running.

*What the fuck are you doing, princess?*

Where does she think she's running to? There's nothing down at that end of the beach besides sand and palm trees. Beyond the cape, there's a series of bays and coves. No roads. No escape route. She isn't even wearing shoes.

Is it me that has her spooked? Or something else?

It's then that I notice him.

I'm not the only one following her.

There's a guy heading in the same direction. I vaguely recognize him. He's a Fitzpatrick cousin. Always hanging around Silas. A bodyguard, maybe.

There's no way in hell I'm allowing him to chase her. It doesn't matter that that's exactly what I'm about to do.

She's mine.

I catch up to him easily. He hasn't heard me come up behind him. I gauge my opponent. He's solidly built, around four inches shorter than I am. Stocky and strong, but flabby.

The kind of guy who's too lazy to hone his body into its peak fighting condition. I grab his shoulder and he jumps. "Hey—" he splutters, startled.

"I'll take it from here. Go back to the party."

He stops, eyeballing me. He must know who I am. There's a calculating look in his eye I don't like the look of. It's shifty. Why's he hesitating? "It's my responsibility to make sure she doesn't wander off."

"Not anymore." *Fucker.*

"She's not your wife yet," he has the balls to say.

Seriously? "She will be, soon enough." He still doesn't move. The guy must be a complete idiot to take me on. He's drunk on his own power trip, like some assholes get. Blinded by getting his way without ever having to fight for it. "I'll say it one more time: fucking leave. Is that clear enough for you?"

He doesn't move, which is enough of an answer for me. I make sure my thumb rests on top of my middle knuckle before my fist connects with the left underside of his jaw, just below his ear. Not quite hard enough to break his jaw. Remy taught me this punch and he's used it on me a few times to show me how to use it effectively. I happen to know it fucking hurts. It stuns you.

He falls heavily to his knees.

It's that easy. "I'll break your nose next if you don't get up now and walk back to the bonfire. Have a drink, whatever the fuck you want. But you're going to leave Vivi to me from now on. Understood?"

I guess my message has finally gotten through his thick

skull because he scrambles to his feet, with effort, rubbing his jaw. He gives me an I'll-kill-you look before he heads back toward the party.

*Not if I kill you first, sunshine.* I get this feeling I'm going to have to do exactly that. This guy's got grudges that go all the way down to his bones, I can see it in his eyes. My guess is that he's feeding off Silas's power like a parasite, coveting it. I've fought enough men in my time to be able to easily read the complexities of their anger. I could be a goddamn shrink at this point.

Once I'm satisfied he's obeyed me and he re-joins the crowd, I head in the direction Vivi took. I can't see her in the darkness, despite the brightness of the full moon. I'm beyond the torches. The fronds of the palm trees make a thick canopy.

*Where are you going? And why?*

I check the sand for footprints, crouching down to take a closer look. I find her trail. I can tell from the distance between her footprints that she's moving quickly, not quite running but close. Her footprints don't travel in a straight line. She's checking to make sure no one's following her. There's a dark smear of blood on a blade of sea grass.

This is strangely unacceptable to me. *She's spooked. She's hurt. She's bleeding.*

I round a small cluster of coconut palms and I see the white of her dress, like a ghost, around fifty feet ahead of me, disappearing around another tree.

I'm getting closer and she detects me.

"Stop running," I call out.

She's fast but I'm faster. I catch up to her easily and—as gently as I can—I grab her around the waist. She screams like a banshee and punches at me. She's fighting me. In the scuffle we both lose our balance. I catch my weight so I don't crush her. Once she's underneath me, I use my body to hold her to the ground. I'm so much bigger than she is, I'm completely caging her, pinning her in place.

"Help!" she screams. "*Someone help me!*"

I hold my hand over her mouth to muffle her screams. Her arms are mostly restrained by the weight of my body but she's trying to push me off. Which is never going to happen. She's so small. So incredibly vulnerable. "Stop screaming, Vivi. It's me."

This doesn't appear to comfort her. She stops screaming but her eyes are like saucers and I can feel her racing heartbeat.

"I'm not going to hurt you, okay? Calm down."

She stares up at me, her golden irises almost completely swallowed up by the black of her pupils.

"I'm going to take my hand away but I don't want you to scream," I tell her. "Okay?"

This is the first time I've touched her and my senses are reeling.

Flecks of glinting gold in her eyes give her a magical look, like she could be a mythical creature from the rainforest. She's scared and a part of me hates this fear. But another part of me likes it. Because it's a starting point. It's something I can work with. This is where she starts to learn that fear is the best kind of anticipation.

"No screaming," I remind her.

Slowly, because I know she's not going to obey me, I lift my hand.

"Get *off* me, you—" I put my hand back over her mouth, muffling her cries almost completely. I weigh at least twice what she weighs. I let my weight settle just a little more heavily, to make a point. To let her feel me.

She's glaring at me, half terror and half hatred darkening her eyes. I watch her wide eyes, waiting for her heartbeat to calm. "I said no screaming. I'll get off you as soon as you listen to my one, very reasonable request. No one can hear you anyway."

It's impossible not to notice that her dress is pulled up and her knees are apart, clasped to my hips. Only the tiny layer of her panties protects her. Blood rushes to my cock, thickening it. The soft core of her body cradles my thick length. All I'm wearing is a frayed pair of swim shorts and it wouldn't surprise me if half my cock has found its way out of them, like a heavy, heat-seeking missile. *It would be so easy to push her panties aside and slide deep inside her. There's not a damn thing she could do to stop me.*

"Are you going to stop screaming?"

More glaring.

"Give me a sign, princess."

She nods once, barely.

I take my hand away.

She doesn't scream.

"Good girl. See? That wasn't so hard."

"*Get off me.* I hate you, Wolf Ramsey!"

This hits me in a way I'm not expecting. She hates me? The little virgin is mad at me. Okay, with good reason. But it's so mild, her anger. So very unthreatening. "Really?" I pretend to be offended but her kittenish rage is sort of … adorable. It entertains me. It makes me want to change her mind about me. And it gets me fully, painfully hard. "I just saved you."

"*Saved* me? You didn't save me, you *tackled* me! You're an ego-inflated *bully*, just like all the rest of them."

"The rest of who?"

That insolent pout really is something. *Her mouth is so fucking perfect.* "No one. It's none of your business."

"Actua—"

"And don't tell me you think it *is* your business! It isn't! I'm not marrying you! I refuse to do it. They can't force me and neither can you. I don't care about the curse. Now get off me!"

The little minx is worked up. I get that and I understand why, obviously. Soon I'll do something about it. First, I need to get a grip on how fucking dazzling she is. I can't remember ever being so … *enthralled* by a woman. Not like this. Not completely and absolutely riveted by every small detail. I contemplate the color of her lips for a few seconds. A rosy pink, as soft and silky-looking as the petals of a rose. Her lips are the exact color of my wildest dreams. I don't know why I fucking say that, but they are.

"Did you hear what I said?" she seethes.

"I heard you. It would be hard not to. You're yelling and I'm right here."

"That's because you're on top of me! You're crushing me! Let me go, you … you …"

I wait for it, grinning because riling her is the most fun I've had in a while, and I happen to know she's safe from me —for now—even if she doesn't. I get the feeling she doesn't usually react as much as she is right now, to anything. She glides through life with her feathers all in place.

I want to ruffle her. I want to make her *feel* as much as I'm feeling. "Go on. Say it. Give me your worst."

If looks could kill. But she won't give it to me.

"Aw." I'm genuinely disappointed. "I'll get your rage out of you one of these days."

"You won't get a chance to! I'll be gone. I'm leaving."

I watch her, more intrigued than worried about her threat, if that's what it is. "Where are you going?"

"Anywhere but here."

"What's wrong with here?" She doesn't say it but it's clear enough: *I'm* here, that's what's wrong with it. "What's your plan? Do you have a destination? An escape route? A ride?"

She squirms, trying to get loose. I let my weight rest just a little more heavily.

"Do you or don't you?"

"I'm working on it!"

"That means you don't."

"I do! I'll figure it out. Let me go."

I finger a strand of her dark hair that catches the silver-gold of the moonlight. It's as smooth and silky as a feather. "Princess?"

"Stop calling me that! I'm not a princess."

"You are," I insist. "And I'm going to make sure you're treated like one. You know what I think?"

"No! And I don't care," comes her petulant reply. Which makes my cock throb hotly.

"No?" I wait for her wide eyes to meet mine. "You know when you will care? You'll care when you're lost in the forest and you're hungry and you don't know how to forage because you've never had to do anything for yourself in your entire life, especially out here. And you'll *really* care when a feral pig with razor-sharp tusks is chasing after you and you don't have big bad Wolf here to protect you. Isn't that right? Which means you could get hurt or even killed. Even if nothing chases you, the rainforest is thick and it's easy to lose your way. The nearest road is around twenty miles south and you'll have to climb steep cliffs to get to it. I've done it and it's not an easy walk. Especially since you don't have shoes. The rocks between the bays are jagged coral and volcanic rock. They're difficult to climb even when you're prepared and you know what you're doing—which you obviously don't. And you're hardly going to hunt and fish with your bare hands."

More glaring.

"So, how about we come up with a new plan."

Steely silence.

"How about I carry you back to the beach instead." I don't ask it. It's what's going to happen.

"I don't want to go back to the beach."

"Why not?"

"I just don't."

"Is it because of that asshole chaperone who was following you?" I can read the flicker of panic at the mention of him, and it tells me all I need to know.

"He was following me?" She's scared of him.

*The fucker is toast.* "I took care of it. I'm going to help you up now, but I want you to promise not to run. Because then I'll have to chase you again and I'll easily catch you and we'll have to do this all over again. Which *I* wouldn't mind but you're the one complaining."

She's still breathing hard and I can feel her full, soft breasts pressing against my chest with each inhale.

Her scent is like nothing I've ever experienced. Flowers. Lemons, maybe. And something else. The scent of her fear, like morning dew mixed with virgin's blood. I don't know. Whatever the cocktail is, it's blowing my head off. "Do you agree not to run?"

"What do you mean, you took care of it?" There's relief in her question.

"Well, I almost broke his jaw. If I'd broken it, they might have called the rescue helicopter to take him away and that would've ruined the party. So I went easy on him. But I threatened to break his nose if he didn't leave you alone for the rest of his natural born life."

She likes this. She's relieved by it. "You did?"

"He wasn't happy about it, but he listened. At least for now."

We're both quiet for a few seconds. My monster hard-on

is cradled snugly between her thighs. She's so warm and quivery, I'd bet money she's wet.

*Fuck, she feels good.*

Everything about her is mesmerizing me. I'm a beast of amped-up fascination.

Her lips have a puffy plushness to them that makes me feel downright depraved. I want to devour her mouth. Which is a first for me. I don't kiss women. I never have. It always felt much more intimate than I ever wanted to get.

Vivi Fitzpatrick is a different story altogether. Not just because she's about to become my wife, but because my craving to taste her and own her and possess her is the most intense thing that's ever happened to me. "Promise me you won't run."

"Wolf?"

"Yeah?"

"Please don't …"

"Don't what?"

"Don't hurt me."

This shocks me, even though it probably shouldn't. There are tears in her eyes. One paints a shiny line down the side of her face. That single tear breaks some fucking thing inside me. I literally can't handle her tears. Slowly, I swipe it with my finger. Her skin is as soft as the finest, most delicate silk. I lick her tear and she watches me do this, wide-eyed. It might be the tear or the terror in her or the commitment to her I've already made, but that salty little taste of her transforms me into a person I barely recognize. And it occurs to me then that maybe we're not doomed.

Maybe my parents and Remy's stories turned out to be catastrophic because they disobeyed the curse. Vivi and I aren't going to disobey it. We're going to follow its course due north. Maybe love doesn't have to be tragic. "I'm not going to hurt you, Vivi."

"It's just … you could. So easily."

"But I'm not going to." When she's ready for me, I'll show her all the things I can do to free her—physically as well as existentially—but that's a conversation for a different time. Like tomorrow night. For now, I'm already dedicated to making sure she's never threatened. It's up to me now to keep her happy and comforted. It's up to me to make sure she can live her life in ways she never has before. So I lift myself off her and I—more carefully than I can remember doing anything—help her sit up next to me. "Don't cry, princess. You're safe. I'll make sure of it."

She glances back toward the direction of the beach.

*What did he fucking do to her?* My blood is lava in my veins. "He won't follow you. I told you I took care of it. You've got me now, to make sure you don't have to worry about anything or anyone."

At the comment, the look in her eyes gets softer, almost hopeful. She *likes* this assurance. I find myself wanting to promise her the moon and all the stars.

"I'll protect you with my life," I tell her. It sounds dramatic as fuck and it is. But it's true. It's what I do for my family.

She just told me she's refusing to marry me. But I've still got tonight and most of tomorrow to change her mind.

# 8

# Vivi

*HOLY HELL!*

I'd scream but he'd hold me down again and force me to
obey him! I'd run but he'll chase me and catch me. I'd
scream but no one else can hear me. I'd tell him again how
much I hate him but he's just offered me … safety.

If I can believe him.

Something tells me I can. Which makes me hate him
even more because I'm so far out of my element here and I
don't *want* to need him but I do. In the deep, rasped assurance in his voice, I can hear that he's telling me the truth.
Like Echo and Remy, the truth means something to Wolf
Ramsey. He might be as rough as they come, but I don't
think he'd lie about something like that.

So I sit here for a minute to try to catch my breath and
figure out what to do next. Adrenaline is pumping through
my veins, as though I've just been zapped by a Wolf

Ramsey-shaped lightning bolt. I hate this even more. That his fire has lit me and somehow turned me into a hot mess of twisted confusion.

*God.*

*His body.*

*The way he was pressed onto me*—into *me, almost*—*huge and hard and … something was happening to me … something is* still *happening …*

How does he so easily stoke my basest urges? My common sense is telling me to run a mile from him but my cravings almost *want* him to pin me down again. To give me more. *I'm scared and I'm shaken, but I'm also … wet.*

Wolf's large, warm hand eases around my ankle. He lifts my foot off the sand. I try to pull away but he's expecting it and his grip tightens. There's a cut on the top of my foot and a small smear of blood. "Hold still," he says. "You've cut yourself."

"I'm fine. It's nothing."

He ignores this. His thumb brushes my skin, as rough as a cat's tongue. And then he leans in and lightly sucks the blood from my cut.

Shocked, I try to yank my foot away again but he holds it. "What are you doing?"

"You're bleeding."

"*So?* You can't *lick* me. That's … it's dangerous."

"Is it?"

"You don't even know me. You don't know anything about me or where I've been."

His teeth flash white under the moon's glow. "You're

honestly the cleanest person I've ever seen. The risk seems low to me. Besides, soon enough you'll be my wife—if you'll have me, that is." The last part is a joke he finds funny. His eyes are light, like he's feeling the effects of his lightning bolt too. "If there's anything to worry about, I'll be deep-diving into it tomorrow night anyway, so I figure what the hell. I hardly need to protect myself from my own wife."

*Oh my God.* "I told you. I'm not marrying you. I'm not marrying anyone."

It's outrageously intimate. There isn't much blood, but still. He releases me and he lays back in the sand, propping himself up on one bent, brawny arm. It's hard not to stare at the impressive shape of his shredded body, fully bare except for his weapons belt and a pair of swim shorts that clearly show off how freaking big and … *holy shit*. I force my gaze back up, to the flat, quilted outline of his abs. The pronounced V that's sort of fascinating to me.

The contours of his muscles are illuminated in the moonlight, as though Mother Nature is intent on showing off one of her greatest masterpieces.

"You said you don't believe in the curse," he says. "Why not?"

"I don't think it can hurt me. I don't care about it."

"Yeah? Why's that? Everyone else in your family cares about it."

"My mother died three days after I was born, from complications. I never knew her. My father went slowly mad, in a way that was horrible and heartbreaking to watch. He hated me because I looked so much like my mother, but

I wasn't her. He hated that I stole her from him. Everyone in my family has sort of hated me my whole life because it was me who killed her. They don't say that, but I can tell they're thinking it. All my siblings are damaged and none of them act like normal people are supposed to act, because they've never gotten over losing her. Partly because of all of that, I'm basically a prisoner in my own life. As charmed as it might seem to the people on Instagram, it doesn't always feel charmed to me. So I already feel like I've been cursed. I was cursed from the day I was born." I don't care what it sounds like. And it's weird that I'm even telling him all this. I don't usually gush, to anyone. Except Ash, and he always listens but it's from a more distant perspective. He tries to relate but sometimes he can't. Wolf Ramsey is watching me and listening to me intently. He's fully invested in what I'm saying. My decisions and the reasons I'm making them are going to affect his life directly and in ways he cares about. "Since you asked."

"Okay," he says, but not in a judge-y way, which I appreciate. "There's a lot to unpack there, so let's start with your mother. You feel guilty about her death and I can understand why you would. But you need to get over that. Starting right now. It wasn't your fault, obviously. Your mother would be happy you lived and she would have given her life for yours in a heartbeat. I think deep down you know that. It's fucking hard to lose your parents, I get that. I lost my parents too, when I was very young. I don't remember them at all."

I already knew the Ramsey parents died in a plane crash

a long time ago, but I guess I never really thought about how it would affect someone like Wolf. Maybe it's one of the reasons he's had to be so tough. "I'm sorry," I tell him.

"I guess we have something in common, then."

"That might be the only thing."

That lazy grin plays at the corner of his mouth. "There's the feisty little attitude we know and love."

I realize: despite the heaviness of the topic, I almost meant it as a joke. I'm teasing him. That I would be bold enough to do that feels … good. Something about this connection is empowering. Like, somehow, the wild beat of his heart is tuning in to the wildness of mine. This closeness makes my own spark feel like it's gaining momentum, feeding off his raging wildfire.

"As for the part about your life being controlled," he says, "that's a choice you're making. Starting right now, you have a different choice."

"That *you'll* control me, you mean, if I marry you."

His smile lingers. "That you'll control *me*, more likely. I'm already putty in your hands."

"I don't know what you mean."

"I wasn't going to step up and offer to marry you. I had nothing to gain. I was ready to let Knox take the fall, and Blaise. They're older, it's up to them to take on the burden since we, and they, agreed to let Remy off the hook because he was so in love. None of us wanted to deny him that."

"It's kind of … amazing. That you were willing to do that for him. My brothers and sisters wouldn't do that for me in a million years."

A shadow crosses his expression. "It didn't end well, but none of us could have predicted that. Anyway, I'd heard about you. Rumors."

"What rumors? Wait, don't tell me. That I'm inexperienced. Sheltered. Painfully shy, awkward and borderline reclusive."

His smile is hard to read. "Yeah. All of that. And that you have a lot of followers and modeling contracts and so on."

I shrug. But I admit something to him, because I have nothing to lose. And he's surprisingly easy to talk to. "I have an assistant that posts my photos on Instagram. It's her full-time job."

"That's all she does?"

"Yeah."

"Why?"

"I guess it makes money."

"For who?"

"For my family, maybe. I'm not sure. I never see it. But … never mind."

"What?"

"Nothing. It's foolish."

"Tell me. I want to hear it anyway."

"Well, do you know what I wish?"

"What do you wish?"

"That I could use it to help people."

"That's not foolish. Why don't you, then?"

"Because I don't control it. It's funny, now that I've had a few days off from the photo shoots and swarms of stylist teams, what I'm realizing is that I don't really care that much about any of it. None of those were projects or brands or contracts I chose myself."

"That's going to change. I'm going to help you with that. From now on, you're going to create the life you want, exactly as you want it."

I hate to admit it, but despite that wolfish sneer, he could almost be described as kind.

"Most of all," he says, "what people talk about when they mention you is how stunning you are. Your beauty is legendary, whether you know that or not. And I can assure you, the rumors don't do you justice. Not even fucking close."

I roll my eyes a little. "Right."

"As soon as I saw you, I knew I would step up."

"You did? How?"

"I couldn't believe you were real. You're quite literally the most beautiful girl I've ever seen. I felt like the universe or the angel or my ancestors or whoever's in charge of these things put you in my path for a reason. I'm going to honor the curse not only because I have to but because I want to."

That might just be the nicest thing anyone has ever said to me. Again.

"All we need now is for you to agree to it. You wouldn't have to obey *everything* I say, by the way." Even though he's built like a rugged, athletic mountain man, the edge of humor in him is always there, sitting just below the surface of his rough facade, even when the topics are heavy, like now. What I realize is that I like this about him. I can let my guard down with him in a way I would never have expected.

"You just tackled me because I didn't obey you," I remind him. "I don't even want to think about what'll happen the next time I don't."

"I didn't tackle you. I rescued you. There's a difference."

"Rescued me?"

"Yes. From yourself. From getting lost and going hungry." The light sea breeze plays in his thick hair. Like his eyes, it seems to change color with his mood. Now, it's dark with a silvery halo from the moon's glow. "And from that thug who was following you."

I'm used to the flicker of fear at the mention of my cousin. This time, it's more subdued. I can admit I'm reassured by Wolf's presence and his promise. Despite everything, I'm not anxious. I'm not stuttering. I'm still feeling the effects of being held down by his big ... *hardness*. Under all those burly muscles and that wild-man schtick, he's sort of ... fun to be with. His roguishness is endearing. "You really do believe in the curse?" I ask him.

His playfulness drifts. "My parents died because they didn't obey it. Remy's family died because he didn't obey it."

"Or ... things happen sometimes that no one can control," I suggest gently.

"I don't want to mess with it. I can't risk my family being hurt by it even more than they already have been."

"It's *marriage*, Wolf. We don't even know each other. I'm not ready."

"You don't have to be ready. You just have to say two little words and leave the rest to me."

"Leave the rest to you? What does that even mean? You can't expect me to be reassured by that."

His thumb glides over the tender skin of my inner wrist and the light touch sends a zinging current along my bloodstream ... to that warm, wet place where the huge ridge of him was pressed against me. Whatever my sane mind thinks of Wolf Ramsey, my body *loves* his big, buff masculinity. My cravings are reacting to his nearness, even if I don't want them to. "It means I told you I'll protect you and I will. I give you my word. I'm not going to say I won't expect you to obey some of the things I ask you to do. But you'll be free to make your own choices and I'll make sure you can. Within reason. Sometimes you'll have to trust that I know what's best for you."

I almost laugh. "Trust *you* to know what's best for me? Who gets to decide these 'reasons'? And what rules of yours do you expect me to obey?"

"You'll be faithful, that's one thing I'll never compromise on."

"Will you?"

The blue of his eyes shines like sea glass. "Will I what?"

"Will you be faithful?"

He doesn't answer me right away. Which is all the answer I need.

I climb to my feet. "You're dreaming if you think I'm going to *marry* you, then watch you sleep your way across Hawaii. There's no way in hell!"

"Your jealousy is adorable, princess. And to answer your question, yes."

I realize my fisted hands are on my hips. He stands up and looms over me, all six feet whatever of hulking MMA-fighting prime beef. It's impossible not to notice his manly perfection. Even so, I don't care. I mean, the *nerve* of him! "Forget it! If you have to *think* about whether or not you're going to be faithful to our marriage, then it'll never work. Not in a million years! It's ridiculous that you would expect to make rules about *me* being faithful but then you think you can make a different set of rules for yourself."

He's grinning widely now and—goddamn him—he really is sort of stunningly handsome when he smiles like that. "Are you done?"

"No, I'm not *done*! You can take your rules and stick them—"

"I didn't have to think about whether or not I'd be faithful to my wife. What I was *thinking* about was how punishing my fidelity is going to be for you. But don't worry. You'll enjoy it. Or at least most of it."

His eyes are flashing with that dark mischief I'm becoming used to, but then his gaze lands on my bare arm and all the amusement is suddenly gone. He gently grasps my arm. "What's this?" His question is edged with cold rage —so much of it, it scares me.

"Oh. I was … late to the limos. Yesterday. I was running late."

"That doesn't explain why you have a hand print

bruised onto your arm. Who did this?" The realization darkens his eyes. "The bodyguard?"

"I—I was late—*oof.*"

Wolf has scooped me into his arm. He starts carrying me down the beach.

"I can *walk*, Wolf. Put me down."

"You've hurt your foot. It might be sore."

"I'm fine." Then, because he's showing no signs of putting me down, I ask him, "Where are we going?"

"I think you know where we're going."

Okay, I'm not proud of it, but a part of me is waiting to see how this is going to play out and doesn't entirely hate the idea. The bully who's been harassing me for as far back as I can remember might be about to get some payback.

It doesn't take us long to reach the torches and soon we're at the party, which is rowdier now. Wolf carries me over to where Blaise and Echo are standing near the bonfire. They're talking to Aurora and Tatum.

Very carefully, Wolf sets me down. His voice is low, meant for me only. "Wait right here."

I nod. *What's he going to do?*

The music is loud but Wolf's voice is louder as he walks closer to the fire. "Hey, asshole."

Everyone turns to look at him.

"We're done fighting, man," one of Wolf's cousins says. "Have a beer."

Wolf storms over to where Jett is having a drink with some of the other men. Wolf grabs Jett by the front of his shirt and pulls him over to the fighting ring. "Let's see how tough you are now, fucker."

What happens next is both terrifying and … well, more than a little satisfying. My fiancé—and no, I still haven't decided—is getting my revenge for me. He's doing what he promised he would do if I marry him.

Wolf is *really* pissed off, is what it boils down to. I guess he doesn't like other people hurting me, now that we're almost betrothed.

It's a strange feeling.

No one has ever fought for me before. Not even my siblings, since fighting for me would have meant putting me before themselves. The fact that Wolf would be willing to do this makes the thought of marrying him just a little bit easier to tolerate.

The damage to Jett is accumulating.

I find myself lightly gripping Echo's arm.

"God, what's he doing?" she murmurs.

My cousin is definitely no match for Wolf Ramsey.

Only a few punches in, Remy and Enzo and the others are stepping in to try to pull Wolf off. I think they're worried Wolf might actually kill Jett, or at least do some serious damage. I guess now I know why they call him the killing machine. For some reason, the phrase doesn't freak me out nearly as much as it did yesterday.

It takes four of them to pull Wolf away. "If you ever touch, follow or speak to my wife-to-be again, I'll fucking kill you," Wolf growls as they pull him off. "Consider this your one and only warning."

While they're still restraining him, someone hands Wolf a beer and he chugs the whole thing.

"Wow," says Echo. "Is this about earlier today?"

"Partly," is all I say. I don't really want to go into all the gory details. She can probably guess. She sensed right away that I was scared of Jett and that something was off when it came to the way he was stalking me.

"Where did you disappear to, Vivi? Are you okay?"

"Yeah. I just went for a walk."

"Is everything all right between you and Wolf?"

"Everything's fine." As fine as it can be, at least, when you're about to marry a lethal, hot-blooded fighter you met only yesterday.

She smiles. "That's good."

I guess it is, but there's too much emotion for me to process all of it right now. My immediate future is a ticking time bomb that might either destroy me or do something else entirely.

It's late now and the full moon hangs low over the ocean, tinting it with molten glitter. "Vivi, your room is ready," Blaise says. "Wolf wants you to stay in the house. It's been prepared for you."

"Oh. Thanks, but—"

Wolf appears next to us. There's not a scratch on him. He weaves his rough fingers through mine. "Come on, princess. Can you walk?"

"I was thinking of going back up to the—"

"You're staying in the beach house tonight." He looks down at me and his eyes narrow, like he's remembering our conversation in the dunes. *You'll be free to make your own choices. Within reason.* "Let me show you to your new house."

*My new house.*

Wolf starts leading me toward it.

"We'll come see you in the morning, Vivi," Echo calls after me. "Around ten. To get you get ready."

*For my wedding.*

Will I go through with it? Is there a way to escape?

*Do I want to?*

Still holding my hand, Wolf leads me up the steps of the beach house's lanai, where people are still gathered around another fire pit. Some are sitting at a tiki bar that has steps leading down into an infinity pool.

I'm completely charmed by the house. The plantation-style lanai leads into the main living area, which is spacious and open-plan, with a central island providing a divider between the great room and the expansive kitchen.

Not surprisingly, the whole place has a beachy vibe, with sturdy pale-wood beams running the length of the room. White-washed walls have been decorated with colorful art. Gigantic leather couches and rustic wooden furniture create a swanky-modern meets welcomingly-lived-in feel. Wolf's cousins and friends are lounging around, eating, drinking and making themselves at home.

They all look up as we walk in. The conversation quiets for a few seconds as they notice with keen interest that Wolf is holding my hand. Maybe they weren't expecting it: this closeness, already, between the fiercest of the Ramsey fighters and the shyest Fitzpatrick.

*I* wasn't expecting it either, come to think of it. Weirdly, I don't mind the scrutiny and the attention. I have Wolf now, to shield me from it.

"You can redecorate it however you want to," he says. "This house is yours now."

I'm surprised he would offer this. It's not only the most to-die-for house I've ever seen, it's also one of the main hubs of the Ramseys' social scene. "I wouldn't change anything." When his gaze meets mine, I remind him, "Besides, I haven't said yes yet."

His expression takes on an exasperated edge, as though I'm trying his endless patience. "If you'll follow me upstairs, I'm about to convince you that you should."

Wolf pulls me along behind him up the wooden staircase that looks like it's been carved from native Hawaiian wood.

It's a little embarrassing that they're all watching us, but then again, what do they expect? The reason they're partying is because the alliance matches have finally been made. There's a sense of relief in the air and some of the people, including Jagger, who waves at me, have reason to celebrate. *They* don't have to marry someone against their will.

As I guessed from outside, the upstairs is modern and tastefully designed. The entire floor is a giant master suite, with a large bathroom off to one side. The cedar and glass doors that make up the front wall of the main room are folded all the way open. The lanai is almost as big as the interior. There's a hot tub and tropical plants framing a plush outdoor sitting area, illuminated by low blue spot-lights. Beyond them, the moon hangs low over the ocean view.

Against the far wall, which is a painted mural of the inside of an aqua wave, the gigantic king-sized bed has been sprinkled with red rose petals. Several flower arrangements of white peonies have been placed around the room. There's a standing bucket of ice with two bottles of champagne chilling.

"I asked Blaise to get some people to prepare the room for you. They've gone a little overboard."

"Maybe just a little."

Other than the tidiness and the flowers, though, the room is obviously a bachelor pad. One wall is entirely dedicated to weapons. There are racks and shelves with every kind of sword and knife imaginable, as well as circular blades, hatchets and contraptions I wouldn't dare guess at what they might be used for. A locked glass case holds rows and rows of guns, both pistols and rifles.

"Wow," I gasp. "Looks like you're preparing for an invasion."

"We're always preparing for an invasion. Which you already know."

Our eyes meet. I didn't choose to be here and if I thought I could, I'd still run. But I *am* here. And I feel safer in Wolf Ramsey's presence from very real threats that have been a part of my life for as long as I can remember than … well, than I ever have. I'm not used to the relief of that. It's powerful. "Thanks for … standing up for me."

"I told you. I'll kill for you. I'll die for you. It's what I do for my family."

I could point out—again—that we're not family yet, but I hold it. No one has ever said anything like that to me before. I can admit it's reassuring. In an unguarded moment, my throat catches.

Several of the shelves of his bookcase display framed pictures, books and knickknacks. I walk over to take a closer look at the photographs.

There's one of three young boys with their arms around each other's shoulders, on the beach, smiling for the camera, their skin gold with sun. It's Wolf and his brothers, all knobby knees and gap-toothed grins. Wolf and Knox were white-blond children and Remy's hair is brown with a sun-lightened top layer. They look like happy little hell-raisers.

There are other photos of Wolf and his siblings at different ages. As teenagers. Birthdays. Skiing. Surfing. Riding horses. All the photographs capture moments of fun, adventure and what looks like a magical childhood.

In the middle of all the other pictures, in an ornately carved frame, there's a picture of a young couple. The woman is dark-haired and stunning. She looks almost eerily like Echo. The man is dark blond, strapping and good-looking. I can see Wolf in the shape of his eyes. He has Knox's hair and something about the set of his mouth is Remy's. "Is this your parents?"

"Yes. That was only a few weeks before they died."

"I'm sorry, Wolf. They were so beautiful."

"Yeah. They were."

This room clearly shows two very different sides of Wolf Ramsey. The fierce weapons expert has a softer side. I'm not sure why, but the carefully-placed photographs of his family comfort me. He's wild because he grew up on the land, with no parents. He's tough because he's had to be, for a lot of reasons. But he's also capable of caring deeply for the people in his life.

"I had something couriered in today from Honolulu." He seems almost nervous, and it's a new look for Mr. MMA Killing Machine.

"What is it?"

He takes a small box from where it's sitting next to the photograph of his parents. I hadn't noticed it until now.

"I'm afraid I'm a traditionalist when it comes to things like this," he says. "My family is superstitious as fuck, for better or worse. So you'll have to bear with me." And then Wolf Ramsey gets down on one knee and he opens the small duck-egg blue box he's holding. Inside, there's a ring. Two delicate gold bands are held together by a circular row of diamonds that have been set into solid gold nests. It's very unique. I absolutely love it. "It has seven diamonds. Seven happens to be my lucky number. And tomorrow is the 7th. It's a good omen. I hope you show up for me."

He takes my hand, and he slides the ring onto my finger. Somehow, it fits, sitting there like it was made for me.

"Vivi, I know this is sudden and not what you were expecting. I wasn't expecting it either. But I promise to make sure you're safe and well-protected. I'll do my best to give you a happy life. I might not always get it right. In fact I think it's a given that I'll fuck it up on a regular basis. But I'll learn. And I'll give it everything I have because I don't know how to do things any other way. Our marriage will break the curse. It'll be charmed by the stars in the sky, I can feel it. I can feel them guiding us from afar. Everything I have is yours now. My body will shield you—and pleasure you in ways you never dreamed possible, I can promise you that. My land and my sea will feed you. I'm asking you to take all of it and let me prove to you that you have nothing to fear with me. Only wide open dreams and everything Paradise has to offer. Princess, marry me."

*Wow.* It's quite a proposal.

I can't quite gush out a yes—because I only met him yesterday and I really do wish we had more time. I can admit there are enigmas to Wolf Ramsey I want to unravel. I don't hate the idea of getting to know him. One day, maybe I actually *could* fall in love with him. It's true that my body seems to come to life whenever he's close to me. So … I can't quite bring myself to say no either.

"You don't have to answer me yet." That twinkle in his blue eyes really is mesmerizing. "We've got some time." He stands and leans one brawny, inked shoulder against the wall. He's a good six or seven inches taller than me, his shoulders wide and strong. He's also doing that *thing* again, where he emits those supercharged alpha male pheromones that make me very … *aware* of him. "But there is something I need to try." Holding my gaze in a deep blue challenge, he murmurs in a low command. "Don't move."

He pauses, maybe to test me.

"Do you want to know something?"

I *do* want to know. I want to know more about what goes on inside his head. "Okay."

His eyelashes are dark and thick, his eyes a clear, clear blue. "I've never kissed anyone before."

This surprises me. "You haven't?"

"No."

"But you've …"

The light in his eyes dances. "I've …?"

"You've been with women." It sounds foolish. Of course he's been with women. Legions of them, no doubt. It's hard to identify the small ache in my chest. It's surprisingly hard to think about them.

"I've never kissed a single one of them."

"Why not?"

"Because I never wanted to. I never wanted to get that close to them."

Without meaning to, I roll my eyes. "You were getting pretty close to them anyway."

"It's an animal urge. But not an emotional one. Kissing wasn't something I ever wanted from them." I don't want to hear about what he wanted from them. He lifts my chin lightly with one finger until I'm looking into his eyes. "But it *is* something I want from you."

I don't know if it's jealousy. How could it be? "Who says I'd kiss you anyway?"

His amusement at the churlishness in my reply is spliced with heat. Wolf slides a warm hand around the nape of my neck. He tilts his head slightly and contemplates my face, his eyes resting on my parted lips.

Slowly, he leans in and eases his mouth over mine, settling in with insistent pressure. It's sudden but at the same time I've never felt so *ready*. I'm mad and confused and turned on. My cravings for him are beyond my control.

He tastes like dark hunger, smoky lust and warm sun. He tastes like wild dreams and stormy pleasure. I don't know how to describe him. He lights up my body in a way I've never experienced.

I've been kissed only once before, by Ash: a brief, barely-there touch.

This is something else altogether.

Wolf makes a low groan, like he's almost overwhelmed. He deepens the kiss, forcing me to open to his demand, to take more of him, to let him in.

His aggression sends channels of fire into my body, lingering and curling. I feel it in the tips of my breasts and in the low pit of my stomach. I go instantly, shamelessly wet.

*God.*

The taste of him is crazily intoxicating.

I can't help it. As he kisses me, stroking my tongue with his, I draw him into me, gently sucking.

He reacts with a growl. "Fuck, baby, I'm so fucking hot for you I can't take this." *Baby.* He lifts me and carries me over to the bed, setting me down so I'm laying back against plush pillows.

I'm nervous. I don't know if I'm ready for whatever he's about to do but at the same time I *need* him to do it.

"We're going to wait until we're married tomorrow before I make you mine. I want to follow the rules for you. I want the best possible karma we can get. But tonight, I need to taste you. Lie back. You're going to like this, I promise."

He crouches over me, licking his tongue into my mouth in erotic, greedy plunges. With each invasion, I feel him in the core of my body, where a soft, slippery pulse takes hold. I'm drowning in sensation.

*His tongue. His scent. The heat of his big, lusty dominance.*

Just a few short hours ago I was terrified. A part of me is still terrified. But the cravings he's forcing me to feel override all that. Feminine need courses through me, hooking itself in, pulling me along for the ride.

Wolf takes one of my hands, then the other, raising them over my head. I feel the tug of something around my wrist. Both wrists. When I try to move them, I can't.

*Holy shit. He's tied me to the bed.* "What are you—"

"What's your safe word, princess?" His blue eyes glint darkly.

Safe word? "*Fuck,*" I gasp.

He laughs. "'Fuck' is your safe word? That's the worst safe word I've ever heard."

"No—"

"That's no good either. Too obvious. You need something you don't use all the time. Like, I don't know, pineapple."

I'm almost engaged against my will and now I'm tied to a freaking bed with a gigantic, outrageously virile Ramsey fighter pinning me under the weight of his huge, hard body. Even so, I stop to consider this. "Pineapple?"

"Yeah. Pineapple."

"I can't use pineapple."

"Why not?"

"It's my favorite fruit. I eat it all the time."

He's watching me with absorbed amusement. "It's my favorite fruit too."

"It is?"

"Yeah. Something else we have in common."

"What's your safe word?" I ask him.

His smile is compounding the whole effect of his beastly sex appeal. My body has a mind of its own. I can feel a soft trickle of moisture wetting my panties. "I don't need one."

"Why not?"

"There's nothing you could do to me that I wouldn't want you to do."

"Untie me."

"No."

It's making me irate, that he seems to be enjoying himself immensely. So I test him. "Pineapple."

My husband-to-be-if-I-decide-to-say-yes is a devil. He makes no move to obey me. "You only use your safe word when it gets too intense for you, or too painful. When I'm pushing past your boundaries. We don't even know what your boundaries are yet. Let's find out." Like this is the most fun he's had in ages.

*Help me.*

I feel more hot than panicky but I need to know. "What are you going to do?"

"Whatever I feel like doing, gorgeous. You're at my mercy now. And I am *hungry*. Damn, I've been wanting to taste your sweet little pussy ever since I saw you last night, standing there in that tight outfit like you were put on this earth to drive me insane." *Oh my God.* "Well, I can give as good as I can take, princess. That's something you should know about me right off the bat. I'm fucking *starved*. Are you ready for me?"

"*No.*" Even though I think I might be.

Wolf's fingers draw a circle around my nipple over my dress and a soft moan escapes me. "If you're not ready then why are these sweet little cherry nipples already poking out like they want to be sucked on? I'd bet a million dollars your panties are soaked right now. You want me to find out, don't you, baby girl? You want me to see how wet you are for your husband-to-be."

He pinches my nipples and I moan even louder, something that sounds like *no I don't.*

"That's why you're tied up, sweet. You don't know what you want yet. But I'm going to show you. See, when you give up control, when you're helpless to resist and you're completely dominated, it means you don't have to make decisions. I can make them for you. You can just relax and leave everything up to me. You have no choice but to let me take care of you. It's going to make the pleasure so much more intense for you."

I gasp again as the pressure of his fingers twists and squeezes.

"Do you touch yourself when you're alone? Do you make yourself come? What does my little virgin princess like?" He doesn't seem to be expecting me to answer and I *can't* answer. I'm too overwhelmed by how good he's making me feel. "Let's find out. Relax for me. Give me everything I want."

Wolf peels my dress down over my breasts, releasing the bouncy fullness of them.

He groans. "Holy fuck. Look at you. You're fucking perfect."

He takes my breasts in his rough hands and squeezes them, rubbing his thumbs over the hard, painfully-sensitive peaks.

*Holy hell.*

"You want me to suck on these juicy nipples, don't you, baby? You want me to lick you and bite you." He licks the tip of my nipple and I think I'm about to die or cry or melt into a puddle.

Watching my eyes, he makes me wait. "My princess needs it *bad*. The question is, how bad? Show me what you want from me."

My body is a total traitor. Without meaning to, I arch up to him, feeding my nipple to his mouth. His eyes flash and he takes the offering, sucking hard on the sensitive peaks. One, then the other, swirling and flicking with his tongue.

"*Ohhh.*"

He does it again, biting me gently. My pussy quivers and I moan again, even though I'm trying not to.

Something's happening. A warm throb is taking hold inside me that feels like a lava melt of sensation that's getting ready to overflow.

"Damn, you're a hot little thing. You *love* how big and rough I am, don't you, princess? You want your big alpha Wolf to give you a taste of my power. Your primal instincts *crave* what I'm about to force you to do."

*Oh my God. They do.* I'm almost panting. The warm melting rise is so close to … something. It's maddening. Crazy. I *need* relief.

"Beg for it, sweetheart. Say, 'Wolf, eat my wet, pink virgin pussy 'til I'm coming very, very hard.'"

*Eat?*

I'm ridiculously in the dark about stuff like this. Because I really was sheltered. I mean, I guess I've heard of what he's just described. I just honestly never imagined it happening to *me*.

"I could probably get you off just like this but I need to taste you too fucking bad. I can't take this."

He moves lower, his strong hands roughly roving up my thighs, pushing my dress all the way up to my waist, revealing the white lace of my panties.

"Look at you," he murmurs, like he's spellbound. He rubs his fingers over the saturated silk of my panties and I'm half mortified and half losing my mind with need. The feel of his fingers there is … way too good. "You're *soaked* for me. You want me to *devour* you, don't you, baby girl? You want me to feast on this wet, sweet nirvana until you're coming all over my tongue."

I gasp and squirm as Wolf peels my panties off with his teeth.

He exhales and the sound is somewhere between a hiss and a growl. "So fucking pretty." There's not a hair left on my body that's not on my head. Details like that are managed by my beauty teams, and have been since I hit puberty. As used to being groomed and undressed as I am, I'm not prepared for *this*. The shocking level of intimacy is on a whole different level. He's murmuring, removing my dress completely. "So ready for me to do all the filthy, beastly things I'm about to do. Lie back. Let me taste all this. I need it now."

I almost start to protest because isn't this sort of crossing a line?—but he's already there, pushing my legs apart and pinning me in place.

Wolf licks his tongue over my soft, aching flesh and it's the craziest thing that's ever happened to me in my entire life. I just never, ever knew anything could feel so good.

I can't think, I can only feel him, licking into me, finding my clit and sucking on it with his greedy mouth. His tongue pushes into me. He's playing with me, feasting. Biting. Sucking. Savoring me as he takes what he wants.

I feel a rise inside myself, of blooming pleasure that's so powerful I don't even know what to do with it. It's going to overflow. There's a breaking point he's pushing me over the edge of. He's about to change my world.

But then, he slows.

He stops.

His head lifts, and his wicked mouth is shiny with wetness. "You're mine now, princess. You can't give me a taste of heaven and not give me everything. I'll hunt you down if you try to leave me. Marry me. Say yes."

I'm breathing hard. I don't want him to stop. *"Please,"* I gasp.

"Please?" His low laugh is infuriating. "Please stop, Wolf? Or please eat my perfect pussy like you're starved for me. Which is it? Say yes to me. You're too damn pretty. And horny as fuck, all slick with the sweetest honey, just for me. I need to feast on my prize."

His tongue laves tenderly against my clit, swirling it, applying the kind of pressure that, if he would just keep going and do that once more, it would shatter me.

He knows this.

But he won't give it to me.

I squirm to try to get closer. Maybe I can do it myself. *I need it so much.* I think I might go mad if he won't give it to me. *"Wolf. Please, Wolf."* I'm almost crying.

"First you're going to fall in love with what I can do to you," he murmurs against my pussy. "Then you're going to fall in love with how good I can make you feel." Another extremely lewd lick. "And then you're going to fall in love with the life I'm going to help you create for yourself and for us and our little beach babies. Because sometimes it's good to have help with things you haven't been able to conquer yet. I'm going to be the one to do that for you." His tongue slides inside me, then out. "Now that I've had a taste of you, there's no way in hell I'm letting you walk away. Say yes and I'll give you everything you want. But once you say yes, there's no turning back. You need to make sure you can keep your word, like I've promised to keep mine." Another flick. His fingers glide over the moisture, exploring me in a wildly intimate way.

With two fingers, he taps. *Right there.*

He does it again and the lava is brimming so close to the top of some out-of-control peak, I need to reach it more than I need my next breath.

His tongue licks me lazily, opening me like he's carefully arranging the petals of a flower.

"Say yes, princess, and I'll give you what you need. All of it. Every day and every night."

Another, harder tap.

*One more. Please. One more.*

He waits.

I literally can't take this. I'm going to die of raw need if he doesn't give me more. *"Yes, Wolf."*

"Yes?"

*"Yes.* I'll marry you. *Please. Yes."*

A soft *bite,* and I'm *so, so close.* "Are you sure this isn't a clever ploy to get me to eat you right over the edge and then you disappear and leave me standing at the altar? What do you say, baby? Are you for real?"

*"Yes.* I'll marry you. *I will.* I do. I promise."

There's a pause that feels almost emotional. "That's my good girl. Now you can get your reward. You ready to come for me? Right now? How bad do you want it?"

"*Bad. Please. Please.*"

"It's times like these when the real you shines through, did you know that? This is where the shy little people pleaser finds her true self and the real freak comes out. Show me. Relax, move, open, grind that sweet pink pussy against my face. Let yourself be free, gorgeous girl. I've got you."

So I do it. I stop resisting. My knees fall open and my body goes pliant. I arch and give myself to him fully. I let myself surrender.

"That's my good little girl. Now get ready for your life to change, in ways that are better than you ever imagined. I'll meet you on the other side of your boundaries."

It's then that Wolf Ramsey shows me exactly what power he was talking about. His fingers stroke into me, finding a sublime trigger that forces the pleasure peak to a ludicrous summit. His mouth latches onto my clit, milking it as his fingers rub and grip.

It's happening.

The spasms start and I'm riding the heat, until the magnitude of sensation tips me over into a tidal wave of nearly unendurable pleasure. Waves of it wrack through my body, exploding, over and over. I writhe, just to cope with it. I can barely hear the animal moans I'm making through the crashing bliss.

Wolf rides it with me, his mouth and his fingers working the ecstasy, prolonging it. Spinning it into another wave. And another.

Until I'm riding a dazed, spent high.

My eyes are closed, my body heavy and reborn. I'm

floating. I feel the touch of his fingers. Something hard and hot. There's a wet, rhythmic sound and a growling groan. Warm wetness rains onto my pussy, coating it in pulsing beats. He smooths this wetness, swirling it and dipping it barely inside me. Gliding it over my clit, he uses the silkiness to rub me there until I feel myself slide into another orgasm, my inner muscles clamping voluptuously on the emptiness.

"You're mine," comes the low whisper. "This pussy is mine. Marked by me and claimed by me. Only me. I'll follow you anywhere you go."

I feel his weight on top of me. There's a tugging at my wrists as he unties me. He kisses my lips and I can taste *myself*. His feeding frenzy on my own pleasure. The taste of it on his mouth and the warm wetness of his claim connects me to him more than anything has, to anyone, ever. I can't explain it, I can only feel it.

"Good thing the music's loud," he jokes.

My eyelids are too heavy to open more than once, to see him staring down at my face, his eyes dark as he kisses me again.

"Keep your word, princess. Show up for me."

And then he's gone.

# 9

# Vivi

I SLEEP LIKE THE DEAD, with no dreams, just a deep, restorative bliss, teased at the edges by the soothing rhythm of the waves right outside my window.

His bed is comfortable. Like, *insanely* comfortable. Even now I feel like I'm floating on a sea of cushiony clouds. I open my eyes and see that the sun is low and the sky is clear. A light sea breeze touches the gauzy curtains. It's going to be a perfect day.

I'm naked, sprawled under a velvety-soft sheet.

My body feels … okay, *amazing*. As though it's glowing from the inside out with the memory of all that surging, exploding pleasure. I feel more beautiful than I can ever remember feeling.

*Wow.*

I've heard of orgasms, obviously. I don't know why but I've never really thought much about what they might *feel* like. I'd never really … searched for one before. He asked me if I touched myself and I really haven't. A few times, but not often. Even then, I never even got close to reaching that crazy summit he forced me to climb … and then to tumble over into the most intense pleasure of my life.

Oppression isn't sexy. My life is so carefully managed and scheduled by other people, I never know when I'm being watched. I don't think there are cameras in my room but I don't really know that for sure. I don't trust Silas enough to rule it out. And I wouldn't dare try to order a vibrator or something like that online. I'd be caught out immediately. I can just imagine Silas questioning the item-ized credit card purchase—if I had somehow been able to find one. Or Lana Lee's scathing commentary.

How have I lived like that for so long?

Why have I allowed it?

All that's going to change, starting now.

One, he promised me it would. Two, I'm going to make sure *I* take charge of things like that. It's time. In fact it's long overdue.

I can see that so clearly now. The distance from home Paradise is providing me with is making everything clearer. The bullying. The over-scheduling. The basically-locking-me-in-my-room-for-half-my-life. The control.

Fuck all of them.

Wolf's assurances are empowering me. Not only that, but the orgasms he gave me are having a strange effect on me. I feel like one of those video game characters that's fully charged and boosted with health.

That's what he's given me: power.

I'm *alive*. I have a glowing soul and body that's capable of receiving mind-blowing pleasure … and *coming extremely hard. Twice.*

I've discovered myself.

In this moment I feel weirdly, wildly happy.

There's a soft knock on the door.

The door opens.

Echo, Blaise and Perri let themselves into the room and they're carrying a picnic basket of food and a tray holding four travel mugs of coffee.

"Hi, honey," Perri says. Gently gauging whether or not I've been destroyed by my husband-to-be or am still intact. She lifts my hand and inspects my ring. "Wow. It's very you, Vivi. It's whimsical and unique."

I can't bring myself to thank her for the sort-of compliment. I no longer need her approval.

But she's right: it *is* me. I don't know how Wolf Ramsey knew it would be. Maybe it was a lucky guess. Or maybe it's him too. Maybe we're a better match than we might have expected.

Something tells me Blaise and Echo know that whatever relationship Wolf and I have, at this point, still hasn't been consummated. My guess is that they're as superstitious as Wolf and they know he'll want to save that particular detail for the wedding night. Just a guess, but their concern this morning is all about getting me to the altar on time.

I sit up, leaning against the pale wood headboard of Wolf's modernist four poster bed. I prop a pillow behind my head and pull the sheet up to cover myself a little more thoroughly. I glance at the pieces of fabric Wolf used to bind my wrists, hoping they don't notice them. Then again, it hardly matters.

Echo gives me a once-over as she sits down on the bed next to me. All three of them are staring at me even though they're trying not to.

I'm sure my hair's a bird's nest. My dress has been tossed onto a chair next to the bed, inside out. I have no idea where my panties are. I can feel that my cheeks are flushed.

I can't bring myself to worry about what I look like. I'm too peaceful.

Perri walks through the open doors onto the lanai. "This house is insane." She looks down onto the beach. "Oh, look, some of the fighters are already practicing."

"Is Drake down there?" Blaise asks her.

"He's in the ring," Perri comments, "getting pummeled."

Perri seems unusually upbeat. "Who's Drake?" I ask her.

"Our cousin Hunter's friend from Maui." Echo hands me a cup of coffee. "He's a professional surfer."

Perri's smile is coy. "He and I had … well, a meeting of the minds last night."

My eyebrows lift. "What?" Here I was, thinking she was pining from a broken heart.

"I decided to get back on the horse." Perri takes a sip from the mug of coffee she's holding. "I guess it was obvious to everyone except me that I never even remotely had a shot with Knox."

I'm a little shocked that she would rebound so quickly, after all the drama.

Echo is kind. "I'm sure you would have if his soulmate hadn't turned up when he was least expecting it."

Perri glances back to the fighters. I can hear their grunting from here. "Poor Drake. The guy with the eagle wing tattoos on his back is annihilating him."

"That's Nero," Echo informs her.

"Vivi," Blaise says, "your design team is ready for you. Your head stylist is chomping at the bit to get her hands on you."

"Lana? I'm surprised she waited up at the castle instead of insisting on climbing into your dune buggy with you."

"It wasn't easy to persuade her," Blaise admits. She's standing in front of Wolf's bookshelf where all the photographs are displayed. "I haven't been up here since he first built this house three years ago. I've never seen some of these pictures." She snaps photos of them with her phone. "I wish they could be here today. Who would have thought that three of us would be getting married before the end of the year."

Echo looks up from her phone. "Three?"

"I told Tristan about what happened with Knox and Cassidy." Blaise is dressed in a pair of fitted off-white pants and a matching tank top made from cotton and soft suede that I can recognize by now as one of Echo's designs. Blaise is tall and toned, with the body of an elite athlete or a warrior queen. She has that vibe to her, of someone who could lead armies or slay dragons. And Echo's designs for her channel that detail. "I told him the Ramsey-King alliance is sealed now and they can satisfy the curse so I don't have to. We're getting married, Echo. He's flying in today and we'll make the announcement soon. Don't tell anyone yet, though. Today is about Vivi and Wolf."

Echo goes over to Blaise and gives her a heartfelt hug. "Blaise. I'm so happy for you."

Blaise's eyes are shiny. "I can't believe we can really be together."

Echo explains, "Blaise has been secretly seeing this guy who lives on the North Shore of Oahu for over a year. He's gorgeous. He's an artist and he owns his own gallery."

Seeing Blaise's tearful relief makes it clear to me that I'm doing the right thing, at least for Wolf's family—wait, have I decided?

*You promised him. Last night. You told him you'd show up for him if he would only keep … eating you until you came so hard you saw stars.*

Is it too late to change my mind?

*Do I still want to?*

I've never seen any sign of vulnerability in Blaise before. She's always in control of every situation and her family leans on her as a steadying force. She's the kind of person who would anchor you and guide every decision you make. But this whole thing has obviously been weighing very heavily on her.

Knox and Cassidy can make the Ramsey-King alliance,

but Blaise would still be next in line to secure the other match, being second oldest.

It's because of Wolf—and me—that she can marry the man she's in love with.

I mean, I'm glad I can do this for her. I'm glad Blaise will—*might*—get her happily ever after. And I'm glad Knox and Cassidy will get theirs.

But in many ways I feel numb.

Will I get mine?

I mean, the orgasms were … yes, life-changing.

But it doesn't change the fact that, in just a few short hours, I'm going to be married and irrevocably bound to a man I've known only a few days. *Whose unholy vigor has already given me the most intense experience of my life, by a magnitude of around a trillion. And that was just a brief warm-up to what's going to be happening tonight.*

My wedding night.

I'm scared. But after last night I'm also … *curious*. And terrified. And still drifting on a lingering high from the effects of … *his mouth.*

*God.*

I can feel my face flush even more at the memory of … *his tongue.*

*His hunger, which could only be described as freaking voracious.*

*The warm pulse of his wetness.*

I can only imagine what's in store for me tonight.

I gave him my word that I would show up.

I could still change my mind, of course. Disappear. Take one of his guns for protection—not that I've ever been taught how to use one, which is another thing I want to fix. I should know how to defend myself. This time, I could prepare myself more carefully for the journey. I could sell the ring on my finger if I had to.

If I thought I could get away with it, would I do it?

Wolf would follow me and find me. He promised me that.

If Echo, Blaise and Perri weren't here as my chaperones, would I quietly walk down the beach and try again?

Maybe I would.

I wrap the sheet around myself and head to his bathroom to take a shower. The shower is made of smooth sandstone and takes up half the length of the room. It looks out over a picturesque waterfall. I rinse myself. Touching myself where he touched me. I'm still slippery with his claim and my own pleasure.

*I want more of it.*

What keeps me here more than anything else is the craving.

*I want more of Wolf Ramsey. I want him to give me everything he promised he would.*

What I find myself thinking is this: *if I have to marry him to do it, then so be it.*

FROM THERE, my wedding day is a blur.

I can vaguely appreciate that the air is balmy and the breeze is soft, that the mood is festive and that everyone around me seems to be having a fantastic time.

I float through the preparations as though watching them from a buffered distance.

My dress is divine, with delicate seashells embroidered into its fitted bodice. Tiny white pearls and pale pink shells are sewn into the detailing, giving the whole thing a shimmery, Venus-born-from-the-seashell effect (which is what Echo said she was going for, and it works). The hem of the satin floor-length skirt is gathered at the front with seven pieces of carved white shell. Seven white feathers are sewn into the tail of the train. Echo said she asked Wolf if there was anything he wanted to be added to my dress and that was his request: sevens. My hair is long with a wave at the sun-lightened ends. The lace veil is pinned into place with a tiara encrusted with delicate pearls and glittering diamonds.

Echo, Blaise, Tatum and Perri are my bridesmaids. All four of them are wearing dresses made from varying shades of purple silk. Their bouquets are pale, purple-pink roses. Mine is white.

The enthusiasm of everyone around me pushes me forward on what feels like a conveyor belt of forward momentum. I want to slow it down. I wish I could stop time and decide for myself if this is really something I want.

But I can't slow it down. I can't run and I can't hide.

And it's time.

Paradise's small chapel sits on top of a hill next to the castle. It has a magical view.

Silas, Malachi, Enzo, Jagger and Stone are waiting for us

at the door of the church, to escort the five of us down the aisle. The double doors are open and I can see that the small church is crammed full of people.

A quartet plays Bach's Cello Suite No. 1. My mother's studio has, in one of its walk-in closets, shelves of classical music on vinyl. I used to go through the stacks when I was a child, listening to them one by one, feeling like they were connecting me to her through time. This piece was always one of my favorites. No one here could have known that, since I've never told anyone.

It feels like a good omen, that they'd be playing it now.

Today is the seventh. There are seven diamonds in my engagement ring. Wolf talked about his superstitions and about creating as much good karma as we could get. I don't happen to be superstitious at all, but I can feel, here and now, that the scene and the mood and the slant of the sunlight *does* feel auspicious. If I could ignore the fact that I've known Wolf Ramsey for a grand total of two days, I might even say the scene felt as close to perfect as such a thing can get.

I can't see the altar from here, or my husband-to-be.

Aside from Stone's bruised face and his two black eyes, the men look outrageously handsome in their tuxes.

"You look stunning, Vivi," says Enzo. He's much taller than me and his eyes are the same color aqua as the sea behind him. All the men in the alliance families are tall, and big. Well-built men with striking eyes, near-legendary hand-someness and that edge of danger that clings to Enzo now like a second skin. If I was as superstitious as my almost-husband I might even say these men are the chosen ones. Ruthless but also riveting. Enzo's look could be described as GQ-model meets hot gangster. Even so, I'm glad it's not *him* I have to marry. He's calculating and cruel, according to my brothers. Then again, so are they.

Jagger grins at me, the blond flicks of his hair catching sunlight. "If I'd known the extent of it, *I* would have volunteered. Is it too late to steal you?"

"Yes," Echo and Blaise say in unison.

Silas offers me his arm and I'm glad he's the one giving me away. Our eyes meet and I see my brother in a different light today. The newly discovered live wire that seems to have plugged itself into my soul has the urge to lash out at him. *You should have protected me. You should have lifted me up instead of pinning me down.* Very soon, I'll no longer be his to control. My power will be my own.

The music changes.

They're playing the wedding march.

"My little sister scrubs up pretty well." Malachi kisses my cheek. I look up into his amber eyes, so similar in color to my own. The two of us look more alike than any of our other siblings. Do I hate him? No. In many ways he was just doing his best to survive, like I was. Except that he chose— and was allowed to choose—to sleep his way across the islands to cope with his demons. He offers Echo his arm. "Let's do this. You ready, Vivi?"

"Yes." As ready as I'll ever be.

Echo and Malachi go first. Then Blaise and Enzo. Jagger and Tatum. Stone and Perri.

Until it's my turn.

I follow Silas's lead and we enter the church. The interior of the chapel is serene and idyllic, with whitewashed walls and a wooden ceiling with criss-crossing beams. Large stained glass windows recreating Kauai's landscape decorate the scene with shards of colorful light. It's full to capacity. Several hundred people are packed in here and every single one of them is staring at me. Some of them gasp and murmur.

I'm glad for the thin barrier of the veil.

And there he is.

Standing next to his brothers, tall and broad-shouldered in his tux. He looks handsome and noble, like he's a prince of this island, and I guess he is. A subdued power and a wild masculinity cling to him. With his vivid blue eyes, his build and the ultra-confident way he holds himself, he seems larger than life. His eyes are glued to me, watching me as Silas leads me down the aisle.

I blush as our gazes lock. I know what we're both remembering. *How hard I came when he licked me.*

The terror I've felt at random moments—yesterday, last night, this morning—is gone.

That glimmer of mischief in him. The memory of his perfect mouth. His rapt expression now, as he watches me walk up the aisle toward him, reassures me. Not completely, but enough.

Wolf Ramsey looks staunch and triumphant. Starstruck. Relieved. And drop-dead gorgeous.

Something about the combination makes me—for the

first time right here and now—*want* to marry him. Kind of desperately. My groom and I, somehow, click.

I like that I can almost read his thoughts. A conversation passes between us without words.

*You showed up, princess.*

*Yes. I showed up. I'm already a little addicted to what you can do.*

Remington Ramsey is stoic and handsome but the sadness behind his expression is closer to the surface today. Maybe the wedding dress is reminding him of all he's lost.

Knox Ramsey's expression is much dreamier. His eyes are fixed on his own bride-to-be, whose flaxen hair catches the reflection of the stained glass window from where she's sitting in the front row.

Silas places my hand in Wolf's. Then, in an unusually caring moment, he places his palm on my arm. *Thank you for stepping up. For going through with it.*

Which—I'll be honest—kind of pisses me off. I almost want to make this marriage the happiest in history just to spite him and show him that I'm not doing this for him. I'm doing it for myself.

Wolf steps forward and lifts my veil. He leans to whisper in my ear. "I've never seen anything as beautiful as you, princess. You won't regret showing up for me, I promise you that."

There he goes again with the growing list of nicest-things-anyone's-ever-said-to-me. With an edge.

Wolf takes both my hands.

And then it begins.

The minister is a prodigal, solemn version of the

usually-boisterous Ramsey cousin. He might be in his late thirties. He glances at the open Bible in his hands, then at us. "The alliance marriage vows are not to be taken lightly," he tells us. "The union is an irrevocable bond never to be broken. Sacred vows, sealed with blood and body, forged by fate."

*Holy hell. I can't believe I'm doing this.*

But as Wolf recites his vows, I find myself riveted by the husky resolve in his voice. "I, Wolf John Ramsey, take you, Vivienne Sofia Fitzpatrick, to be my lawfully wedded wife. With this ring, a symbol of our unending marriage, I vow to honor and protect you from this day forward, to have and to hold you, for as long as we both shall live."

He slides the gold band onto my finger.

And then it's my turn.

I glance at Remy. Knox. Silas.

Wolf. Who's gazing down at me. Waiting.

There's a flicker of unease in him, at my hesitation, followed quickly by determination. I have no doubt he'll do anything to marry me. He has to. *And he wants to.* I can see it in his devil-blue eyes.

"Repeat after me," says the minister. "I, Vivienne Sofia Fitzpatrick, take you, Wolf John Ramsey, to be my lawfully wedded husband."

And so I do it. I repeat the words that will seal me to Wolf Ramsey for the rest of time, praying that he'll prove himself to be the best version of himself in all the ways he's promised to be. "I, Vivienne Sofia Fitzpatrick, take you, Wolf John Ramsey, to be my lawfully wedded husband."

The minister continues. "With this ring, a symbol of our unending marriage, I vow to honor and obey you, from this day forward, to have and to hold you, for as long as we both shall live."

I begin. "With this ring, a symbol of our unending marriage, I vow to honor and … love you, from this day forward, to have and to hold you, for as long as we both shall live."

Wolf's smile at my edit is … absolutely heartfelt. And it makes me fall just a little bit in love with this fierce, gorgeous man. I remember something he said to me. *I felt like the universe or the angel or my ancestors or whoever's in charge of these things put you in my path for a reason. I'm going to honor the curse not only because I have to but because I want to.* As unlikely as it is, what we're feeling in this moment is genuine and it seals our bond more than the rings ever could.

"I now pronounce you man and wife," the minister proclaims. "Wolf Ramsey, you may seal your vows with a kiss."

I look up into the eyes of my new husband. I'm struck again by the vibrance of them, not just in color but in the intensity of his life-force behind them. He's going to be a handful, no doubt about that.

Wolf bends to kiss me, his lips barely brushing mine. But then he settles in with more pressure, touching his tongue to my lips, opening them, reminding me of his hungry feasting last night. I open to him, feeling his effects everywhere. It's hardly the place to get wet for him. Then again, maybe it's the perfect place.

The minister clears his throat.

Wolf breaks the kiss, grinning at me, then the minister.

The ceremony is done. Knox, Remy and several of his cousins are patting him on the back and I'm led by my imposing new husband through the throngs of Ramsey well-wishers to the grand hall of the Ramsey castle, where the party has already started.

# 10

# WOLF

It was right around the time I first tasted the girl who was about to become my wife that I started wondering if maybe I am capable of falling in love after all.

Actually I don't need to wonder.

She's nirvana in human form. I never knew a person could be so fucking *ideal*. I wasn't prepared for the extent of it.

It's an unnerving kind of perfection that feels like it's been tailor made just for me. Of course I'm aware that she's gorgeous and everyone sees it, but the way all the details of her converge is literally the kind of cocktail that has my head spinning.

Her eyes are wide and the color of amber, her eyelashes long and curved. The way she looks out from under them is shy but with that sassy undertone that's possibly my favorite thing about her.

The slaying appeal of her gives me an eerie feeling. *Mom? Dad? Great great great grandfather Nathaniel? Are you out there somewhere? Did you send this girl to me to make up for all the angst? The loss? The grief? For forcing us to live with the curse hanging over our heads our whole lives? Is this my reward for stepping up?*

The band plays a song and we dance to Can't Help Falling In Love. I'm not sure who chose this song. I don't really care. I guess it fits because I don't know what the fuck is happening. I hold her close to me as we dance and I'm staring down at her. Her lips are full and glossy and I lean in to kiss her because I know how good she tastes and, even if I could resist her, there's no reason to now. She's mine.

The room is watching and everyone cheers but I barely notice them. I'm too smitten with this vision of gorgeous-ness that happens to be my new wife.

Her angelic face only gets more beautiful the more I stare at it. I plunge my fingers into her long, silky hair and wrap it around my fist. Her body is flush against mine and I keep her there so she can feel how fucking hard I already am—not great in the middle of our wedding reception but it can't be helped.

She's so damn *beautiful*.

I'll wait out the next couple of hours while we dance and toast the marriage and cut the cake. We'll do everything by the book to keep the wedding karma rolling along with no bumps.

Then she's mine.

The little nymph with the fire in her eyes and the candy-pink pussy that tastes like sweet, juicy need. I can't say she tastes like my wildest fantasies because I'd never thought to fantasize about her.

I honestly never thought much about marriage and children until Vivi and the dilemma that swirled around her showed up. Before her, I pictured myself in my thirties, maybe knocking up a few women on purpose just so my bloodline would be out there running around in the world, making waves. But now, that scenario sounds nightmarish. The logistics would never have worked. I would have wanted to keep the babies with me and raise them in Paradise. Which means I would have had to fight the women for them or invite them along too—not something I would have ever considered with anyone I've met so far in my life.

Until now.

My fascination and my new obsession are stuck in overdrive.

I can't believe this little goddess is *my wife*.

She's going to carry *my babies*. The thought is maddening. Because I can't wait to get started.

*I want to breed her like a wild, feral animal. I want her to be full of my flooding cum until she's round and full with my baby.*

*Fuck.*

It's a monumental shift but there it is. I've never craved anything so badly in my life.

My world, suddenly, revolves around this cute-hot little nymph who's going to be the bearer of my *children*. My sole purpose now is to keep her safe. I need her healthy and comfortable. I need her well-fed and naked and relaxed.

Wet and ready. And so happy she'll give me anything I want.

Is it because she's my wife that I'm reacting to her this way? Is it because I'm so mired in the superstitions surrounding the curse that my psyche has cast a spell on me, tricking me into seeing her as a supernatural-level force of beauty and fertility?

*No.*

*It's because she's the one.*

And I'm up to the task of making sure she'll receive everything I want to give her. "You're perfect," I tell her.

She smiles but then her mouth quirks. "Not even close. Ask anyone in my family."

"I don't care about them. I care about you. Trust your husband. If I say you're the most beautiful girl in the world, then you are. And the bravest. The sassiest. And the sexiest."

She laughs and rolls her eyes and the sound is the lightest I've heard her make yet. I try not to think about the lusty moans she made as she was coming in my mouth. *Keep it together, Ramsey. You'll be back in heaven again in a matter of* … two hours is going to be my limit. Maybe one.

Her laughter is real and it lights up her face. She's gorgeous when she's surly and petulant but her levity takes it to a whole new level. She's so damn pretty I can't help myself. I get this strange sense of vertigo but in one direction only: toward her. *I love the sound of her laughter.* I listen to it, in awe of her, and her amusement rubs off on me.

I'm grinning at her and this makes her laugh even more.

Which makes me laugh. Which makes her laugh even harder, until she's almost breathless with it. Something in us aligns. We're in this together and we're overcome by the weight of it but also the connection. It digs into us right here on the dance floor in a shared, unexpected moment.

"You're crazy," I tell her, holding her closer. Her wild heart beats next to mine.

"You're very good at telling me what I want to hear."

"I've just never seen anyone who's literally flawless. How is that even possible?"

She gives me a beguiled smile. "It isn't."

"Show me, then. I keep looking for flaws but I can't see a single one."

"Trust me, there are plenty."

"Like what?"

"I'm too shy, for one."

"Shyness isn't a flaw."

"It is."

"You're only shy because you've been forced to live under someone else's thumb your whole life. That's over now. You're good now. I'll hold you like you're both breakable and explosive. I'll love you like it's dangerous to drop you. I'm going to lift you up, princess, until you're shining brighter than the sun. You don't know your own power yet. But I do. I can see it."

Her smile softens. "Stop doing that."

"Doing what?"

"Saying the nicest things anyone's ever said to me. You've got a knack."

"That's my job now. I'm going to give you the whole fairy tale. Your smile and ..." I lean closer and whisper in her ear, "... those moans you make when I'm sucking your clit and fucking you with my tongue ... " I hold her gaze as she blushes and we keep dancing— "I'm going to fill my life with them. Your laughter, your safety and most of all your pleasure are my only priorities. Because you're stunning and sweet and I'm going to make all your wildest dreams come true."

Her cheeks are pink. She's remembering. She's turned on and she's also touched. She *loves* being praised and told all the things about herself that she should already know, but doesn't.

"Do you want to know how I'm going to do all that, baby?"

She blinks at me, but there's an eagerness in her that's making me feel downright twisted.

"I'm going to start by giving you on-call stellar orgasms. *Lots* of them. As many as you can handle. The kind where you cry and moan and you can't remember your own name because nothing's ever felt so fucking good."

More heat rises to her face but she smiles and her little white teeth are blowing my mind.

Softly, I murmur, "Are you wet for your husband? Is that candy-sweet pussy coated with honey, just for me?" More blushing. We both know she is—and fuck, the thought of her, all wet and ready for my thick cock to force its way inside the tight, slippery nirvana of her body as she comes is working me into a barely-controlled frenzy. I try to keep my cool but I'm being too obvious. One of my cousins whistles from a nearby table.

The next song starts and other people join us on the dance floor but I'm oblivious to them. I'm completely captivated by my wife.

Two days ago, when I first saw her, I was dazzled by her beauty.

Yesterday, when I chased her and she fought me and I *felt* her for the first time, the effect she has on me forged itself into me like an electric shock button is wired inside my chest, zapping me whenever I look at her. It's physically painful.

Last night, when I kissed her for the first time, my new addiction began to consume me. At this point it's basically burning me alive.

"We deserve each other," I tell her.

"Why's that?"

"I can't do anything by halves. I fight hard, I live hard and I don't second guess the things I can't control."

"Like …?"

"Like this."

"This? What 'this' do you mean?"

"This marriage. Everything that's happening here."

"You could have stopped it, Wolf. You didn't *have* to step up."

"It was destiny. I could feel that."

She laughs lightly and shakes her head. "Destiny. The curse. Karma. You act like those things made your choice for you."

"They didn't make my choice but they showed me what was meant to be."

She's not convinced. "We'll see."

"Yeah," I say, forcefully. "We will see. *You'll* see, more importantly. You'll see that you deserve someone who's sure about this. About you. No half love. No inconsistency."

"I don't see how you can know that when we're only two days in." She's protesting but her eyes round with a pooling hopefulness. She's bound to me irrevocably now and she wants so badly to believe me.

"You deserve someone who appreciates you. Things aren't supposed to be perfect but sometimes they just are. Sometimes they work out in ways you never thought they could because you want them to."

She eyes me warily but she's leaning closer. Her lips are parted. Her eyes shine. "You better be as real as you keep telling me you are, Wolf Ramsey."

"Oh, I am, baby. You just wait." I hold her closer so the hard length of me presses hotly against her.

She *feels* me. Her hips barely pitch forward in a reflexive plea.

Her responsiveness is rocket fuel to my open flame. She's watching me as I whisper promises. She's drinking all of it in.

It takes every ounce of self-control I have not to sling her over my shoulder and carry her away right now.

Jagger taps me on the shoulder. "Can I dance with your wife, Ramsey?"

"Not a chance in hell," I growl. I'll kill him or anyone else who touches her.

Jagger laughs and wanders off. "Don't try to dance with Vivi, anyone," he jokes, "unless you're prepared to die a painful, bloody death while slow-dancing to Shania Twain."

He's not wrong. This is new territory for me. I'm almost dazed by how fiercely protective I feel.

*Mine.*

We dance and I can bear the scene only because her supple body is pressed up against me. We eat and drink. The speeches and toasts are made. The five-tiered chocolate cake with vanilla icing is cut and served with raspberry sauce and everyone takes a piece for good luck. And the party revs up.

But I've held out long enough.

I thank them for coming and they cheer as I pull Vivi by the hand. My low husk is only for her, "Come on, little wife. It's time for bed."

# 11

# Vivi

A DUNE BUGGY with white ribbons and a *Just Married!* sign draped along the back is waiting outside. Wolf carefully places me in the passenger seat. Something in him has changed. I can see it in his eyes and feel it in the thrumming tension of his body.

We're *married* now. Our bond is cast in stone—or as close as these things get. We can't ever get divorced, according to the rules of the curse, which I know Wolf will take very seriously.

His dedication to me feels real. He won't let anyone else near me and his words are addictively romantic. The big, fierce Wolf Ramsey is a sweet talker, who knew?

Being pressed up against his hard body all night, dancing and being fed sugary cake and sparkling champagne by him, I'm brimming with a new kind of high. I know how good he feels. I *want* to surrender to what he can do. He's my husband now. I can't escape him. What I wasn't expecting is: I don't know if I want to.

Our emotions are raw. Whatever our conscious minds might think of this whirlwind of an arranged marriage, our basest urges have accepted that we're magnets who can't resist each other's pull. Our bodies are hot with anticipation.

We pull up next to the house and he parks the buggy in front of the steps of the lanai. "Stay right there," he says.

Then he walks around to the passenger side of the dune buggy and scoops me into his arms.

And then my new husband carries me up the stairs.

"Welcome home, princess." Wolf kicks open the door and carries me over the threshold. I already know he's a traditionalist when it comes to all things superstition-related and he wants to do it properly. I have to admit, so far, everything about my wedding day has gone without a hitch. I can't really imagine how any of it could have been more beautiful or more perfect—aside from the elephant in the room a.k.a. I hardly know my husband. Or that, only a day ago I was half-terrified of him.

I'm not terrified anymore.

Okay, maybe a little bit terrified.

I'm Mrs. Wolf Ramsey now and there's a comfort in that because I know he'll protect me. He's already proven that. After a lifetime of feeling powerless, with him as my new guide, my life has taken on all the glow of a phoenix rising. It's almost jarring how different the horizon looks now. And I recognize the new, fiery glint. It's the recklessness I knew was inside me the whole time.

Wolf Ramsey has lit my flame.

*I'm going to give you the whole fairy tale.*

*Your laughter, your safety and most of all your pleasure are my only priorities.*

*I'm going to make all your wildest dreams come true.*

Can I believe him?

The house is empty of people and has been cleaned and decorated with flowers and a *Congratulations Wolf and Vivi!* banner. There are balloons and flowers everywhere. Low lamplight illuminates the space.

"Shit, they really went all out." Wolf carries me up the stairs. The bed is covered in crisp white sheets and plush pillows, sprinkled with white rose petals. Fresh arrangements of cut roses have been placed around the room. Their fragrance mingles with the salty sea air. Lit candles burn inside glass globes.

"Wow," I muse. Everything is so thoughtfully done, not by decorators who are getting paid to promote their own brand so they can put it on Instagram, like I'm used to. This house has been prepared for us by people who *want* us—and me, specifically—to feel at home here. The flower arrangements are white and purple, to match the color themes of our wedding. Everything is cozy and luxurious. The sliding doors to the lanai are open, offering their view of the night sky and the moon's reflection on the rippling water. More lit candles have been artfully placed on the outdoor tables and around the hot tub.

If I were ever to try to imagine a space I would want to

become one with, and start a marriage to, and live my life in, this is it.

I'm nervous about what's about to happen here but I'm also high on adrenaline and champagne.

And I'm *married* to a hot hunk who gave me my first two orgasms—which I still haven't recovered from—and has promised to give me more, starting now. And who also says things like, *I've got you. You're perfect. I'm going to lift you up until you're shining brighter than the sun.*

I mean, as much as I wasn't expecting the plot twist of my weekend and didn't exactly choose this, it could definitely be a lot worse.

My body feels supple and young. He's been feeding me all night with his lightning bolt touch. Every cell in my body is buzzing.

Wolf sets me down gently on my feet next to the bed.

*God, I hope I'm ready for this.*

My new husband is definitely ready. The huge length ridging in his pants that's been pressed up against me for most of the night seems to have doubled in size. He took off the jacket of his tux earlier. Now, he peels off his shirt and tosses it onto a chair as though it's been constricting him. His muscles look even more pumped up tonight, with pent-up tension, maybe. I'm not *that* naïve. He's half crazed with lust—it's radiating off his broad, sun-dark shoulders in waves—and his intensity both scares me and thrills me.

"You're in for it tonight, golden-eyed girl."

*Oh God.*

He's wearing the thick leather weapons belt around his waist that he's never without, aside from the twenty or so minutes it took for us to recite our vows. His tatted-up chest and arms add to the savage energy of him. His ink only accentuates his mountain-man-with-a-tropical-island-twist vibe. A sun with curved rays. Cresting waves. A hunting knife. The spiral-patterned band around his sculpted upper arm that I recognize from our wedding reception as part of the Ramsey crest.

The sheer size of him, along with his guns and his ink and his knives, should be intimidating. And it is. But my fear is edged with a primal excitement. I mean, the veined, suntanned arm porn, the tantalizing arrow line of hair that disappears below his belt buckle, the dark-lit eyes and mean-ing-filled glares all night, and crashing through the middle of it all, the laughter.

I'm sheltered but even I can see that dreams are made of him.

His fingers glide over my bare shoulders. Slowly, he unzips my wedding dress. All I'm wearing under it is a tiny pair of white lace panties. Wolf eases the straps over my shoulders, letting the dress fall to the floor. My full breasts bounce lightly as they're freed from the built-in support of the bodice.

"My wife is a goddess." Challenging me with the garish jewel-like glint of his turquoise eyes and his white teeth, exposed in a half-snarl.

He looks bigger and more powerfully built than I've ever seen him. Carnal and dangerous. And here I am, mostly naked, quivering from my feverish response to him. He circles me, letting his rough fingers trail across my skin in an unhurried claim.

"*Mine*," he murmurs. His fingers brush the soft surface of my nipples, pinching lightly. Under his touch, they bead into taut pebbles. His thumbs graze and my breath catches. Watching my eyes, he rolls and tugs the sensitive tips.

I exhale a soft breath.

"I'm going to take it just slow enough, but barely, and give you just a little more than you can handle. You already know it's going to be the best feeling you've ever had. You're ready."

*Am I?* It's hard to speak. I'm concentrating on staying upright, keeping my knees from buckling under me as his fingers tease.

His gaze holds me captive. "You're desperate for what I'm about to do, little wife."

*Okay, yes.* The heat of his touch is burning me.

"Say it," he commands. "Tell me what you want."

"I want you," I whisper.

"Well, that's good, princess. Because you're going to get me. All of me. My wife *always* gets what she wants." He plumps my full breasts with his strong, warm hands and he lowers his head, sucking my nipple into his mouth.

I gasp, like I'm coming up for air from under water.

He laps and suckles, squeezing my other nipple with rough fingers. Then he switches sides and sucks strongly on the punished bud, getting it wet, biting gently with his teeth. Until both my nipples are slippery and swollen from the hot work of his mouth. He takes them between his fingers and grips them more tightly—painfully—and the pleasure-pain shoots to the low pit of my stomach, causing a wild bloom of heat. Fresh wetness coats and softens my pussy. My moan has the edge of a sigh to it.

His eyes darken with a predatory glint. "Good girl. Feel me."

"I feel you, Wolf." I feel *everything*.

He removes his touch from my hot, sore nipples. He feathers his fingers down my stomach. Circling me again, he traces the swell of my hips, and lower. "Did you know pain triggers an endorphin load that heightens the intensity of pleasure?"

*Oh God.*

His fingers slide over my saturated panties.

"For your first time, it's going to hurt. But I can give you so much pleasure you won't care about pain." His fingers nudge and pinch at the lips of my pussy through the thin fabric. He traces his fingers over my ass, easing my panties into a thong, which he pulls gently, creating pressure where my pussy is bound by it. And it *is* painful, in a way that could almost be described as … maddening.

"My perfect wife needs me to take her over the edge," he purrs into my ear. "Are you ready to make this marriage official, princess? Say it."

Dirty talk is a new one for me. I don't answer him right away, mainly because his fingers are rubbing along the bunched-up thong, pulling it tighter.

"I said how bad do you need your husband to make you come hard and get you nice and soft and ready for me? I'm not giving you anything until you beg me for it. Say it."

"*I need you.*"

The hint of a smug smile. "How bad?"

"*Bad.*"

There's triumph in his sneer. "Good little wife. I'm going to reward you for that."

He lifts me easily and lays me back on the bed, crouching over me. His kiss is raw and open-mouthed, full of his hunger and his dominance.

I open to him, submitting to him completely. I whimper into his mouth.

"Fuck, you're sweet," he growls.

Moving lower, Wolf takes his time, kissing and licking a trail down my throat. He circles my nipples with his tongue, then works his way down my stomach, licking, biting and tasting as he goes as though I'm a lavish buffet laid out for his pleasure.

Catching the edges of my panties with his teeth, he pulls them all the way down. He takes off my gold high-heeled sandals, easing my knees wide. With eyes the color of Hawaiian ocean water at midnight, he gazes down at me. "*Look* at you. I can't believe you're *real*. My wife was made for me."

Wolf adjusts my position with his calloused hands. He binds my ankles with padded leather cuffs he attaches to the bed frame. Then he ties my wrists with the silk ties. He's so huge and strong I know that even if I protested he could easily dominate me. So I just go with it.

I'm naked, splayed and tied up.

"Outside our marriage bed," he says, pinching my nipple until I squirm, "with my help, if you need it, you're going to fully control every part of your life. But in our bed, you're mine to take care of."

He bites gently on my nipple, increasing the pressure. It hurts. A lot. *What the hell have I gotten myself into? I can't escape him now.* The sharp bite of pain feeds itself directly to my clit, centering there. It's a confusing zap of electricity. "*Ow.*" At my protest—or whatever it is—he releases the bud, taking my other nipple between his teeth. Again, he slowly bites, harder this time, waiting for me to react. The pain is stronger this time, jolting my pussy with heat. My inner muscles flutter. "*Wolf.*" I moan his name, not because I want him to stop. I moan because if he keeps doing that I'm going to come.

His tongue licks the ridges he's made with his teeth. "You're hard-wired to crave your dominant alpha male, baby girl. You can't fight biology. You want your big, strong mate to protect you. You want to feel assured that your husband has your back as you live your life, which I will. But what you crave from me most of all is to provide for you and the babies I'm going to give you. When I tie you up, and spank you, and do whatever I want to you to give you plea-sure, you'll *feel* my power. You know I'll take care of you out there because I'm so fucking good at taking care of you right here, when you're at your most vulnerable. It's all related."

"It is?" is all I can manage.

"Yes. It is. You can be a successful, modern woman when you're taking the world by storm. And you can still get off on submitting to your husband. When I take control like *this*,"—a strong suck on one nipple as he pinches the other and *oh my God, I'm so close*—"you know I can satisfy your deep need for security. I'm going to prove it to you right now. You're going to give me everything I want. Say 'touch me, Wolf. Eat my pussy. Bite me and make me come hard.' Say it."

"Touch me, Wolf."

A crooked, barely-their grin. "'Touch me and *eat my pussy*, Wolf.' Come on, little wife. You can do better than that."

"*Eat my pussy, Wolf. Please.*"

"That's my good girl. You're torturing me something crazy, Mrs. Ramsey, with these perfect creamy tits and this wet little virgin pussy. You *know* you're torturing me. I think you're doing it on purpose. I think my baby is *dying* for her husband to fuck her so good and so hard she can only cry and moan thank you, for all the orgasms that are about to change her life." *Holy hell. I mean, talk about big dick energy.* He fumbles with his belt. Wolf unfastens his pants and grips his —*Jesus!* I felt it last night when he was on top of me and I felt it tonight as we were dancing. But it's a shock to finally *see* it.

I'm wide-eyed but also … awestruck.

*Wow.*

*It's huge.* And thick. Surprisingly hard-looking, standing so rigidly out of his pants that it rests upright against to his hair-dusted stomach. The length is veiny and ridged, the top rounded and shiny with a slick of moisture. It looks heavy and brutal. Hot-looking and so engorged it must be painful.

The sight of my husband's gigantic cock does something to me. I'm embarrassingly inexperienced, I'll be the first to admit. I'm also female. My reaction to it feels primal.

I want to touch it.

I want to *taste* it.

*I want to please it.*

My body responds to my husband's massive, leaking virility. My tender nipples bead even more tautly. Instinctively, my back arches and my knees fall open wider so he can see more of me and … access me. I want to offer my wet pussy to that big, meaty *thing* like I've never wanted anything.

I should be scared. I don't know why I'm *not* scared. I've been scared of so many things in my life.

But under his worshipful gaze, he's right: I am powerful.

*I* did that to him. He wants *me*. He *chose* me.

I used to crave safety. Now, all I'm craving is *to taste it. To feel it. To make it come.*

*Whoa.*

I'm not myself. I'm a mess of need that's sprung up from some lusty, hidden well inside myself I never knew existed. My inner sex goddess has woken up at the sight of that giant beast and she is *hungry.*

Wolf reads my body language and his eyes narrow, half with amusement, half with ownership. "I know, baby girl.

You want all this and you'll get it. But first we need to get you very, very ready for me."

His rough palm slides over my thigh. Slowly, he slides his fingers over the lips of my pussy. Then he holds his fingers up and they're shiny with moisture. Watching my eyes, he licks his fingers. "How did I get so fucking lucky? My wife is dripping with nectar."

Leaning closer, his hot breath fans over my swollen, aching flesh. I squirm because I already feel like I'm starting to come.

Wolf's tongue laves slowly over my silky folds, opening me. He thumbs carefully, rolling sensitive flesh to reveal my clit, which he touches with the tip of his tongue.

I don't even know where the noise I make comes from. A whimper of need. It's a delicious suffering. A tiny tease when what I want is for him to eat me like the ravenous animal he is. I wish I could weave my fingers into his hair and grab fistfuls of it. I wish I could pull him closer.

*"Please, Wolf. Do it now."*

He chuckles against me. Then he slides a finger inside me. There's a stretching sensation but I'm so wet he uses the moisture to slide deeper. Pin-pricks of pain entwine with warm sensation as he adds another finger and curls and slides them along an insanely responsive place inside me.

"Here it is," he murmurs, prodding deeper. "My wife's virginity. Right here."

I can feel the barrier he's gently pressing against with his fingers. I guess I'm glad it's indisputable. "You can believe it, then," I gasp.

"Princess, everything about you screams virgin. I never doubted that."

"My family doubts me. I'm surprised they never asked for proof."

He eyes me darkly. His fingers slide from my body. In a sudden movement, he reaches for his belt and pulls a large bone-handled hunting knife from its holster. "You're worried about *them*? That they somehow won't be satisfied by your blood? I'll give them all the proof they want."

I stare at him in shock. "What?" *What the hell?*

I'm reminded of how strong he is, all burly muscles, with his gigantic cock standing stiffly, leaking milky moisture while I'm tied up and completely at his mercy. "I can't have my wife distracted by anyone else's idiotic concerns. I need you fully focused on enjoying the ride."

Wolf runs the blade of the knife along an inner vein of his arm. Pressing the blade deeper, he draws a small, clean line. A trickle of blood pools. Then he sets the knife aside.

He touches his fingers to the blood of his wound. "My blood for your blood. My pain for your pain."

He paints his blood to the skin of my upper thigh. The hot, silky glide of his fingers spreads a molten awareness through my veins, infusing me with heat, as though I'm absorbing some of his crazy-ass life force.

Wolf withdraws his touch, reapplying his paint. He smears some onto the sheet between my legs. When his fingertips touch my pussy, I can't move, or breathe. His fingers stroke, prodding lightly, parting my intimate folds to stain me with his blood.

"What you need to remember is that it doesn't matter what they think anymore." His thumb circles my nub as slippery fingers probe deeper in a languid rhythm. "It matters what *I* think. And I think you're perfect. You're strong and you're more courageous than anyone else in your family. You're flawless. You need to start owning your own power. Trust your husband. Your pleasure is my duty. Relax now and let me give it to you."

My hands are fisted into the sheets and I can feel my breasts rising and falling with my heavy breath.

He slides open a hidden drawer from under his bed. "I've never used this drawer. I've collected some things but since you're the first woman I've brought to this bed—"

"I am?"

"Yes."

That seems unbelievable. "Why?"

"Most of the people in Paradise are related to me. I don't invite other visitors here."

I feel sort of ridiculously touched by this. *It's mine and only mine. It's ours.* "Why not?"

"Because they'd never leave. This is my sanctuary. I never wanted to share it."

"I'm ... I'm glad you didn't."

"I was saving it."

Despite everything—the manacles on my wrists and ankles, my spread-eagled legs and sore nipples and sticky desire and this over the top intimacy, these words, coming from my bad-ass husband, are sort of ... outrageously sweet. "Why?"

"I don't know. I never thought I'd get married. Maybe a small piece of me was secretly hoping I'd find someone to share this house with. I guess I was, even though I didn't realize it. And now you're here and it would be a shame to waste the opportunity to take our wedding night to the next level."

"W-what level?"

"The one where you learn to trust me implicitly. Until your sense of well-being both inside and outside the bedroom becomes unrecognizably better. Letting go can trigger biological effects that last for days or even weeks. It's a deeper way to explore consciousness, power and control over every aspect of your life."

*Okay, wow.*

"I didn't know it, but I've been saving this place just for you. And I didn't even know you yet. I should get some points for that."

"I think you already have all the points you need," I point out with a gasp.

He almost smiles, and this adds a new layer to the dominant-alpha-male-about-to-take-his-new-wife's-virginity vibe. The glint in his blue eyes is downright dangerous, which excites me more than it scares me.

Against all odds, my new husband *is* safety. It's a complicated, addictive safety, wrapped up in a hot, rough, dirty-talking package.

Our gazes are locked and I can feel the pull of him. It's not just the masculine beauty. Or the after-effects of the vows we took only a few short hours ago that will bind us for the rest of our lives.

This gaze is soul-connecting.

I *like* him. He's hot and tough and protective. At the very heart of him is a roguish sense of humor entwined with a perceptive, thoroughly-male kindness. The combination is … I'm not going to say it's making me fall in love with him. But I'm drawn to him. Deeply. Which, all things considered, is a relief. "What's in the drawer?"

"Experiments. To see how hard I can make you come."

*Oh.*

He holds up a blindfold. "Let's see where your boundaries lie, princess."

"But—"

"Quiet." The command is unconditional and it coats my pussy with fresh wetness. It's stunningly erotic, being laid out for his pleasure and his domination.

He secures the blindfold over my eyes.

The mystery of what he's about to do lights my body up. I want to bite him and taste his skin and rub myself against him. I feel sort of delirious with anticipation.

I freeze as the lightest, softest touch grazes the sole of my foot, tickling me.

"What is it?" I breathe.

"A feather."

The touch traces languidly over my ankle and up my calf, barely a touch at all. All my concentration centers on that soft, gliding line. A fluid, sensual path along my thigh, my hip, circling my navel, to my breasts. As the line traces across my skin, its touch seems to burn me and brand me with fiery, penetrating neediness.

My body is on fire. I feel like I might go up in flames just from the soft, enticing feather-light touch.

A devil-edged growl. "Let's level up."

A long, torturous moment of desperation.

Something else touches me. This touch is more solid. Heavier.

"What is it?" I manage to breathe.

"A small whip with a triangular leather tip."

I cry out as the leather slaps against my nipple, shocking me and sending a sharp bolt of sensation straight to my clit, which pulses with warm, spiky pleasure.

"Your sweet little clit is poking out for me, baby. I think it wants to be spanked."

*Oh God.* The touch of the leather whip glides up my calf. To my thigh. Circling closer. Sliding over my swollen pussy, petting me and parting the intimate flesh.

He taps lightly.

I flinch and moan.

"I need your pussy soft and ready to take all of me. I want you coming when I make you fully mine."

He taps again.

A soft squeal escapes me.

It's too much. If he does it again, I'll fall over some cataclysmic edge. My release is sitting there on its precipice, simmering hotly, *so close.* The magnitude of it is daunting as hell.

"You ready, baby? Say it. Tell me how much you want me to spank your pretty little clit again."

*Holy hell.* "*Please.*"

"Do you still hate me?" I can hear the triumph behind his low question.

*Damn him.* "*No. No.* I don't hate you." *I need you. I need what you're about to do to me.*

"Not even a little?"

"*No. No. Not at all.*" *Please,* I want to scream. *Please do it again.*

"So you like me then?" I can hear the amusement in his voice, the sadist.

"Yes. I like you. A lot. Please. *Please.*"

A dark, satisfied chuckle. "All right then. Good enough for now. Hold on, baby. Here we go." The swell begins even before the whip touches me. I know it's coming and my body blooms. When the leather taps my slick, hyper-sensitive nub, a torrent of pleasure erupts through my body in violent, voluptuous bursts.

Wolf's mouth is there, latching onto it, licking into it, humming with his greed, spinning me into a state of … I don't know. It's hard to describe. Transcendental relief, maybe.

I'm crossing a threshold. The old me never knew anything could feel this good. The new me now knows what pure, exploding bliss feels like and I'll never be the same again.

My mind goes dark and quiet, able only to comprehend the wild, clenching rapture.

With my inner muscles still rippling, Wolf climbs up my body, kicking off the rest of his clothes and laying himself over me. And I can feel him. The heavy, solid bulk of his cock, pressing against the slippery pleasure. He holds himself there, easing off my blindfold.

I blink up at him, dazed. His face. His hair. The inked pattern ocean waves licking up his neck.

"Eyes on me, baby."

*God, he's so beautiful.*

"That's my good girl." Gazing into my eyes, he rubs the broad head of his cock back and forth against my clit. Another wave of my orgasm washes through me. He uses the spasms as an invitation, riding them, easing the head of his cock inside me. Diving deeper into each ripple. And deeper. "*Ohh, fuck, baby girl.*"

I whimper because even though I'm still sort of coming, *it hurts so much*. He's too big. *It'll never fit.*

"You can take it," he murmurs. His body is practically vibrating with tension and I get the sense that this is so insanely good for him he's having trouble controlling himself.

*He's still not even halfway in.*

"I'm about to break through, little wife. I can feel you." I almost wish I could stop him because *what if I don't freaking survive this?* "Relax for me. Let me in. *Oh, fuck.* You're so fucking *tight*, princess."

His fingers slide against the pucker of my ass in a sweet, skating rhythm. It feels … good. More than good. And when his thumb mimics the same rhythm over my hyper-sensitive clit, I slide into *another* climax.

Wolf grips my ass, using the milking clenches of my pussy to thrust his big cock into me. I cry out as he breaks through the fragile barrier, sliding deep. I'm being split wide open. I'm totally impaled, so fully stuffed I can hardly breathe.

He holds himself still, dropping his head. The brush of his thick-silk hair against my skin is a welcome softness. He seems sort of mindless. We're both breathing hard. I want to scream. Silent tears wet my sweat-damp hair.

After a few seconds, he lifts his head. There's empathy in him, spliced with pure male power. "You'll get used to me." I can read in him that my protests are futile. "That was the part where I can't stop it from being painful. But it's all pleasure from here on in."

"*I can't do it.*" More tears pool and spill.

He smooths back a strand of my hair and wipes a tear. "You're already doing it, baby. You've done it. And now it's time for another orgasm. We're going to come together."

"*I can't.*"

"You can." His eyes are lust-drowsed, like he's on the cusp. "And you will." Despite the pain and my tears … I *love* how close he is to the edge. He can barely handle how good this feels.

I want to see that. I want to watch him lose control. I want to be the *reason* he loses control.

Wolf reaches up and pulls loose the ties on my wrists. "Hold onto me." He shifts us and his cock slides even deeper—*holy fuck!* It hurts like hell but there's a dark, hungry edge to the pain now. I cling to him for dear life, digging my nails into his skin because I need to *grip*.

His warm hand slides around the nape of my neck and his thumb rests gently on my throat, like a light throttle. This grounds me. *You'll feel my power when you're at your most vulnerable.* It's true. I can. *I need it.*

Wolf thrusts into me, moving deep in slow, deliberate, rutting plunges. I'm getting thoroughly fucked by my new husband and even though there are fresh tears in my eyes, my focus shifts to the steady drag of his body against my clit as his thick, silky cock rubs itself along a deep inner trigger. Again. And again. It's punishing. It's also rooting out sweet, star-flicked heat, which spreads through my belly, gathering and centering.

"Vivi," Wolf groans. "You were made for me. Nothing has ever felt as good as my wife. You're so beautiful. My gorgeous girl." There's emotion in his deep, rasped growl and it touches something in me. We're one now and it feels that way. *He's inside me.* It's profound and I'm crying for more than one reason.

He rolls his hips as he grips my ass, bruising me as he grinds slow and hard.

The aggressive, ridged friction rubs the pleasure-pain to its breaking point, spilling over in a tumbling flash of agony-edged ecstasy, which shatters into a million swimming minnows of warm, clenching relief.

I'm staring into his eyes as my pleasure milks him tenderly. He growls like a bear as his cock jerks inside me, flooding me in hot spurts. Slippery sounds fill the room as he thrusts. The overload spills and wets my thighs. I cling to him, riding the overwhelming pleasure all the way because I have no choice but to take it.

It lasts for a long time.

We're quiet now, as our bodies remain locked in a secret dance. Until the aftershocks start to calm. My fingers play in his hair. He has such beautiful hair. He kisses my lips lazily.

Then his head dips as his mouth searches for my nipple. I offer it to him, so sated now. I wasn't expecting the peacefulness. The endorphin rush, maybe. The serene sense of profound closeness with another person. I wasn't expecting to feel this comforted by it.

Wolf's lips fasten over my nipple and his tongue slowly traces the outer edge. Keeping the tender bud inside his mouth, he licks me. Steadily. Almost sweetly.

Deep inside me, where Wolf's bulky cock has softened but not completely, my soreness dissolves into a fresh wave of desire.

He moves to my other breast, suckling and stroking with his tongue like he's feeding from me. His fingers slide down my body. He teases my clit in light, rhythmic pinches until another orgasm washes through me, tugging strongly on the hot flesh that's wedged so deeply inside me. He's getting hard again.

Wolf's watching me with a beguiled expression, smoothing my hair. "How am I ever going to get enough of my sweet, hot little wife?"

Through the night, I'm taken beyond any and every

limit I ever knew—or didn't know—existed. After the fifth —*sixth?*—climax I enter a state of physical enlightenment in which my body exists in its own realm, thoroughly base and primal. All I'm able to comprehend is the acute, drawn-out rapture.

At some point my ankles are unbound.

After hours of exquisite torture and unimagined bliss, I'm vaguely aware that he's cleaning me with a cool cloth. Even after everything we've done, the care he gives my sore, punished, blissed-out body is almost shockingly intimate.

I'm covered by the soft sheet.

And I sleep deeply, wrapped possessively in the arms of my savage husband.

# 12

# Vivi

I HEAR the chirp of a bird.

I open my eyes.

It takes me a few seconds to figure out where I am.

But then, I feel a thick nudge deep inside me from behind.

Oh.

*Oh yeah.*

I'm married.

I'm in bed with Wolf Ramsey, my new husband, who very thoroughly took my virginity last night.

*Very* thoroughly.

*And he's still inside me.*

*Wow.*

I'm sore. Like, *really* sore.

Even so, the deep thrust feels—*oh*—*so good.*

I'm curled on my side with my knees pulled up. Wolf's big body is wrapped around mine, spooning me.

*Fucking me.*

Slowly, like he's dreaming me.

I slept *so* well. So deeply. I guess my subconscious likes having an overprotective he-man wrapped around me all night.

"We're really married now," I whisper.

I hear the low murmur close to my ear. "Yes, God help you. There's no getting rid of me now."

There's a small pinging sound near my head. I look to see a cell phone sitting on the bedside table. The screen is lit up and I can see a name illuminated there.

Cheyenne.

*Cheyenne?*

There's a message bubble.

> Call me, you beast!!! PLEASE come visit me!! I'll make it sooo good for you!! I'll give you ANYTHING you want PLEASE xxxx

*What the hell?* "Who's Cheyenne?"

The burly arm that's wrapped around me picks up the phone, powering it off and tossing it. I hear it land on the rug somewhere on the other side of the room. "No one that matters."

"Umm." Well, that's not quite going to cut it. Not even close.

I wriggle away from him. He tries to hold me but I

manage to move enough so that his thick cock slides from my body.

"Who is she?"

I'm on my back now with him very heavily on top of me. He's glaring down at me—all two hundred and whatever pounds of clenched muscle and aroused male ferocity.

His hair, with all its different colors, from dark brown to dark blond at the tips, is mussed-up, framing his face in a halo of disarray. Now that his aggression has softened and is fully focused on pleasuring his new wife, he's ... mind-numbingly gorgeous. Which pisses me off even more.

He doesn't like the question.

His hair falls across his forehead, barely tempering the stormy look of him. "As I said, no one that matters. I made a vow and I don't intend to break it. I am, however, going to need more attention from my nubile little wife, because if I'm going to be faithful—and I am—you're going to have to milk this fucking beast of a hard-on with that tight pussy again because I need you real bad, baby girl."

"Is she a *girlfriend?*"

He pins me with a look of patient exasperation. "No. I don't have a girlfriend. I have a wife."

"But you've ..." I let the question hang in the air. I don't want to ask it. And I already know the answer.

"Princess. I'm not a psychic, am I? I didn't even know you existed. Okay, I knew you existed but I didn't know you were the most gorgeous, delicious little nymphet who's ever walked the goddamn face of planet Earth. Or that you were about to become my wife. *Or* that your honey-sweet virgin pussy was strutting around Waikiki waiting for me to discover it. You can't get pissed off because I slept with women before I met you."

*Women.* "Actually, I can do whatever the hell I want. Get off me."

His eyes are bright with that damn mischief I really don't need right now. "Get *off* you? Because I got a text from some vapid chick I barely remember?"

"Yes!"

He laughs at my expression and—damn him—he's far too heavy for me to push him off. Instead, he holds my wrists with his hands and forces my legs apart with a strong, hair-roughened thigh until my legs are partly wrapped around him. The head of his rock-hard length parts the lips of my pussy. He holds himself there, barely inside me.

I try to wriggle free but it only makes his fat, slippery cock slide deeper.

"How many are there? Why would she be texting you? Are you in a *relationship* with her?"

He's entertained by my jealousy. He's playful. "No, I'm not in a *relationship* with her. I'm in a relationship with you. A lifetime of wedded bliss kind of relationship. Now tell me how bad you want me to fuck you senseless again. Beg me for it. I can feel you quivering, princess. I know you want me to pump my cum deep into this tight, luscious heaven on earth. Just say the word."

"How about two words. *Get. Off.*" But I can't dislodge him.

"That's what I'm trying to do, sugar pie. But it's more fun if we both get off at the same time."

"I *mean* it, Wolf." But my body remembers everything, *the traitor!* I'm already wet from the last time he came inside me, even though he cleaned me after. I'm also wet because he's so damn sexy and he feels so insanely good. And he's not waiting for me to agree. He doesn't need to. My body is agreeing for me.

His thickness slides deeper. There are pinpricks of pain but the burn gets lighter each time he does this.

"How many times did you sleep with her? Why is she texting you? Where does she live?"

Wolf blinks down at me innocently. "I'm not talking about this with you." *And deeper.* "None of it matters."

"Of course it *matters.* When was it?"

"When was what?"

"You know what. *Her.* When?"

"Baby—"

"When?"

His grip tightens and his cock is stretching me and forcing me to take more of him. I gasp and my eyes sting with tears. Not because it hurts. But because I hate the thought of … her. Them. *He's mine now. They can't have him.*

A tear pools and spills, drawing a warm line down to my hair.

"Poor baby," he croons, but the devil is in him. "My overreactive princess is jealous." He kisses my mouth lightly. I can tell he *loves* my jealousy.

I turn my head away.

"Do you want to know something?" His deep voice is rasped.

"No." But I want to see where he's going with this.

He meets my glare. "I love that you're my wife."

*Oh.*

Okay, it's a beautiful thing to say. But I'm wary. He knows how to say exactly what I want to hear exactly when I want to hear it. It's what he does. And the L word takes me off-guard. Then again, he didn't actually say he loved *me*. "You might change your mind about that. You've only known me for three days."

"So? I can love that you're my wife if I feel like loving that you're my wife." He licks my bottom lip.

I don't react. "You don't even know me."

"I know the most important things about you."

"Like what?"

"Like ... that you make the cutest little moans when I slide my cock deep, like this."

*Oh hell.*

"Your favorite fruit is pineapple. Your middle name is Sofia. Your favorite color is ... let me guess. Purple."

"No."

He smiles at my churlishness. "What is it, then?"

"Red."

One eyebrow lifts. "Yeah, I can see that. You're fiery. Passionate. Moody."

"I'm not moody."

He exhales a laugh. "You're *so* moody. One minute you're laughing at me and the next minute you're scowling."

"I don't scowl."

"You're scowling at me right now."

"Only because I have a very good reason to." But a part of me likes this game. We've jumped in at a ridiculous deep end and now we need to learn how to swim. We need to figure out how to make a marriage out of a forced, glorified business deal that involves … well, so far, hot sex and not much else.

"It's not a good reason," he tells me. "Because it means nothing. You'll soon learn that I don't break my word. And I definitely don't break my vow. Guess what my favorite color is."

I don't want to indulge him. But he's waiting for it. He thrusts a fraction deeper. "Blue," I breathe.

"Good guess."

"It is blue?"

"Of course. Blue is the best color. Kauai ocean blue. What's my lucky number?"

"Seven."

"Yes. That's why your ring has seven diamonds. And your dress had seven feathers sewn onto it. You looked so damn gorgeous in it, baby. I've just never seen anything as gorgeous as you. Everything about our wedding day honored the curse. We can't help but have good luck. What's your lucky number?"

I don't really have one. Except, maybe I do now. "Seven."

He's genuinely pleased by this. "It is?"

"Yes."

"Since when?"

"Since yesterday."

My heavy, overbearing husband is touched by this. He's also turned on by it. His cock is very hard and it's a crazy juxtaposition, that his expression is so charmed but his manhood is so rigid and forceful. "You need to learn that you have nothing to worry about, sweet. I'll prove it to you. See, when you materialized out of thin air when I was least expecting you, with your tight green dress and your golden eyes that were shooting their fiery little daggers at me, I already knew I was ruined for anyone else. It was that easy for you. And I mean fucking *ruined*." He thrusts again and I cry out because he's so damn big and now he's fully rooted inside me. Even worse, I'm already starting to come. "I'm already addicted to how damn good you feel. You're basically all my wildest fantasies wrapped up into one squirming, juicy, petulant, pouting little package. I couldn't have dreamed you up. Here you are, scowling at me and all I can think of is how lucky I am to have found you."

*Wow.*

"I love that you taste like nectar of the gods and the sweetest honey. I love that you said yes to me."

Another deep thrust and—*oh God*—the pleasure rise is already near its summit. "I didn't really have a choice," I protest.

"Of course you did. You made that choice when I was eating your pussy, remember?"

"Oh yeah."

"You made that choice because you're hot as fuck for me."

I can't really deny it, since I'm on the brink of what's shaping up to be yet another life-changing orgasm.

"Because you know how good it feels when your big bad Wolf fucks you hard. I love the sounds you make when you're about to come. Like now. I love how tight your pussy grips me. I love how you fight it but you know it's futile. Admit it, you're ruined for anyone else too. There's no one else for us, baby. You're mine. I'm yours. No one else matters anymore. Now stop arguing with your husband over someone I never cared about. Let me make you feel good. Hold on to me. Wrap your legs around me."

*My husband is a sweet-and-dirty-talking blue-eyed devil.*

I obey him because the pain—and there's a lot of it—is spiked with a greedy kind of pleasure that won't take no for an answer.

"I love that you're my wife and I can take you with no barriers between us. I've never done it like this before and I can tell you, it's a game-changer."

"What? Really? You've never …" I can't bring myself to finish my question. *You've never had sex without a condom before?* Because I hate thinking about him with other people.

"No. Never. People want to get their hooks into me anyway they can. I couldn't let that happen."

"But you don't mind … my hooks?" I might be teasing him, I don't know. I'm too full of him to think clearly and I'm feeling inexplicably emotional about what he just told me.

"You're my *wife*. I fucking *love* your hooks." His cock slides out a fraction before driving back in. And in. Forcing me to take all of his impossibly thick girth. "That's what I'm trying to tell you, baby. You hooked me the minute you pouted at me and blinked those long eyelashes at me like you were put on this earth to torture me." Long, low strokes that rub my clit while his deep length caresses every trigger I own.

He releases my wrists to grab my ass as he grips me and fucks me, ensuring he's as deep as he can get as he buries himself inside me, over and over, growling a dark hum.

I can only surrender and do my best to survive him. He holds his depth each time he plunges deep and the measured drives tip me over a ludicrously high peak. Waves of pleasure flood me, clenching tightly around him. Each wave feels so unbearably good I moan because I can't stop myself. *God. Oh. God. Wolf. Yesss.*

I don't even recognize the sounds I'm making. Wolf is groaning too and his cock jerks in sync with my own rhythm. *You're so fucking sweet baby oh fuck ooohhh fuuuck.* The throb of him spins me into another, even stronger orgasm. My body *loves* that he's filling me up with his jets of liquid heat. My pussy tugs his bulk with each burst, like it wants to milk every drop from him and take it deep inside.

We ride the rush all the way, locked in a writhing, thrusting, sweaty clinch.

Until I'm boneless and spent. Drifting on a dazed, blissful tide.

I go pliant. My eyes are closed.

I can hear him but I'm inside a rapturous haze. *That's my girl. Nothing has ever felt as good as you. We're sworn to each other now. Don't doubt me.*

Wolf pulls himself from my body and I feel the spilling gush. I let him kiss my lips and suckle my nipples. I'm too blissed-out to move. My legs are still spread, my pussy rippling. I'm more submissive than I've ever been. Using his seed, he circles and plays my clit until I come once more as his fingers push his spilled cum back inside me. My body sucks on his fingers as he does this, almost embarrassingly eager.

"You're so full of me, princess. Maybe we've already made a baby. I want to fucking *breed* you. I want you full and spilling with my cum until you're knocked up with my babies."

My eyes blink open slowly and I watch him. *Wow.* I didn't mention it. We didn't talk about protection. Clearly, he's not worried about possible consequences. The total opposite, in fact. "I've had the shot, Wolf."

"What shot?"

"You know. Birth control."

His irises visibly darken. I don't know how he does that. "Why?"

"I—Silas made us get it. You know ... because of the curse."

"It was *Silas's* decision?"

The fury in his voice shines a light on how wrong it is, for Silas to have laid down the law on that detail for me and my sisters. Especially since he went and knocked up someone else while he was hell-bent on making sure the same thing didn't happen to us. It should have been our choice. For my sisters, it's probably a good option. For me, it was an extra caution, maybe. To ensure the sacrificial lamb could be put to good use if the situation called for it.

"The days of Silas controlling you are over. We can talk about this. I'm not going to force you to go off birth control until you're absolutely ready to. But I want to give you babies. Lots of them. How long does the shot last?"

"Three months. Sometimes longer."

"When did you get it?"

I think about it. "Close to three months ago, I think."

"Good. It'll wear off soon."

"It doesn't always happen right away. Besides, I'm only twenty," I remind him. "We've got time."

"Time is never guaranteed. My family has learned that the hard way and so has yours. Besides, for us, it doesn't matter. I'll take care of them. I'll take care of you. You can have nannies or whatever help you need. I've got more money than you could ever spend. It wouldn't stop you from doing anything else you want to do."

"I'd like to travel some more."

"We can take our babies with us. Let me get you pregnant. I've always thought five would be a good number."

"Five?"

"Or maybe seven. For good luck."

"*Seven?*"

We're interrupted by the sound of voices. Down below,

outside on the lanai. "Hey, lovebirds, time to get up. Our flight leaves in two hours." It's Malachi's voice.

And others. Remy and Blaise.

Wolf climbs out of bed and grabs a pair of jeans. He pulls them on, doing his best to stuff himself into them. I have no benchmark for this kind of thing but he seems to bounce back exceptionally quickly. He should be sated for now but he's already regaining momentum. He straps on his weapons belt.

I don't want to go back to Seven Mile Beach yet. "Do we have to go with them?" It seems strange that we're "we" now. I'm surprised by how much I like the sound of it.

"No." A new tension has settled over him. "The alliance rules say we're supposed to live at your family's estate. But we're entitled to a honeymoon."

He clearly doesn't like the idea of leaving, and neither do I. I love this house. I love this room. *Welcome home*, he said, and it already feels that way.

The thought of going back to Seven Mile Beach and dealing with Silas, Jett, Lana and all the demands of my family and my management teams is depressing. The past two days, even though they've been a seriously wild ride and a roller coaster of emotion, have also been … the best of my life. Which might be pathetic but it's absolutely true.

I've found myself. And I want to be alone with my husband, to explore this new side of myself and to get to know him better. "I wish we could live here."

"We will. But we'll take care of business there first.

Remy, Silas, Enzo and the others have discussed it and we've all decided that it makes sense to divide our time between both. Knox and Cassidy are going to live in Paradise too. We have jets and helicopters now. The old rules are outdated."

I know Wolf takes the alliance documents seriously and I'm relieved that he's willing to work around them. "At least the name of the place is Seven Mile Beach." He's surly and I don't blame him. "There must be something I can like about it."

There's a knock on the bedroom door.

"Vivi?" It's Tatum's voice.

"Shit," comes Wolf's irritated murmur.

"What time is it?" I ask him.

He picks up his phone from where he'd tossed it. He powers it on and holds it up. "Messages deleted." *Messages? There was more than one?* "It's almost noon."

"Vivi?" Perri's outside the bedroom door too. "We're leaving soon. Can we come in?"

Wolf lays the sheet over me. Then he walks over to the door. He's long-limbed and lean. Absolutely shredded. Shirtless. His hair's a mess and his eyes are light this morning. He looks big, masculine as all hell and utterly delicious.

*And he's mine.* I'm still adjusting to how much I like this. I wasn't expecting to.

He opens the door and my sisters stare up at him, wide-eyed. Their cheeks get pink—and it takes a lot to make my sisters blush. Wolf steps back and motions with a sort of irritated flourish for them to enter.

"I'm going to go talk to Remy," he announces grumpily, before heading down the stairs.

My sisters burst into the room.

Still overwhelmed by the intensity of the night, I wrap the sheet around myself and start getting up. I need a shower. But I freeze when both my sisters gasp a low shriek. I glance at what they're staring at.

The bed is stained with blood. Mine and his.

Proof. *My blood for your blood. My pain for your pain.*

"Holy shit, Vivi," Perri whispers, alarmed. "Are you okay?"

Actually I've never felt better in my life.

"That *brute*," Tatum cries. "You've been ravaged!"

Yes, I have. I don't bother mentioning that I … enjoyed it. A lot.

At least they'll accept that this marriage is well and truly legit. I don't want anyone doubting me and my hot, beastly sex god of a new husband.

## 13

After my family's shock wears off and they all leave for Honolulu, Wolf takes me out on his boat.

It's moored offshore in the scenic cove that surrounds his house. He lifts me into the dinghy that's tied up on the beach.

"I can walk, Wolf."

"No. It's my job to make sure you don't hurt yourself in any way whatsoever. I need you safe, rested and so happy you have no choice not just to thrive but bloom into the most wildly exceptional version of yourself. You'll hardly remember the old you ever existed. It's also good luck to let me carry you across every new threshold. Especially houses and boats."

He charms me. Coming from such a rough, rugged beefcake-type, his gushing praise hits me like a shot of warm adrenaline cut with Wolf Ramsey's own brand of hundred-proof aphrodisiac. I can admit I love how *nice* he is to me. It makes me smile when I'm not expecting to. "Your superstitions are over the top," I tell him, but I know why. A part of him wants to make sure we have better luck than his parents and his oldest brother.

He places me on the cushioned seat of the dinghy and starts the motor.

It's not long before we're pulling up next to what looks more like a yacht than a sailboat. "This boat is huge."

"This is Lucky," he tells me. "She's a sport fishing yacht. And I have to insist that you once again allow me to be a stickler for tradition. Don't move, baby." After tying the dinghy to the back of the yacht, he scoops me into his arms and carries me aboard.

Considering how new our relationship is and how we've gone from zero to sixty in a matter of days, it's surprising to me how familiar we feel with each other already.

Partly because having sex non-stop will do that, I guess. But maybe even more than that, what I like best about my new husband is that I can trust him. For all his ferocity and his in-your-face masculinity, he's honorable. He's a big, sexy tomcat. His word is also his law. I find this amazingly comforting.

I'm not used to it. My own family doesn't operate that way. They'll change their mind, or their priorities will shift because there's money to be made or it's an opportunity for publicity that ends up being more important to them than whatever they might have half-heartedly promised yesterday.

Being able to trust Wolf appeals to me like nothing else could. My husband is hot. *And well-hung AF.* He's also a decent human being. It's a potent combination. He's fiercely protective of his own—which I now happen to be, in the most profound way imaginable. He understands pain but instead of letting it get him down, he uses it to channel his own sense of duty and honor. His intentions aren't underhanded or devious. Instead, they come from a place that's all about staying true to his family, his land, his home and his word. These are the things that are important to him.

Not publicity. Not projecting an image that's only half true. Not promoting his brand. He couldn't care less about any of the things that have shaped my life for as long as I can remember.

I *love* this. And I feel very at home with him because of it.

This is true of all the Ramseys. Remy is noble and the kind of person you immediately respect. Blaise's strength and fairness make me wish I could get to know her better. And Echo is one of the kindest people I've ever met.

Wolf has all those same traits, even if they didn't sit on the surface of my first impression of him. It took me longer to see them, but now that I have, they seem larger than life.

When I first met him, I was terrified. I knew he was lethal in the fighting ring. I know he's probably killed people —which, unfortunately, isn't that uncommon in the alliance families. Silas has. Stone and Enzo too, most likely. Because of the threats, sometimes there's no choice. I also know that, before me, Wolf slept with a lot of women (I don't want to think about how many) but he always ghosted them. Every single time. I vaguely remember hearing that about him and he admitted it to me himself.

None of it *sounds* honorable. From a distance, it would be easy to assume the worst. Which I did.

But what I'm realizing is that, as morally gray as he seems from a distance, up close and personal he's not like that at all. For everyone else he's morally gray but for me—and only me—he's a white knight in shining armor.

Because of circumstances mostly beyond our control, he's my husband. And he's saved the very best of himself for me.

*I love this.* It makes me feel close to him. It makes me want to return the favor.

Wolf carries me on deck.

The yacht has a large, stained-wood deck at the back with seven deep-sea fishing rods lined up in a rack. There's a cushioned bench with a compact built-in fridge next to it. A chrome ladder leads to an upper deck, which has seats and a table under a roof and a glassed-in indoor area.

He takes me into the main cabin.

"Wow." I'm used to luxury but the Ramseys always take it a step further. Every detail isn't just there to impress, it's there to create the best possible experience. There's a differ-ence. Their aesthetics are next level. There's an expansive lounge with leather couches, a round table with built-in chairs, a flat-screen TV, a bar with stools and a galley kitchen. Windows run the length of both sides of the room.

"There are three bedrooms downstairs." He sets me

down. Next to me, a bottle of champagne is chilling in a bucket of ice and there's a platter of fruit, bread, chips, crackers, sliced meat, dips, nuts, olives and cheese that's been prepared for us. He pops the cork and pours us two glasses.

"How did you manage to do all this?" I happen to know he's been busy.

"The boat's been fully stocked with food and drinks in case we wanted to use it."

"That's nice of your family."

"We've sealed an alliance marriage. Everyone's happy, not just for us but for themselves. We've let all of them off a very large hook they've been worrying about for a long time."

"I guess so."

He clinks his glass against mine. "I know so. Come on, I'll give you a tour then we'll take her for a spin."

Up a narrow staircase, the upper deck has another seating area and a jacuzzi. We enter the small glassed-in room, where there are a lot of high-tech control panels and a large shiny-wood steering wheel. He pats one of the plush raised leather seats. "Take a seat, princess. I'm taking you to Pirate's Cove. One of my favorite places."

He pulls a metal lever and there's the metallic, clinking grind of the anchor being raised. Then he starts up the boat and we sail parallel to the shoreline.

It's magical. The day is clear and the sky matches the sea.

So much has happened over the past few days and at

such lightning speed, it's nice to just relax and enjoy the moment.

The palm trees, the white sand and the blue water are dazzling, but I'm distracted. Wolf is dressed only in a pair of worn, low-slung jeans and his belt. He's shirtless and bare-foot, steering the yacht. His sculpted, inked muscles flex gracefully as he moves. The old me would have been intimi-dated by the strength coiling through his powerful body. The new me knows what those strong, calloused hands can *do*. And that ass really is a work of art. I mean, I'm allowed to appreciate a prime specimen of masculinity when it's my own *husband*.

He notices me watching him. His slow smile … well, it hits me right where it always hits me.

All I'm wearing is a skimpy pink bikini and a gauzy white beachy wrap-around dress that ties in the front. I'm already aware of a certain dampness he so easily inspires.

"My wife is checking me out."

I blush. "I'm just enjoying the sights."

"If you can tear your eyes away from my ass for a split-second, you might notice that we're in one of the most beautiful places in Kauai. This is Pirate's Cove." We're slowing to a stop and I look out to the most idyllic bay I've ever seen. Swaying palm trees line the beach. The water is so clear I can see the fish.

Once the yacht stops moving, Wolf lowers the anchor. "We're going to stay here tonight. I'll set up a couple of lines and see if I can catch us some dinner. We can swim, sit in the jacuzzi, whatever you want. Unless you're desperate to jump my bones immediately, in which case we'll move that to the top of the list."

I feel shy. But that ridge in his jeans is sort of … reminding me of how good it felt when he—

"Fuck, I've created a monster." He's grinning at me with that hungry blue glint in his eyes I'm now becoming familiar with. He comes closer, pulling the tie of my dress until it falls open. "All right, then. If my wife wants this cock then she gets it. You should see how pretty you are with your cheeks all pink and your perfect tits just begging to be teased." He thumbs my nipples until they bud. "Take it out," he says.

"You mean …?"

"You know what I mean. Do it. You want it, come and get it."

I think about the text he got this morning. The other women who wish he was theirs. *What do they do to him?* I'm new at this but I feel like I've got the gist of what he likes. It's really not that hard to figure out.

*I'll make it sooo good for you,* she texted him.

*I* can make it good for him. I can make it better than good. I'm his freaking *wife.*

Just three days ago, I was a timid, obedient virgin on the cusp of a fiery awakening. And here it is. Right here. My competitive spirit has kicked in. So I take a step closer. I run my hand over the huge, hard bulge. I squeeze gently, cupping his big arousal, massaging him through his jeans. He groans.

I open the button at the top and lower his zipper carefully. Sucking in a breath when I feel the silky hardness of him, I wrap my hand around his hot, hard length. Carefully, I pull it out.

*Wow.* This is the first time I've held it in my hands. I explore the veiny ridges, gliding my fingers over the milky moisture that's leaking from the head. I use the slickness to coat his silky bulk.

"*Ah, fuck,* baby. You feel too good." Wolf places his hands on either side of my head, weaving his fingers through my hair, wrapping it around his fist. He doesn't kiss me so much as devour my mouth. Our tongues tangle and slide.

I want to make him feel good. I want to make him feel *so* good, he forgets about all the girls who came before me.

I keep working his cock as he kisses me. He's long and broad and smooth, veins snaking along his length like a roadmap I'm learning. I use my fingers to squeeze and glide and explore. He growls a low oath and more moisture leaks from the tip. I think he might be getting close already. His jeans and his belt drop and he kicks them away.

The seat is behind him and I push against his chest. Breaking the kiss, he lowers himself onto the seat. His knees are apart, his gigantic cock rigid and engorged.

The sheer size and unapologetic heaviness of his thick shaft really is sort of intimidating ... but I'm so damn *hot* for him, it overrides any residual fear. I'm hungry to get close to him. I want to *feel* him and please him.

"Take off your top," he orders me.

I play coy, feeling shy but also powerful. I want to get

him very, very hard. I want to see if I can make him lose control.

I let my wrap fall. I unclasp my bikini top, letting it fall away too. My naked breasts feel full and sensitive under the blue burn of his gaze.

"Look at you, sweetheart. I never stood a fucking chance, did I?"

I give him an empathetic pout. "Poor Wolfie," I whisper and his eyes darken. I want to rile him and provoke him. More milky liquid pulses from his colossal manhood.

"Take everything off so I can see how wet my wife is for my big cock."

I hook my thumbs under the sides of my bikini bottom and I slowly lower it, stepping out of it.

"Turn around and bend over," he commands. "Show me that perfect pussy. Let me eat you this way and get you nice and ready to take me." A week ago all this would have shocked the hell out of me. Now, I'm on my husband's wavelength. His dirty talk is exactly what I need. I might have been a virgin only yesterday but I'm also ... eager. Insanely so. I don't want to just lie back and take it. What I want to do is drive my husband crazy with lust.

So I do it. I turn, leaning forward, holding onto a railing. My feet are hip-width apart. My gaze is shy but not entirely. *Fuck those other girls. He's mine. I'm going to give him everything he wants and more.*

"Touch yourself. Dip your fingers into that sweet honey, baby. Show me where you want me." His voice is low and rough.

I don't just obey him, I *feel* him. I work my own sensuality, feeding off his heat. I arch my back so he can see more of me. Using my fingers to gently open my pussy, I dip them into the warm wetness. I'm still sore. I'm also *very* wet.

"Fucking hell, I can't take this. Get that sweet little ass over here. Let me taste you, baby."

His fingers grip my hips and he pulls me closer, eating into my softness, fucking me with his tongue. It's incredibly erotic, offering myself to him like this as he gnaws and licks, groaning with a sort of gluttonous hunger as he feasts on me.

My pussy starts to quiver with the overload of pleasure and he senses that. "Come here. I need to get inside all that gorgeousness. Climb onto me. Fucking ride me, baby."

We've never done it like this before, with me on top. I'm not sure how it will work but I turn and climb onto him, straddling his hips until his huge shaft is pressed up against me, from my clit all the way to my navel.

"Sit down onto me. Feed me into that tight, wet pussy. I need you so bad."

I hardly recognize myself because I'm sort of feverish to take him inside me. I want to ride him and fuck him. Sitting up a little, I guide the slick head of his cock, using him to caress my clit in rhythmic, pressing glides. I could come if I kept going. I *will* come.

"Fuck yes, princess. Use me. Ride me hard."

I can tell my frenzy is turning him on beyond belief. I can feel the throb of him. His chest rises and falls with heavy breaths.

I ease the broad head inside me, moistening his length with my wetness, impaling myself by slippery, star-studded degrees. He's so big it's hard to take him deeper. But I'm determined. I can already feel the fluttery ripples of my orgasm waiting there. I bounce down onto him, then I sit up, bouncing again, letting my body adjust to the bulky invasion. Little by little, it's working.

Wolf's eyes are glazed with lust as he watches me. His fingers grip me as he helps me take more of him, thrusting deeper with each of my bounces. He groans.

I *like* that he's losing control. I *love* how overcome he is. My husband is almost mindless as I bounce again. And again, until the thick length of him is fully rooted inside me. It's the first time I've taken him that it isn't bordering on *too* painful. This time, it's easier. The pleasure is closer to the surface. And I need more of it.

I rub my nipples against the hair-dusted surface of his chest. I kiss his lips as I ride him, arching and torturing him with wriggling teases, squeezing him to pull him deeper. "Do you like this, husband?"

"You're a little minx, baby. You *know* I love everything you give me. Nothing, ever, anywhere has ever felt as good as you feel, sweetheart. But you know that too, don't you?" He's watching my face, his brilliant eyes half-feral and half-drowsed with pleasure. "For being so new at this, you're a natural."

"I want to make you come hard," I whisper, squeezing myself around his big cock.

"You are, baby girl. You are."

I'm still learning but I let the sensuous pleasure of my body guide me. I might not be experienced but my crazy need for him knows exactly what it wants. He feels so good. Each time I squeeze and bounce, I can feel the rising tide climb higher, closer and closer to my tipping point.

Wolf's mouth fastens onto mine with primal need as he grips me and thrusts harder. I suck on his tongue as I squeeze my inner muscles around him. Wolf makes a low sound. His body shudders and his cock jerks violently inside me. The jets of his release pulse inside me, setting off my own nearly-excruciating climax. I squirm into it, riding him and working his pleasure as he groans and bucks deeply into me.

After the waves start to calm, Wolf holds me close and kisses my neck. His length is still buried wetly, deep inside me, and I can feel the trickle of moisture wetting my thighs as he softens just slightly. His eyelashes are a silky tickle against my skin.

He holds my face with his hands. Then he gazes into my eyes. "Princess?"

"Yeah?"

He doesn't speak right away. He tucks my hair behind my ear. There's an unsettled edge to him. "I love my wife."

I blink at him.

"Don't say anything." He rests two fingers against my lips. "Don't tell me how it's too fast and I don't know you well enough. I thought I'd experienced pleasure and beauty in my life before, but they were nothing compared to how it feels to be inside you. When you milk my cock with that tight little heaven on earth, baby, you fucking *own* me. I'm addicted to the feel and the taste of you."

He's talking about loving *it*. Not me.

But then he says, "I'm your husband so if I want to fall in love with you I will. And I am. So don't tell me I can't."

It takes me off-guard. The delivery is sort of insufferable but also so unexpectedly sweet. "I wasn't going to."

There are tears in my eyes. Because, after only four short days, I feel closer to my new husband than I've ever felt to anyone. What I'm realizing is that I might be just the tiniest bit in love with him too.

LATER, we go down to the rear deck. Wolf baits two of the fishing rods and casts them, placing them in the holders. He's standing close to the edge. He's put on a pair of swim shorts which fit him in a way that shows off his body in all its built, buff glory. Now that I'm no longer scared of him I can fully appreciate how beautiful he is. His shoulders are wide and square, bronzed with sun, tapering down to his lean waist and that killer ass. His legs are long and muscular. I've never seen a more perfectly formed man.

He catches me watching him and he smiles slowly as he sets the last of his fishing rods. "Damn, girl. You've had three orgasms within the hour. My wife is insatiable."

All it would take is a light touch. And I can't resist.

Very lightly, I push him.

He's not expecting it. He loses his balance and falls into the clear water.

It's honestly the funniest thing I've ever seen in my life and I laugh like I haven't laughed in a long time. Maybe ever.

Surfacing with a flick of his hair, he climbs up the ladder with mischievous revenge in his eyes. "You are *so* in for it right now."

I scream and run into the cabin but he catches me easily and he lays me onto one of the couches, opening the short silk robe I'm wearing. "You're getting me all wet!" I laugh and he licks my pussy, eating into me. He growls *so, so wet* as he pushes my legs high and bent. I open for him, giving him anything and everything he wants. He takes his big cock in his hand and rubs the head against the mess he's made of me, sliding all the way to the hilt, until my laughter gives way to moans as he makes me come hard. Again. And again.

And with each burst of pleasure Wolf Ramsey gives me as he growls his words of devotion, I fall just a little bit harder.

THE NEXT FEW days pass in a blur. We make love. We swim. We catch fish. Wolf cooks for me, teasing me because I've never actually cooked for myself before and I have no idea how to do it. He teaches me and he feeds me. We drink champagne and get drunk. We laugh. We make love again.

I lose all track of time. Our schedule is ruled only by our cravings and our bond, which strengthens and entwines with each passing hour.

Wolf ties me up and takes me to the very brink of what I can handle, obliterating my boundaries. He tells me he's taking it easy with me, at first, now, learning what I like. I don't know if he'd even listen to my safe word if I needed to use it.

He seems very skilled at taking me to the point where I *almost* use it but not quite. I sometimes wonder if I'll ever need to.

Something tells me I will, when we're not in this secluded bubble of solitude and connection, where no one can bother us or intrude. When we're alone in this idyllic place, nothing can touch us. We can relax without the outside world threatening us with its storm clouds.

But we can't stay here forever. We're due in Seven Mile Beach in two more days.

For now, we savor the time we have to just get to know each other.

We're in the kitchen of the yacht. I'm sitting on the counter and he's feeding me grapes. We've made love twice already this morning and we just went for a swim. We're hungry.

Wolf is teaching me how to make pancakes. He thinks it's funny that I've never learned to cook. "So then you add some vanilla and you mix it all together like this." He shows me. "Tell me. If you could do anything you wanted with your life, what would it be?"

"Anything?"

"Anything. Except I think we can rule out chef."

I laugh.

"Seriously. Paint me a picture of your dream life."

I think about it. "What I'd really like to do is to help people."

He positions himself between my spread knees. His big cock slides against my stomach. "You can help me right now," he murmurs lecherously, dipping his finger into the pancake batter and touching it to each of my nipples. Then he proceeds to suck it off in lusty pulls.

"You've had enough help." I'm laughing but I push at his head. "Stop that. You're getting me all sticky."

"I like you sticky." He dips his finger again and touches it to my pussy. I try to push him away but he grips me and pulls me closer. His mouth is there, eating into me. "Wolfie needs breakfast."

He brings me to the very brink, but then he stands, lining himself up and pushing inside me. I'm still adjusting and it always takes me off-guard. The size and squirm-inducing thickness of him.

"Fuck, you feel good, baby girl. Like heaven. So sweet and tight. You're mine."

I *am* his. I don't question it. I don't need to. It doesn't matter that it's happening so fast it still sometimes makes my head spin. I don't overthink it. I can't, when he feels this good. I wrap my arms and legs around him as he slides deep.

He winds his hand around my hair, pulling tight. As he

fucks me slowly, he kisses my neck, licking and marking me with little love bites. "Tell me more about your plans."

"Can I tell you a secret?" I breathe. We do this. Since we have sex practically non-stop and have since we got married, we often have rambling conversation while we're doing it.

"What secret?"

"You can't tell Silas."

"Why would I tell Silas anything?"

"I started—*oh God*—I started a charity a while ago. I haven't done much with it yet. My cousin manages it for me. But I want to take it over. There's a lot more I could do with it."

"What kind of charity?"

"There's a fund for helping kids go to college. One for funding medical research. Another one that funds children's programs. Stuff like that. It probably sounds lame or idealistic—"

"It doesn't sound lame at all."

"It just seems like a waste to not at least try to—*oohh*—to try to do something more meaningful with all the money we have and not just spend it on ourselves."

"I'll help you."

"You will?"

"I already told you, it's my job to make sure you get everything you want and do everything you want to do."

He pulls back his hips and drives forward. His hands won't allow me to retreat and his next thrust has me crying and digging my fingernails into his back. Every time he goes deep, my legs wrap more tightly around him and I arch to take more of him. "*Wolf. I'm so close.*"

"I know, baby." His forehead touches mine and our mouths crush together desperately. "Who do you belong to?"

"*You, Wolf. You.*"

"Come for me. Squeeze that tight little pussy around me and make me come. Let me feel you."

"*Wolf. Oh God. Oh fuck—*"

The spasms explode through my body, tugging him in voluptuous bursts as his cock throbs and jerks, pumping his liquid warmth deep inside me. He holds me for a long time, whispering to me as our orgasms spiral into each other. *You're a beautiful dream. I'll do anything for you, do you know that? I didn't know anything could feel this good.*

There's something very primal and life-affirming about getting fucked by a massive, virile beefcake while he simultaneously whispers the sweetest words you've ever heard in his low, lust-drowsed growl.

*I love this about him.* The contrasts. The staunch male physicality wrapped around a true, emotion-filled beating heart that knows all about pain, just like mine does.

We wait until the wild pleasure calms, both stunned into silence. His kiss unhurried and all I can think about is how amazed and thankful I am that he's mine.

My husband.

I know I could never settle for anything less than this. And I'll never have to.

Wolf Ramsey has surprised me in every possible way.

*But will it always be this easy and this good?*

After a few minutes, he pulls himself from my body and cleans me. As he does this, my stomach makes a small rumbling sound.

He smiles. "Pancakes are coming right up."

"Be careful you don't burn anything important."

He wraps an apron around his waist and I laugh because he looks so ridiculous, all buff and rough in the tiny apron—and nothing else. "Sometimes I think you only like me for my gigantic dick. I feel used."

I throw a dishtowel at him.

"Careful, or I'll have to take you over my knee. Just sit there obediently for five seconds. I know it's a lot to ask."

"I never agreed to the obedience clause."

"That was a clever dodge. And I liked the edit."

A shared memory infuses the moment. Of us, standing at the altar holding hands while we vowed to honor each other for the rest of time. Those words have power. They've spilled over into the beginning of our lives together and we can feel them.

I promised to love him.

*I think I do. I think I'm falling for my husband.*

I love being with him. He's fun and funny one minute and darkly dangerous the next, in a way that never fails to stoke my desire for him into a wild, blazing bonfire.

As the hours turn into days, I feel myself blooming. I never knew I was capable of being so uninhibited. He makes me feel free to be *myself*—and it's a version of myself that's new. He invites me to open to him like a flower seeking sun. To embrace the parts of my personality I never have. The *eccentric* parts, which had never been allowed to fully indulge themselves before.

We spend hours talking about our lives and our dreams and occasionally the things that hurt the most. We have a surprising amount in common when we talk about *those* things, most of all.

Wolf and I both know how it feels to have huge holes in your life where the most important people should have been, but never were.

Now, he's swimming and I'm waiting on deck for him. *I miss him.*

"Hey, beautiful." He's climbing up the ladder with a spear gun in one hand and a knife between his teeth. I'm on a towel on the deck, laying on my back, sunbathing naked.

Tied to the end of his speargun are two very large fish. He sets them on the table of the small outdoor kitchen and takes the knife in his hand.

"There's something I need to show you." He opens a compartment near the fishing rods and pulls out a leather pouch.

He comes over to me and I can detect a current in his tone that's new. Our impending deadline is weighing heavily on both of us. I don't want to go home to Seven Mile Beach. Wolf wants it even less.

He crouches over me, straddling my hips. I don't even mind that he's getting me wet. I'm hot from the sun and I'm happy he's back. I missed his big, sparked presence that infuses everything with safety. He takes the pouch and wraps the strap around my upper thigh, fastening it there. "What is it?"

"It's a knife. A very sharp one."

Wolf slides the small bone-handled knife from its holster. Reaching for my hand, Wolf places the handle of the knife in my grasp, wrapping his own hand around mine. The knife's tip glints in the sun.

He touches it against the skin of his side, just below his ribs. I almost tell him to be careful.

"Here," he says. "This is where you strike. Gouge deep —and put some effort into it. Muscle is more resilient than you might expect. Up and in. Twist and slice. Like this." He twists the knife in our collective grasp to show me the motion. "Show me."

"Why would I need to know this?"

"In case you're ever threatened like this. You can never be too safe."

There's a tension in him that's more pronounced the closer we get to our deadline. He hasn't let me out of his sight since we said our wedding vows. But we can't spend every second together for the rest of time.

Wolf lets go of my hand, watching me. He's waiting, so I mimic the movement he showed me.

"That's good. But harder. Deeper. You have to *want* to kill and you'll need to if you're ever in this position. Never aim small. Do it again."

He's more satisfied by my second attempt.

"That's better. You're going to start wearing this all the time. Under your clothes. When we get back, I'm going to teach you how to use firearms. And some other weapons that will be useful if you ever need them. Has anyone taught you how to defend yourself?"

"No."

He shakes his head. "Unbelievable. But we're going to fix that."

The threats we face are real. I know that as well as he does.

Holding his weight with his arms, he leans down and kisses me lightly, like he can't resist.

"You're a very good kisser," I tell him. "Not that I have much to compare you to." His kisses are always full of lusty adoration. Wolf doesn't just kiss, he *tastes*. He *devours*. He's feeling it. And so am I. "You've really never kissed anyone before me?"

"No." Maybe it's something in my expression. "Why? Have you?"

I make the mistake of hesitating. "No."

"What the fuck?" His eyes flash as he bears down on me. "You kissed someone else?"

"No."

"You're not a very good liar, sweetheart."

How is he this perceptive? "It was nothing. Honestly. It was hardly a kiss——"

"Who was it?"

"No one."

"Tell me who it was."

"Wolf, it was nothing. It was the lightest, most innocent thing."

"Who?"

"It was … my friend Ash."

"*Ash.*" Like the word leaves a bad taste in his mouth.

"It was me who kissed him. It was barely even a kiss at all. I was just … curious."

"When?"

I blink up at him. He's not going to like this.

"When was it?" he asks again.

"It was … the day I came here. *Before* I met you," I point out.

"Show me."

"Show you what?"

"Show me how you kissed him."

I sigh. "You really want me to?"

"Show me."

"Okay, then. Let me sit up."

He allows this, holding me on his lap. Wolf is watching me and I can tell he's very unhappy about this new revelation. He's practically seething and he's hot to the touch.

I lean closer and brush my lips against his in a barely-there touch, just like I did to Ash. It seems unreal that my life has changed so much since then. And that *I've* changed so much since then.

"That's it?"

"Yes. That's it."

"Did he kiss you back?"

"No."

"He must be the stupidest motherfucker on earth. How do you know him?"

"He's a friend."

"If he's just a friend you wouldn't have kissed him. Did you want to take it further?"

"No." It feels strange to be admitting all this. "I don't know."

I know by now that my husband won't rest until he gets every detail he wants. "Are you in love with him?" Like he's bracing himself.

Did I once believe I was? Maybe, but that was a different version of myself, a naive, less complicated version who had no idea what being swept away by a tidal wave of passion feels like—or even that such a thing existed. "No, Wolf. Not that way. I loved that he was my port in the storm. I loved that I could talk to him when there was no one else who would listen. He made me feel like I wasn't so alone."

I'm surprised when my husband is borderline sympathetic—in an I'll-kill-him kind of way. "Fair enough. But you have me now. You're not alone. You can talk to me. *I'll* listen." He will too. He does. "Does he live in Waikiki?"

"Yes. At Seven Mile Beach. He works for my family."

"Then I guess *Ash* and I will have a few things to discuss."

"It wasn't Ash's fault. It was mine."

"Do I have to worry about you trying to run off with this fucker when we get back to Seven Mile Beach?"

Would I? I was so desperate to. Before. My husband doesn't like the time it takes me to consider this. But I'm honest when I look into his eyes and tell him, "*No*, Wolf." As much as I value Ash and his friendship, now, it would be like running off with a mild-mannered little lightning bug when you've experienced a trillion-watt pleasure-lightning bolt. There's no coming back from that.

"I used to think Ash might be the one for me," I tell him, my voice low and soft. "I wanted him to be. But he never quite was and it bothered me. He once told me I'd find the one who was meant for me and it would be worth the wait. At the time I was sort of upset by that because it didn't feel like I would ever find the one. But now I think Ash was right. It *was* worth the wait."

My husband is drinking in my words but it does little to tone down the brimming fury. "You're not going to see Ash without me there. Understood?"

I feel that light petulance creep back into my mood. Here we go. Here's the part where he makes his demands and tries to control everything I do.

"I said, do you *understand*? Unless you want Ash dead, you'll honor my request and you'll do it willingly."

"Don't be a bully," I tell him.

"I'm your husband," he says simply. "You're mine now. All of you. Everything."

"You don't trust me?"

"I trust you. It's *Ash* I don't trust. You're too tempting, and it's my job to make sure you're not put in a position where he might be tempted. I don't want him—or anyone else—getting any ideas when I'm not around. Which they will, because you're the most beautiful woman in the world. *I'm* the one who tempts you now, sweetheart. No one else.

You've already agreed to that when you said your vows. Are you doubting them now?"

"*No*. God. You don't have to go postal over it."

"Postal? *Postal?* Oh, I'll go postal, don't you worry about that."

"I said I'm not going to do anything like that again, okay? I hadn't even met you yet. You can't be mad."

"Of course I'm *mad*." He says the word like it's childish and doesn't touch the sides of how he feels.

"I said my vows, just like you did. I'm yours now."

"Damn right you are. And I'm still counting *our* kiss as your first." Churlishly. "Because that one was hardly a kiss at all. It was fucking lame, if you ask me."

I'm glaring at him. I'm annoyed, but also touched by his rampant jealousy. He *cares* about me. More than anyone has ever cared about me, for *me*.

I'm also sort of … crazily turned on by my husband's big, buff maleness. I'm sitting directly on top of his hard, silky cock, which is pressing against the lips of my pussy and wetting my thighs with its leaking moisture. "It doesn't count," I say, to placate him. "It was nothing."

"You're dreaming if you think you're getting off that easily." His voice is low and soft but he's lifting me and turning me. One thing I'm learning is that I can fight him all I want but when my husband is determined to have something, he's too strong to argue with. He always gets his way.

Still, I struggle as he positions me. "What are you doing?"

"Reminding you."

"Of what?"

"That you're mine."

"I didn't even *know* you yet, Wolf." I huff a light protest because it's so ridiculous that he's mad about this, but he's maneuvered me so I'm laying across his lap with my ass up and my head on a folded towel. "*Wolf—*"

"It's my duty to make sure you feel better than anyone else ever could." He pulls my wrists behind my back and wraps a leather cord around them. "I'm your husband."

His hand is on my backside. "I *know* you're my—" He slaps my ass. Hard. "*Ow!* You don't need to *punish* me!"

"I'm not punishing you. I'm rewarding you. I'm showing you how deep my mad devotion goes. You're sweet and sexy and irresistible to your ravenous husband, did you know that, baby girl?" With his other hand, he uses the wetness to work two of his fingers inside me. He starts pushing his fingers in and out in a languid rhythm. He spanks me again and this time the pain spreads and melts into the warm, wet rhythm he's stroking with his fingers. Wolf rubs the warmth in, and in, until my whole body is igniting with heat.

Wolf slaps me again and I squeal and squirm but I can't get away from him. *And I don't want to. What he's working up to feels too damn good.*

"I'm too obsessed with my perfect wife to compromise." His next spank is perfectly placed. It hurts but the pain is double-edged.

Below the pain, like warm water under cool ice, pleasure

spreads, sprouting little wings that tease me toward a hot, crazy climax.

"You belong to me now." He does it again.

And again.

"And *only* me." I think about using my safe word but I'm too needy. The pain of each strike is melting into a spiked, molten rapture. Again. And again. Until the pain and pleasure merge into one sweet burn that spills over into tight, sudden spasms that make my whole body quiver and wriggle.

I come very, very hard.

"Who are you coming for, princess?"

"*You*, Wolf," I manage to moan. "*You*."

"That's right. Because you're mine."

"I *know*."

"Don't ever forget that."

"I *won't*."

He makes me come again.

Then, he unties my wrists and pulls me up to him, carefully brushing the damp strands of my hair back from my flushed face and the tears that have wet my cheeks.

"This face," he rasps. "This sweet, angelic face that killed me at my very first sight of it. These golden eyes the color of warm honey. This pouting pink mouth. I knew it would be my downfall and I was right. I love everything about you, baby girl, so much it hurts. Do you feel me?"

It's whiplash-fast. This marriage. This attraction. This wild love affair. "I feel you." And I do. Under the rising moon over the darkening water, which rolls with a sea change, I *feel* him. I don't know what will happen when we return to real life as a married couple. But here and now, I feel *everything.* The gift he's given me of this fiery, powerful submission for him and only him has transformed me into a technicolored version of myself that's full of magical energy that somehow makes me feel downright invincible.

But even I know that's one thing I can never be.

"Now," he says, his voice husky with dark lust and hot-blooded emotion. "Give your husband a *real* kiss."

## 14

IT FEELS strange to be home.

We're in the back of one of our limos, turning into the long driveway of my family's estate. I see the whole place in a new light now, as though I'm viewing it through Wolf's eyes. After the untamed, wide-open beauty of Paradise, Seven Mile Beach seems closed-in and overly manicured. There are none of the scenic vistas that are so much a part of the landscape in Kauai.

Our beach looks smaller than it did two weeks ago and the buildings, against the backdrop of high-rise hotels and condos in the distance, are oppressively close together.

In the end, we spent almost two weeks in Kauai and almost a full week in Pirate's Cove, as a sort of honeymoon.

We went to Knox and Cassidy's wedding at the castle. Wolf was one of Knox's groomsmen. It was a gorgeous wedding and the two of them are so wildly in love with each other it made the whole scene doubly romantic.

Wolf says he'll take me on a trip anywhere I want to go once we've met with Silas and Enzo and taken care of business at Seven Mile Beach. I told him I'd love to go to Italy.

We know where we want to spend most of our time, at his—*our*, he keeps reminding me—house on the beach in Paradise. In fact he calls it mine. Either way, it already feels like home.

"Do you always travel by limo?" His question is gruff, like this mode of transportation irritates him.

His warm hand rests on my bare thigh, under the hem of my skirt. It almost feels strange to be clothed. We've spent the past two weeks naked or wrapped only in towels.

The weight of his hand is comforting to me now. I'm irrevocably *his*. He's imprinted me with his aggression, his growly possessiveness and his surprisingly intense affection. It's a potent combination.

My husband is big and fierce-looking in the interior of the car. He's wearing jeans and a black shirt that strains against his muscles, showing off his ink and his dark tan. He's not happy to be here at all and I can't really blame him.

What amazing eyes he has, like someone's shining light through a layer of blue sea glass. In Kauai, he fits the gaudily tropical scenery. In Waikiki, he seems downright otherworldly, like a sea creature who wandered onto dry land.

I'm watching him, so distracted by how stunning he is in

this foreign setting, I have to think for a second about what he just asked me. "I guess so. Don't you?"

"No."

"How do you travel?"

"Motorcycle, usually. Four wheel drive dune buggy. Horseback. Boat. Sometimes helicopter."

I did notice it: the Ramseys don't show off their wealth. If anything, they almost mask it.

Unlike my family.

My siblings might as well have *I'm rich, suckers!* tattooed across their foreheads.

"This is just temporary, Wolf. We'll go back to Kauai soon. That's where we'll live, we've decided that."

My phone pings with a barrage of incoming texts. There hadn't been reception on the boat. I didn't even bother to charge my phone, for an entire *week*. In my former life, this would have been unthinkable.

While we were in Pirate's Cove, I was too distracted by having hot sex with my punishing beefcake of a husband 24/7 to worry about it.

But now I'm wondering who's been trying to get a hold of me, besides Lana with her demands. Or Perri, once she discovered my Instagram numbers—a detail that feels even more empty and irrelevant than before. Once we got into the limo, I plugged my phone into the USB port and it's just now recharged enough to turn back on. The screen lights up from where the phone is resting on the seat next to me.

Ash. A whole string of messages. There are also 37 missed calls.

My husband bristles, reaching over me and picking up my phone. "What does *he* want?"

Wolf holds the phone up to my face until it unlocks. He scrolls through the messages and I watch him do this.

I could protest, or tell him it's none of his business. But of course it *is* his business now. And I think about how I felt when he got that text from Cheyenne.

> Vivi, pls call me as soon as you get this! I've found something out that you're REALLY going to want to hear about. I heard about what happened. I can't believe it's true. Call me. I hope you're okay, honey

> Vivi!!! I REALLY need to see you as soon as you get back. It's URGENT!!

> Are you back yet?? Are you okay? I hope you're okay

> I thought you were coming back last weekend?

> I'm worried about you. Pls call me

> Are you okay? Pls let me know

> VIVI PLS CALL ME

"Wow. I'm going to …" I glance at Wolf.

"Go right ahead. You can put it on speaker."

It's not worth arguing with him. Ash is clearly a sticky topic but I need to talk to him. I want to let him know I'm still alive. My husband will just have to deal with that.

I press the call button.

Ash answers on the second ring. "*Vivi.* Holy shit. Where are you? Are you home yet? I've been *so* worried about you."

"I'm fine, Ash. How are you?"

"I'm freaking *out,* of course. I've been going insane with worry. Are you okay? Can you come see me?"

"I'm okay." I'm reborn, enlightened and, if it's possible to fall in love with a hot, ferocious MMA fighter mountain man after only knowing him for two weeks, then I might be that too. "What's the urgent thing you needed to tell me about? I got your texts."

"Vivi, you won't believe this. It's *major.* But I don't want to tell you over the phone, in case it's tapped."

"Tapped?"

"When can you come see me? It's important. Are you back?"

"We're almost home. We're on our way in from the airport. Can you at least tell me what it's about?"

The "we're" gets Ash's attention. "I think I should wait until we talk in person. How soon can you get here?"

The limo is pulling up to the front door of our estate. "I'll come now. I'll need to … uh … well, I'm going to need to bring my new husband."

Ash is quiet for a few seconds. When he continues, it doesn't sound like he realizes he's on speaker. His voice is low. "I am *so* sorry to hear about all that, honey. Social media is blowing up with all the news and speculation about what's happened. Malachi and Aurora gave an interview. I can't believe you got *chosen*. So you're actually, like … *married?*"

"Yeah. I am." My husband is watching me, his eyes burning like aquamarine embers.

"I can't believe you went *through* with it. That whole arranged marriage thing is so insane! They're saying Knox Ramsey is engaged to some girl who's actually the secret lovechild of Jethro King? I mean, what the hell?"

"Yeah, it's pretty crazy," I agree.

"And then for you to get *forced* into marriage like that, just out of the blue?"

"It was definitely unexpected."

"Is he … as rough as they say he is? I mean, *God*, Vivi. *Wolf Ramsey?*" Like he can't imagine anything worse. Only two weeks ago, I wouldn't have been able to either.

Wolf's mouth quirks. "The one and only," he confirms.

Ash falls so silent I wonder for a second if the line's been disconnected.

"Ash? We'll come see you, okay? Just wait there."

"Oh," comes the muffled, mortified reply. "Okay."

My phone continues to ping with incoming messages. "It might be a little while because I'm getting a bunch of texts from Lana, Gabrielle, Perri and Silas," I tell him. "I'm sure we'll get ambushed as soon as we get inside. But we'll come as soon as we can."

"All right."

"See you soon, Ash."

I end the call.

"He's right," Wolf says. "Your phone has been tapped."

"What? How do you know that?"

"There was a clicking sound in the background of that call."

*Shit.* "But why? Who would have tapped it?"

"Any number of people, princess. You've been a target your whole life. We're going to need to be more careful with you."

It's jarring, to think that someone's been snooping on me, and for who knows how long? I think about all my phone calls with Ash. The texts and messages. I poured my heart out to him so many times, about how I wished I could be free of my family.

Maybe Silas or Jett already knew about my relationship with Ash and allowed it because they could get more information out of me by listening in. Maybe they saw it as a way of keeping track of my plans.

Wolf takes my phone and searches through it for a few minutes.

"Here it is. In your folders. A couple of layers in. It's a spyware app. Someone's been listening in on everything you do."

*Those assholes.* "How would they have even put it on there?"

"Who gave you your phone? Did someone set it up for you?"

Of course they did. "Someone on my family's staff gave it to me. Maybe six or seven months ago."

"Well, they've tracked you by GPS, watched everything you've been doing, had access to your camera and listened in on every conversation you've had."

*Goddamn them.* It's creepy and upsetting. But not completely unsurprising.

"There," he says. "I've just deleted it. We can reset the phone to factory settings, in case there are other tracking systems hidden somewhere. Even then, I wouldn't trust it. We'll get you a new phone. In fact, we'll deliver this one back to Silas tonight. It'll send him a message, if it was him, that we're aware and we'll no longer allow it." He powers the phone off and slides it into his back pocket.

It's unfamiliar, how reassuring it is to have him here with me. Looking out for me. *Helping* me. Like it's us against the world—or, more specifically, us against the people who have kept me very carefully caged, monitored and controlled for as long as I can remember.

Wolf's phone buzzes and he pulls it out of his pocket, answering the call. "Silas."

I can hear my brother's voice through the line. "We need to meet."

"Sure. I'm putting you on speaker." By the tone of Wolf's voice, it's obvious he's not intimidated in the least by my brother. And I guess he shouldn't be. Physically, he's stronger. And he has just as much power as Silas does, now that we're married. Come to think of it, so do I. Technically, I'm just as high-ranking as both of them now.

For the alliance families, there's a ranking system that's written into the original documents. I never paid much attention to the rules but I'm familiar with them. Silas talks about them all the time.

Before the alliance marriages are sealed, the oldest of each family gets to make the final decisions about all matters relating to the alliance. But after an alliance marriage, the new member of the family becomes an equal to the most senior family member. And so does their spouse. Which makes Wolf as powerful as Silas. And, by default, this makes *me* as powerful as Silas too.

I guess the idea was to make sure the marriages would create a solid bond across the families that would give new members the power to keep their own family's interests aligned with their new family's. That way, both families become more deeply entwined.

But I wonder if it'll be that easy.

The two colliding battleship forces of my oldest brother (and his bodyguard) and my brand new volatile husband was always going to be anything but smooth sailing.

"The first order of business," Wolf says, "will be to fire the asshole bodyguard who tried to follow Vivi. I want him gone."

"You mean Jett?" Silas asks.

Wolf reads my expression. "Yeah, that's the one. It needs to happen immediately. I'll escort him off the premises myself but if I do that I might end up killing him with my bare hands."

"I can't fire him, he's my cousin," Silas tells him.

"He's not really our cousin," I point out, and ... it feels good. I don't have to answer to my brother anymore. He can't boss me around. *And neither can Jett.*

"True," Silas replies. "But he's as loyal as family."

"Not to me, Silas."

Maybe my brother isn't totally to blame. Maybe he really doesn't realize how bad things have been. "All I ever asked him to do was keep you protected, Vivi."

"My wife had bruises from where he grabbed her arm, Silas." Wolf's tone is as cold as ice. "You allowed that. But I won't. Do you want me to be the one to fire him?"

"I'll do it," Silas replies.

"Make sure he's gone today. If I see him I'll get rid of him myself."

There's a long pause. I'm expecting more of a fight but Silas is no fool. He knows Wolf will follow up on his threat. "All right," Silas agrees. "I'll do it now."

My heart is beating fast. The relief is indescribable. Like a weight I've been carrying around my whole life has been suddenly lifted.

"And no more tracking Vivi's phone," says Wolf. "She's off-limits."

"I didn't track her phone."

Wolf is wary. "I just deleted a spyware app."

"I don't know anything about that," Silas insists. "I'll see if I can get to the bottom of it."

"So will I. And I don't want her being followed. She's my responsibility now and you and your security team can leave her the fuck alone."

It's safe to say that Silas probably hasn't ever been spoken to like this in his life. But my husband is obviously a force to be reckoned with, even for my brothers. I'm surprised when Silas says, "Understood."

"Good."

"Anyway, I'll see you both tonight. At the party. It's something Tatum was putting together. To welcome the two of you back. Malachi and Aurora will be there too."

"All right. See you then." Wolf is scowling as he ends the call.

I'm shaken and my husband can read this.

"Vivi?"

"Yeah?"

"I'm your rock now. I'll protect you and fight for you. You don't have to worry about them anymore. You've got me now."

I'm not expecting it and for some reason this simple assurance, after everything he's just done for me, breaks down some wall inside my psyche. The one that's been working overtime to hold back all my fears and insecurities so they don't completely overwhelm me.

I don't even mean to, but I crawl onto his lap and I hug him. Like, a *real* hug. The restorative, whole-hearted kind of hug that brings tears to your eyes and makes you sigh. The kind I've been craving my entire life. "Thank you, Wolf. Stay with me. Please don't leave me."

He holds my face and—maybe more gently than he ever has—he kisses my lips. "I'm not going anywhere. I'm your shield. Your own personal berserker." This makes me smile through my tears. "Nothing's getting through me, sweetheart. The only thing I care about is getting you back to our safe haven where you're so happy and relaxed and you feel so good, all you want to do is let me love you the way only I can."

*Wow.*

I think I love him.

*I do. I love him.*

I'm so used to being scared, the sudden absence of fear in his presence is the best feeling I've ever had.

There's commotion outside the car. People are waiting for us. "And don't you leave me either," he says. "I need you close to me."

"I won't, Wolf."

"Are you ready? Let's get this over with." His expression gets hard and staunch, like he's preparing to go to battle. And maybe we are. "I'll take care of everything, just hold onto my hand and remember how beautiful you are. How strong and powerful my perfect wife is."

I wipe my tears and nod. Someone opens the door.

Wolf helps me out of the limo and pulls me by the hand. He leads me up the front steps, which are flanked by security guards. Behind them, lush tropical plants stand in huge pots and two stone lion statues stare out over the scene.

We walk into the open foyer of the house and several of my assistants rush over to us. There's Gabrielle, who handles my Instagram, Eleanor, who's in charge of my publicity team and Ashley, whose job is to coordinate my schedule and keep on top of all my appointments.

All three of them get wide-eyed at the sight of my big, imposing husband. He probably weighs as much as all three of them put together. He also happens to be armed to the teeth. I'm used to it now but I remember how alarming it was the first time I saw him.

"Welcome home, Vivi," says Gabrielle, but her eyes are glued on Wolf. With his rough good looks, his ink and his sun-burnished muscles, he couldn't be any more impressive.

"Mr. Ramsey, I'm Gabrielle. This is Eleanor and Ashley."

"The pleasure's mine," Wolf replies. The dry roguish-ness is there but he couldn't sound any less enthusiastic to be here if he tried.

We're ushered into a waiting elevator and taken to the third floor, where the fashion studio is located.

"Your IG numbers have spiked again, Vivi," Gabrielle tells me, holding up the Instagram phone. "They dipped below Perri's but as soon as the news broke about the wedding, they've gone through the freaking roof. Your followers are *dying* to get a photo of you two together. They're literally begging."

Eleanor adds, "All the magazines want an exclusive for the wedding photos and a reveal shoot of you two as newly-weds. They're offering astronomical amounts of money, Vivi. We need to go through these offers with you as soon as possible."

Wolf is watching the whole exchange with cool, gruff detachment, like they're speaking a foreign language that takes some effort to decipher.

The doors slide open and Lana is there, waiting for us, along with a brigade of her assistants, with their iPads, phones and garment racks at the ready.

Everyone goes quiet as Wolf and I step off the elevator. He might as well be a Roman gladiator who's time-warped onto the set of Project Runway. Just completely, totally out of place. A tall, shredded sun god walking through a crowd of pale, emaciated fashion slaves.

"*Finally*, you're here," says Lana, stepping forward with her usual in-your-face overconfidence. "I'm Lana Lee, Mr. Ramsey. It's nice to meet you. I didn't get a chance to introduce myself at the wedding with all the last-minute planning that was going on and the chaos. I offered my assistance to your sisters but they seemed to have very definite ideas about what they wanted for the dress. I think the result was sweet. I'm Vivi's stylist. You might have heard of me."

"No."

"Oh." Lana's face is bright red. I've never seen her speechless before. After a few seconds of mute indignation, she recovers. "Well, Vivi, we'll need to get started right away. I want you in the studio ASAP. We have *so* many looks to put together and we're *way* behind schedule—"

"That's not happening." My husband is at least a head taller than everyone else in the room and his striking, stormy presence has everyone absolutely riveted. "Vivi and I will meet with you when we're ready. It won't be today."

Lana glares at him. It's not her style to take no for an answer. Her color is still high when she replies. "I'm not sure you understand the demands of her contracts, Mr.—"

"The only demands my wife needs to worry about are mine." Okay, I guess my husband isn't concerned about niceties. Which makes me wildly happy. "We're going to be reviewing her contracts. If you'd like to work with us on that and Vivi agrees to it, you can. Otherwise we'll find someone who understands my wife's new priorities better."

Lana stands there, agog. "Of course, Mr. Ramsey."

Wolf scans the group, taking his time, assessing them critically like he's surveying an underprepared army of weaklings he's been sent to train. "We're going to need someone who can be on-call to organize the upgrades my wife and I will be making to our rooms here at Seven Mile Beach. This person will also need to be available for anything my wife needs or wants, whenever she wants it. You'll get a substantial raise. Is there anyone here who might be able to handle that?"

Every single person, aside from Lana, raises their hand.

"Vivi? Choose someone."

"Um … Gabrielle?"

Gabrielle gives Wolf an elated, adoring smile.

*Wow.*

"Is that the Instagram phone?" Wolf asks her. I remember explaining to him once that I had an assistant with a phone that was dedicated exclusively to the account. I'd told him that if I could ever control my own life, I would try to do something more meaningful with it. I still don't really understand why I have such a big following or why people are so interested in me. It would be nice to put a platform like that to good use, I always thought. To somehow help people, instead of just making money that gets siphoned directly to my family for who knows what.

"Yes," Gabrielle replies, blinking up at him.

"Vivi will take a look through and we'll let you know what she decides she'd like to do with it from now on." He holds out his hand.

"Oh." She tentatively hands him the phone.

"Is your number listed in the contacts? We'll let you know what Vivi needs."

"Y-yes it is. It's in favorites."

"Good." Wolf glances down at me, and his fierceness softens. "Where's our room, baby?"

His smile is so beautiful I have to concentrate on keeping it together and not making a scene in front of my painfully attractive husband and all the people who are watching us. What I want to do is kiss him. Instead, I gesture to the door of my bedroom, which is right across the hall from where we're standing. "Here."

"Your room is in the middle of … all this?"

My room, Perri's and Tatum's are all located right down the hall from the fashion department's studio. "Yes."

"We're not living here," my husband announces. "We need something more private. What else do you have?"

What else do I have? "I …" I have my favorite place in the estate. I spent years when I was a teenager begging Silas to let me move into it but he always said it wasn't practical. It was too far away and too secluded from the people who ran my life. It was better if I was accessible to my teams at all times. "I have my mother's library. It's at the other end of the estate."

"Let's go." To Gabrielle, as we're leaving, "My wife needs champagne. And she's hungry."

*Bossy much?*

"Yes, Mr. Ramsey. Of course, Mr. Ramsey." *Seriously?* Gabrielle is gazing at him, starstruck, like he's a freaking rock star or something.

With that, we leave them to it, standing there open-mouthed.

Kind of bemused by the effect my husband has on people, I lead Wolf through the palm grove, past the fountains and through the archways, to the other side of the pool area.

To the walled-in garden with its steel gate. It used to have a whimsical wrought-iron gate that was eventually replaced with something more high-tech. But there's an identical old-style one on the far side of the garden, which used to unlock to a sandy trail that leads down to its own secluded sugar-sand beach. I haven't used the trail in years. The key to the old gate was lost a long time ago.

"This is it." I key in the code to the front gate and open it.

The first floor of mother's library is a sunny, spacious open-plan room. Tall sash windows extend from floor to ceiling. Beams of natural light spill across the Italian tiles and Persian rugs. All the other available wall space is lined with bookshelves. The room is crammed full of comfortable leather couches, love seats upholstered with outlandish, colorful fabrics and Scandinavian chairs designed to be the most comfortable in the world. Tiffany stained glass table lamps are dotted around the room. The bookshelves are full to bursting with books, art and souvenirs from my mother's travels, framed photographs and hundreds of vinyl records.

There are several ceiling fans shaped like palm fronds that haven't been used in years. The whole place is frozen in time and, to me, wildly romantic.

In one corner there's a compact kitchen surrounded by a marble-topped bar. Twenty years ago, it would have been state of the art but it hasn't been used since then.

"I like it. It's very you."

It *is* me. At this my heart practically bursts. I'm not sure why. This relationship might be new and lightning fast but my husband *gets* me. Because he wants to. In a few short weeks, he's taken the time to listen to me and learn me, more than anyone else who's known me a lifetime.

"I think we can make it even more you. We're going to clean this up and add onto it," he announces. "We'll need to double the size, at least. For all the babies we're going to start having soon."

"All seven of them," I murmur.

He grins, pulling me closer, his slow smile hitting me in a place that's as emotional as it is physical. Tropical island mountain men who look as good as Wolf Ramsey should be illegal. "Where's the bedroom?"

"Upstairs."

"Show me."

So I lead him to the upstairs. It's around two-thirds the size of the downstairs, made mostly of glass and light wood. My mother's bed is still here, which she hardly ever used. Occasionally she'd stay here when my father was away or when she just needed some time alone. Her desk sits in the corner, empty now. I boxed up all the old letters, notebooks and other keepsakes long ago and put them in one of the closets. I didn't want any of my siblings to take them—but they've never shown any interest in this place. It's dusty and untouched.

I open the French doors that lead out to a roof garden, which has a view out over the private beach. The outdoor furniture has seen better days. Pots are dotted around, full of weeds now.

"We definitely need a bigger bed," Wolf says. "A four-poster California king, I'm thinking." Wolf pulls me close and presses an open-mouth kiss to my neck, gently biting me. "Let's make a baby now."

"We have a meeting, remember?"

"Fuck the meeting."

"Let's just get it over with and find out what's so urgent. If you want to wait here while I meet with Ash—"

"Not happening, princess."

We take the outside staircase that leads down from the roof garden. I'm nervous about the meeting. We don't get as far as the staff accommodation because, as we walk past the pools, Ash is there. He's rolling up towels and stacking them in one of the racks.

My heart is beating fast.

I grip Wolf's hand tightly. "Be nice," I murmur.

"I'm always nice."

Ash puts the towel down that he's holding. His face pales as he watches us approach. He takes in Wolf's size. His gargantuan build and obvious strength. His weapons. The way his arm is wrapped around me in a firm grip of ownership.

Which tightens.

"Ash." I'd hug him but … maybe not. "This is Wolf. Wolf, Ash."

Wolf looks down at Ash. "*This* is my competition?"

Ash's face has gone white. "I never—"

"I know. My wife told me. And you never will." Wolf contemplates Ash for a long moment. "I can see what she saw in you. You're completely, totally unthreatening."

It's impossible not to compare the two of them, given the situation. Ash is in every way a less imposing man. Obviously. He's about as far from an MMA killing machine as a person can possibly get. He's as boyishly handsome as he's always been. His face looks thinner, his already lean body even more angular under his white staff uniform, like he's forgotten to eat much over the past few weeks.

Right now, he looks like he's wishing he could teleport to an alternate universe.

Wolf, in contrast, is blindingly … dazzling. His hair has a shine to it from the sun, which always seems to choose him for its brightest rays. His skin is brown and dusky. Artfully inked. His jeans and shirt cling to his brawny muscles and the effect is somehow festive with warning. *Fuck with my wife and you'll die* is sort of radiating off him and … I mean, how can I not be charmed by my husband's feral loyalty? It's addictive.

"I'd challenge you to a fight," Wolf growls, "but it's

obvious I'd kill you without even trying." Even *I* get goose-bumps from the murderous husk in my husband's low warning. "Which I will if you ever even *think* about—"

"*Wolf,*" I scold him. "This isn't necessary."

What surprises me about my own reaction to the two of them together is that the solace I used to find in Ash's company is … not gone, but completely shadowed by the safety of Wolf.

All I can think about, in fact, is the feel of my husband's strong, warm grip. The rough callouses of his fingers *and how they feel when they're gripping into me, bruising me and marking me.*

I used to wonder if Ash could be the one for me. If he'd wanted it, could I have fallen in love with him?

Three weeks ago, I might have said yes. Because I had no idea what intensity felt like. I didn't know you could *feel* so much. I didn't know you could click so immediately and so totally with another person that it can change the alchemy of your soul. I didn't know you could come so hard it can knock your world off its axis and enlighten you to a different point of view.

I was grasping. Hoping for something that wasn't there.

Now I don't need to.

Ash gave me a shoulder to lean on when I needed it most. I'll always appreciate him for that. But after the dizzying realizations of the past few weeks, I know that Wolf's storm cloud fits me far better than Ash's smooth, clear water ever could have.

Ash holds his palms up, in a please-don't-beat-me-to-apulp surrender. "I get it, man. Vivi and I were never a thing and we couldn't ever have *been* a thing. She's *way* out of my league. Marriage agrees with her, by the way. Vivi, you look, like, *amazing*—totally in a friend-zone appreciation kind of a way. I wasn't expecting it but I've never seen you look so happy. Besides, I … I've met someone."

"You have?"

His expression turns dreamy. "Yeah. At a party two weekends ago, but we've kind of gone from zero to sixty. His name is Thor."

"Thor?"

"Yeah. It's a nickname. "

My husband almost smiles.

But Ash is absolutely bursting with his news. "Now, can I please show you what I found? Both of you? Because you're *really* going to want to see this. Vivi, remember how you sent me that link so I could check out your charity?"

"Yeah."

"Well, I did some digging. Like, a *lot* of digging." Glancing once more at Wolf as though to make sure he's not about to get pummeled, Ash reaches for a bag and pulls out a laptop. He sets it on a table and opens it. "Something didn't add up so I followed the financial trail of your charity and it led me down a few wormholes. *Big* wormholes. So, well, I ended up hacking into the back end of the charity's bank account. Turns out the money has been disappearing, and not in the directions I was expecting."

"What?"

"It's all going into an off-shore account that's located in the Bahamas."

"The Bahamas?"

"Yes. To an account named J&J Winters Trust. Look at these numbers, Vivi. Does that name ring any bells to you?"

"Winters. That was Jericho and Jett's last name before they got adopted by my aunt and uncle."

We all go quiet for a few seconds as the realization hits.

"Holy shit," Ash gasps.

"There's five million dollars in this account," Wolf says.

"Yes," Ash confirms. "And all of it came from the charity. They're stealing the charity's money."

We're absorbing this information, staring at the numbers. The long list of smaller deposits. A few thousand here and there. They get bolder as time goes on. The most recent deposit is for half a million dollars.

"Vivi?" My husband's growl is graveled and focused.

"Yes?"

"Would you like to show me where Jericho's office might be located?"

"Um … okay."

"Do you have access to the main account of your charity?"

"No."

"Why not?"

"It was a trust fund I was given when I turned eighteen," I explain. "But Silas was going to keep it locked until after the alliance marriages were sealed. I couldn't touch it. Jericho found a loophole. I'd told him that I wanted to start a charity with it once I could access it and he said he could help me do that sooner, as long as all the money went into the foundation. It was our secret."

"Ash." Wolf scowls. "You just got a promotion. You're no longer a pool boy. You're going to help Vivi with these accounts and I'm going to deal with Jericho. Are you willing?"

Ash's face lights up. "Um. Of *course* I'm willing."

"Do we understand each other when it comes to my wife and are you crystal fucking clear on the fact that I can and will tear you limb from fucking limb if you ever—"

"*Wolf.*"

"Yes, sir." Ash actually salutes him. "I don't have a death wish. And I'm a fully fledged accountant now. At your service."

If I didn't know better I'd almost say my husband and my bestie have hit it off, in an as-long-as-every-rule-is-iron-clad kind of way. I can detect what might be the beginnings of a mutual respect. "Good," Wolf grunts. "Let's go talk to Jericho."

So I show them the way to Jericho's office, located in its own small building behind the main office block.

And my husband, using what I learn along the way is a Glock 8, a razor-sharp disc with metal teeth called a Widowmaker, a 50,000 volt taser, and all manner of creative coercion to convince my former cousin—who might have inherited the brains of his family but definitely not the brawn—to not only transfer every penny he stole back into the original account but also call his banker in the Bahamas and have his trust account shut down.

Jericho was pleading, bloody, had at least one shiner and had developed a new limp by the time my husband was done with him. But he was still very much alive, which he seemed to appreciate. He promised all three of us he would never return to the state of Hawaii as long as he lives.

From the relief on his face as he hobbled away from Wolf's clenched fists, I believed him.

# 15

# WOLF

My wife's family is dysfunctional as fuck, which I already knew. At least I've got their attention.

The deviant money-laundering cousin didn't even put up a fight. The guy had no backbone whatsoever and caved surprisingly easily. My guess is he's pilfered much more of the Fitzpatricks' money over the years and has created more than one trust. I had the pool kid track him and he's on his way to Miami. We'll keep digging and chances are he'll end up going to jail but as long as he never steps foot onto the Hawaiian islands again, he'll live.

If the meathead asshole cousin isn't gone by now, I figure at this point I have a license to kill. He's lucky I'm allowing him an out. My instincts are telling me I should have ended him when I had the chance.

Silas can be reasoned with. Deep down I don't think he actually cares one way or the other about much of anything except his lifestyle of hedonism and excess. As long as that remains untouched, he's fine.

The very last thing I'm in the mood for tonight is the party the Fitzpatricks are throwing for us, to welcome us back as a married couple and celebrate the alliance matches.

The whole scenario is pissing me off.

I feel big and mean and ready for a fight.

I don't want to be here. This place is like a goddamn cage.

But I figure we might as well get this alliance fuckery out of the way so we can get on with our lives. I just hope I don't completely lose my shit because some dipshit talks to my wife or glances in her general direction. The touch-her-and-die vibes are coursing through my veins with raw fury.

*Everyone* wants a piece of Vivi.

I can't blame them for that. Except that I'm walking a very fine line between heaven and hell because of it. I'm struggling to control myself. I basically want to pummel everyone who tries to get close to her and it's a problem.

I'm a hundred percent addicted to my girl. It's manic, real and borderline magical. My protective instincts are amped beyond overdrive.

Not only that but I'm head over fucking heels in *love* with her and it's heavy, like claws of fire are gripping into my heart.

Experiencing it when I never thought I could has turned me into a twisted mess of obsession.

The music is loud. Everyone is dressed in trendy outfits

they must think are cutting edge or they're straight off the runways.

I recognize most of the people here, but there are new faces too. Friends of the Fitzpatricks. Business associates of Silas's. A few movie stars probably invited by Tatum. Hangers-on from Malachi's wide social circle that extends across the islands.

My arm is securely around Vivi's waist. I keep her close to me. Every now and then, I kiss her so I can taste her lips. Or I take a deep breath of her hair, which makes me dizzy with lust and infatuation. I need it, to feed my addiction and get my fix.

I don't want to be here, but anywhere I can bask in my new wife's presence basically feels like paradise of a different variety.

I didn't think I was capable of this level of obsession but she breaks every rule and crashes through every barrier I've ever known. I'd kill just to kiss her once more. I'd die to taste her again. I'd give up everything I own to fix my eyes on her wet, naked lusciousness. The combination of all of the above is messing with my head in a major way.

My little minx has hooked me, body and soul. My need to keep her safe and *get back inside her* is killing me. She's all I fucking care about.

"I'm going to go get some champagne from that tray over there," Vivi says. "Do you want some?"

"Sure." I'm in a terrible mood. I don't want to make small talk with random people I'm not interested in. I want to take her back to bed so I can feast on her gorgeousness with no interruptions.

The sooner we can get back to Kauai, the better.

I watch Vivi saunter off in her little black jumpsuit that's fitted to the curves of her body and think I might lose my goddamn mind.

My gaze surveys the room to see if anyone's watching her and a few people look up as she walks past them. But they can feel my intensity and their eyes find me through the crowd almost immediately. They already know I'm practically invincible in the ring and when it comes to my wife, they've heard rumors. Or they've guessed. They know I'm possessive as fuck. News travels fast.

I scout the area to make sure the bodyguard has followed his orders. There's no sign of him. Which is a very good thing. Silas hasn't arrived yet.

"Well, well, well, if it isn't Wolf Ramsey." I turn to see who it is.

The last person on the planet I want to see right now, as a matter of fact.

Cheyenne. The one woman who can very successfully throw a grenade into my evening.

"I guess I know why you never called me back," she smiles but it's calculating. "How was the wedding?"

I wouldn't have called her back, wedding or no wedding. I'm sure she's figured this out by now. "Perfect."

Her eyes rove my face, my shoulders, my chest. Lower. To my perpetually-half-cocked problem. She's checking me out. Remembering.

Maybe once I considered her borderline cute, in an excessively I'm-available-come-and-get-me sort of way that, at the time, I must have been able to overlook.

Now that I'm used to Vivi's supernova beauty, which hits me like a punch to the gut every time I look at her, Cheyenne is ridiculously dull. Her hair doesn't have Vivi's curl or the depth of light-catching color. Her eyelashes are fake and caked with black make-up, which has smeared under her eyes and she's obviously not aware of this. Her lips have been pumped full of that plastic shit that makes them look overly swollen and weird. I really don't understand why anyone would want to do that.

And I miss how flawless my wife is. I find her across the room and she's talking to a few people. I start to make my way toward her but Cheyenne grabs my arm. At the exact same moment, Vivi turns back this way. She's holding two glasses of champagne. She's sees Cheyenne and her smile fades.

"Take your hand off me."

The damage is already done. "I read that interview Malachi and Aurora gave. That alliance is so bizarre." Her voice lowers. "You know, they were joking about it but they said the people who are forced into the alliance marriages don't *have* to be faithful."

I brush her off but I have to touch her hand to do this. Her skin is cold. Almost scaly-feeling. A wave of disgust washes through me. My wife's skin is as soft as silk and I wonder again at the impossibility of her. How can anyone be so ideal? My chest aches with longing and with a feral sense of gratitude. *She's mine.* How did I get so fucking lucky?

"Is it true? That you don't have to be faithful? I just wanted to let you know I'm here for you, Wolf. You can come visit me anytime and no one needs to know. I promise I won't tell. Will you come?"

"Cheyenne, you need to fuck off—"

"Cheyenne?"

My wife is back with her glasses of champagne. Her petulant little pout is firmly in place and it pisses me off that she's going to be upset by this.

"Hi, Vivi. I'm Cheyenne." And she's out for blood. "Maybe Wolf's mentioned me? It's so nice to meet you. Wolf and I used to be … well, acquaintances."

Bitch. She's riling my wife on purpose. "But we no longer are." Nothing I say is going to tone down the tantrum Vivi is working up to. I can't really blame her. "We're leaving," I tell my wife.

Cheyenne laughs. "Everyone is *so* jealous of you," she tells Vivi. "I mean, none of us thought he was the marrying kind. We've all be trying like hell to get him to commit but he never would. It's common knowledge he's the hottest bachelor in Hawaii—or was. And that *thing* he does with the tying up and the kink, my *God.*"

I resist the serious urge to throttle her.

Vivi doesn't reply. She's glaring at me. And she throws the contents of both glasses of champagne in my face before storming away. "I hate you, Wolf Ramsey."

Goddamn it. We're back to that?

Her outburst … *hurts. She can't hate me. I'm too in love with her.* I can't handle her anger at all. "For fuck's sake," I mutter, grabbing her arm but I don't want to hurt her and she's able to shake me off.

"Wolf, my offer is always open," I vaguely hear Cheyenne call after me as I follow my irate wife through the crowd of people.

I catch up to her easily. Carefully, I lift her and sling her over my shoulder.

"Don't touch me! Put me *down*, you … you *animal!*"

I'd laugh at her choice of insults if I wasn't so focused on fixing this. I can't have my girl mad at me.

People are staring but I really couldn't care less.

"Hey—" some prince valiant begins to protest, like he has some say in this, but I push past him and carry Vivi out the door.

"I said put me down!" She's hitting my back. Tiny little punches that might as well be the touches of a feather.

I ignore her protests, which there are a lot of by the time we reach our new house. I carry her up the stairs and toss her gently onto the bed.

"Take off your clothes."

"No! As if."

"Do it now or I'll do it for you, my love."

She crawls up to the head of the bed and leans into the pillows, glaring at my endearment.

By now my wife knows I won't hurt her but she's furious tonight. Which is good, considering what I'm about to do. She needs her anger.

I loom over her and easily turn her so I can unzip her jumpsuit. She fights against me but it's a feigned protest. I'd bet money she's turned on by my aggression and I'm about to find out if she's already wet for me. Either way, I'm so much stronger than she is, there's really no contest. "You remember your safe word."

"Fuck you, Wolf Ramsey."

"We decided that one was no good, remember?" Last time, her anger amused me. This time, it has a completely different effect. It fucking *wounds* me. I'm besotted with her —manic with it—and the jab spears into me in a way I can feel. I don't like it one bit but it there it is. "Game on, baby."

"You want to fuck me, Wolf Ramsey? Go ahead. You've fucked everyone else on these goddamn islands. Go ahead and do it, I don't care."

"I'm not going to fuck you, baby."

She shoots a few daggers out of her eyes but I'm enraged and she can see this. She can't help asking it. "What are you going to do?"

"Something I've never done to anyone else before."

Light alarm sparks her eyes. "What?"

"I'm going to make love to you. But first, I'm going to take you over a different kind of edge. And I'm going to convince you that you don't need to be jealous. I've already told you that but you didn't listen to your husband."

"You let her touch you."

"I didn't *let* her touch me. I brushed her off because she's not you, told her to fuck off and spent the two miserable seconds in her company despising her and thinking about how gorgeous my wife is. I'll burn the fucking shirt if you want me to."

"How many of them are there? Hundreds? *Thousands?*"

"I don't remember any of them. You're the only one I care about."

"Please. Spare me the bullshit."

"I don't do bullshit, princess. I've meant every word I've ever said to you. I'm in love with you and I mean it when I tell you you're the most exquisite, adorable, ideal woman I've ever seen or imagined."

She's not the only one who's pissed off. I peel her clothes off roughly. All she's wearing underneath is a tiny thong that rips easily. I pull off my own clothes and reach into my bag that's sitting next to the bed. I pull out a harness.

"Get on your knees. I want you on all fours."

"Why? What's that?"

"Just do it, baby girl. You're obeying me one way or the other. The easy way or the hard way. Up to you."

Despite the drama, she relents coyly and I can see the glistening moisture coating her pussy. She can't deny this addiction any more than I can. She needs me as much as I need her. She's offering herself to me because she can't resist me.

"Good girl." I strap on the harness, pushing her head down so her cheek is resting on the covers, ass up, knees apart. I tie her hands behind her back. "Arch your back." She does and I tighten and fasten the ties until she's tightly bound in this position. *"Mine."* Fully on display for me to take and give whatever I choose.

I strap a blindfold over her eyes.

"*Wolf,*" she whispers. There's fear in her breathy gasp. Uncertainty. But most of all: a needy craving. My sexy little wife needs my hungry mouth. She needs my praise. She's desperate for my hot, bursting fury.

"You're the most dazzling girl, the sweetest, the sexiest, the strongest. I'm going to fill you up with my love and my lust until you're exploding with it. Are you ready for me?"

I take a flogger from the drawer and a few other things, placing them on the bed.

She whimpers as I sweep the light leather tails of the flogger over her slick, swollen pussy. Fuck, she's wet. "You love being bound and submissive for your husband. Look how turned on you are, you dirty girl. I'm going to give you everything you want. More than you've ever had. You're going to *feel* me, princess, so much." I gently flick the whip over her pussy and she moans. "When I tell you I'm ruined for anyone else, I wasn't lying. I'm fucking obsessed with you. I told you my word is good yet you keep doubting me. Why is that?"

I can't stand this. I have to eat her and taste her. It's been several hours of torture and I need the sweetness of her like a drug.

I whip her again, harder this time, and she squeals. Fresh honey coats her pussy and I burrow my face into her, feasting greedily, thrusting my tongue into heaven. I run my tongue over the pucker of her ass, prodding lightly. She squirms and moans but she's too tightly bound to escape me. Then I suck feverishly on her candy-pink clit until she's rocking against me and I know she's close.

I run my hands over her ass, dipping my fingers into her juicy pussy, teasing her g-spot. "Nothing compares to you. You're the most gorgeous angel. You're the one."

Then I remove my fingers, sucking them clean because I'm a fucking goner. I whip her again with the flogger, just enough to sting. She cries out but it's not her safe word. Just compliant ecstasy. So I whip her again. Until her ass is as pink as her clit.

"How much do you hate me now, princess? So much you want me to stop?"

"No," comes the low whisper.

"Did you know I worship the ground you walk on? Did you know I *love* you? And now you're going to find out how much."

It only takes three more lashes. She screams a low gasp and I watch the rhythmic spasms take hold, inviting me in.

"Fuck, you're pretty. Look at you, coming so hard for me."

I take my gigantic, spilling hard-on and hold it to her saturated core. She's still coming and I let the clenches of her body guide me in. With each clench of her orgasm, I slide deeper, barely retreating before riding the next rippling pull further into her. My cock is huge and thick and veiny and she's tight as fuck but she's so wet she takes me perfectly. So damn snugly, like a silky fist. In and in, all the way to the hilt. Until I'm deeper than I've ever been.

I rut her in a way that's both aggressive and tender,

gaining even more depth as I bottom out with each thrust. I have to hold myself still at the deepest points or I'll lose control. I'm riding the high. My release is waiting there like a fucking freight train. When her pussy starts clenching more strongly again with her next orgasm, there's no way I'll be able to hold it.

I reach for a vibrator. It's a rose, designed to give suction directly onto her clit. I flick it on, fingering her engorged little nub and fitting the vibrator there. I use my body to pleasure her, fucking her deep as I milk her clit with the rose, in a synced, persuasive rhythm.

Vivi's moaning my name, over and over.

This is harder than I've ever pushed her before and I'm aware that I'm breaking through both physical and existential thresholds. This kind of pleasure is severe. It can break you wide open.

"Trust me, baby," I croon in a low growl. "Feel me. Come for me."

I feel her next orgasm begin in a rolling surge that racks through her body. Her pussy clamps tightly around my cock, tugging like a slippery vice—*holy fuck*—that leaves me no choice. The pleasure explodes and my cock pumps hot throbs of cum deep inside her, flooding her pussy with my seed. We're locked in a bucking, clenching, sweaty grip.

I have never, ever come this hard or this long.

We ride it all the way.

"Wolf," she cries. "*Wolf.* Pineapple. *Pineapple.*"

I pull myself from her body in a gush and unbind her, taking off her blindfold. I wrap her in a bearhug and pull the sheet over us. I hold her close to me, smoothing her hair, rocking her gently. "It's okay, baby. I've got you. You're okay."

She's sobbing and I wipe her tears with my thumbs.

"I'm sorry," she whispers. "For doubting you."

"Did I hurt you?"

"No, Wolf. That was … the most beautiful thing that's ever happened to me. Ever. By a long shot."

"Me too, sweetheart."

"I'm sorry about before. I was upset to see … her."

"She's no one to me. I told you that. I can't stand her."

"I overreacted."

"You had cause, honey. But you didn't need to. You just never have to worry about anything except how loyal I am and how crazy I am for you. And I mean *crazy*."

More tears leak from her eyes.

I kiss her soft hair. "You know what I think?" I want to fill her up with good feelings. I want happiness to be the only thing she has room for, because there's so much of it. "I think we're soul mates. I think we have been all along and we were led to each other by forces beyond our control. We're the opposite of cursed. As soon as I saw you, a part of me knew I'd been waiting for something even *I* didn't know about until then. You. I didn't think I was capable of loving anyone. But that night when you were standing there by the pool with your sparked eyes and your feisty little pout, I knew. I knew I could."

Her fingers rest lightly on my chest as she gazes up at me.

"I'm in love with you, Vivi." It's the very last thing I ever expected to feel, but I've never spoken truer words. "I *love* you. There's no one else for me now. I've never loved anyone but you. Not even close."

I hold her like she's breakable, for a long time. Until her crying calms into sniffling breaths and she falls asleep in my arms.

I kiss her lips as she sleeps and I marvel at the shape of them and the sweep of her eyelashes against her cheeks.

I once thought love was the curse. I was relieved that I wouldn't be touched by it.

What I realize now is that love *is* where the deepest pain lies—but not in the way I first thought.

Without her, nothing matters. She's worth the risk. She's worth every risk. As long as I can hold her, just like this, and keep her, nothing else matters.

# 16

# Vivi

WHEN I WAKE up I feel different. Like I've been reborn into a vibrantly colorful butterfly who's finally broken free of her chrysalis.

I lay still for a while, watching him sleep.

He has a scar etched through one of his eyebrows, a smaller, faint one across his left cheekbone and one near his temple. They're the only imperfections. His eyebrows are darker than his hair. His mouth is full. He looks younger when he's asleep but his fierceness is still there in the stubble across his jaw, the swarthy suntan and the inked patterns snaking across his big, sculpted muscles. The scars, along with his too-long hair and his deep tan, make him look like a beefed-up pirate.

What an unlikely thing. To find myself madly in love with this almost-stranger after just weeks of what could only be described as a category five hurricane.

I think about the searing intimacy. The pain of his whip and his body that gave way to the most intense pleasure I've ever, ever experienced. It changed me. The fireworks of it literally broke me apart.

I cried a lot when it happened, over things I've lost.

The pieces of me that were heavy and trapped have been set free. It's hard to describe. But the whole world sort of shines with a new clarity.

All the issues I had about my past have literally been fucked out of my system. Which sounds crazy but that's how it feels.

It wasn't my fault that I lost my mother. It wasn't my fault that my father went mad. It's not my fault that my siblings have been damaged in one way or another and don't always act in ways that are in my own best interests, or even their own. I don't need their reassurances or their approval anymore. I'm strong enough now to take control of myself and my life.

Wolf's support has lifted me up, just like he promised me it would. I trust him. And I trust myself.

I think about all the aggressively endearing things he said to me last night.

I love that I can *believe* him.

I love that my husband always surprises me, saying things to me that are nicer than anything I might have expected from the buff, gruff look of him. He's done that since the very first time I met him.

I love that he's all mine.

Maybe most of all, I love the things he can *do*.

*God.*

No one tells you orgasms are super-charged boosts of therapy and empowerment. Or that they leave a new, clear-headed peacefulness in their wake. Or that they teach you things about yourself you never knew. I love the change in myself Wolf has inspired.

I want to show him how *much* I love him.

The tropical air is warm this morning. He kicked off the sheet during the night. I remember him at some point in the night taking me into the shower, cleaning me and making sure I was okay.

His body is big and bronzed and hair-dusted and, even as he sleeps, he's fully aroused, like an offering of male perfection.

My mouth waters at the sight of his massive, engorged manhood. I love that he's always ready.

Wolf so often wakes me up with his mouth, eating into me and making me come, always demanding control.

Now, it's my turn. I want to taste him and drink him. I want his seed to nourish me. I want to please him.

Being careful not to wake him, I wriggle from his hold. I use the silk ties on the bed to bind his wrists. Tight.

When I'm sure he's securely bound, I slide down his body to nuzzle him, gently, seeing how long I can do this without waking him. I tease him with my mouth.

I love the taste of him, musky and drugging. I run my tongue over the crown, drawing a circle around it before centering on the wetness pearling there. I take his huge cock in my hands.

He wakes, straining against the ties. "*Fuck.* Princess—?"

"Right here," I murmur, licking him.

"What are y—"

"I think you know." I take more of him, sucking on the head lovingly, putting effort into what I'm doing.

"Untie me, you little minx."

"Quiet."

This is fun, turning the tables on him, fully embracing the lunatic passion he's inspired in me. My craving for him feels downright savage.

I use the tactics I've learned from him. "You remember your safe word? Oh, that's right, you don't need one. There's nothing I can do to you that you don't want me to do."

"You are so fucking in for it, sweetheart." His voice is low and graveled. But I can hear the surrender behind the pleasure I'm giving him. I love that his wild ferocity is fully at my mercy. I crazy-love when his huge, musclebound body reacts to me in a way that's beyond his control.

I caress Wolf's shaft with my fingers, holding the heavy weight of him, feathering my touch along the ridged length. I can see that this is almost painfully pleasurable for him.

"Princess." But he's not asking me to untie him now. He's watching me. His eyes are the color of lightning striking ocean water.

In this moment, my big, rough husband is completely at my mercy.

"I want you, Wolf Ramsey." I kiss the tip of his cock, letting my tongue dip into the creamy wetness. "I'm yours.

You're mine. This big cock is mine. This seed is mine." I mean, come on, this is all new to me but I'm feeling it. I'm not a virgin anymore. Not even close. I'm Wolf Ramsey's wife and I *want* to be. I can feel my feminine power and I lean into it. "Let me show you how much I want you, husband."

I move to nuzzle against his monster erection and I begin to suckle on him in docile, deferential little draws, kissing his cock, licking, then taking him deeper.

Wolf groans like his heart is breaking. He lays back on the towel, his eyes darker than I've ever seen them. "I'm going to come, baby. Your sweet mouth feels too good."

"Shh," I croon. "Let me have it. Come in my mouth." So I lick him again. I put my lips around the broad end and take him deeper, using my fingers to squeeze and play him as I find an awkward suction. But then, as I practice, I find my groove.

"*Fuck,* I can't hold it."

"Give me all of it," I whisper. "I want to drink you." I increase my pace and the pressure of my hands and I can feel the pleasure of his body begin to erupt. I know he's on the brink, coasting on a wave, riding it. I take him even deeper and he starts coming in rolling, liquid throbs that shoot down my throat and fill my mouth, spilling to wet my lips and my chin. It feels dirty, what we're doing, and it makes me greedy. I swallow as much as I can in thirsty mouthfuls. Then I lick his still-throbbing cock, taking more, kissing him as I clean him.

He's unusually quiet.

When I'm finished, I untie him.

He takes me in his arms and holds me.

"I love you, Wolf Ramsey," I tell him.

His blue eyes are bloodshot and full of awe. "Good. Because you're stuck with me. I'll follow you to the ends of the earth. I'll follow you to heaven itself, I don't care. Wherever you are is where I need to be."

And then he proceeds over the next few hours to get his revenge, devastating me with pleasure in every possible way, as I cry and fly and most of all, fall even more deeply in love with my beautiful savage.

# 17

# Vivi

(NOTE TO READERS: This chapter has a trigger warning for violence including attempted rape.)

MY MOTHER's library a.k.a. our new house is swarming with people.

Gabrielle is managing the contractors and decorators, who are currently buzzing around downstairs, measuring things and scrolling furiously through their iPads.

There's a lot of banging going on from the new additions that have already started. The new wing—which is going to triple the size of the original building, at the insistence of my husband—will be ultra-modern.

After several hours of answering questions and making decisions about everything from the perfect placement of the new couches to swatch colors, I've retreated to the upstairs, which is calmer but not by much. Wolf is pacing the rooftop garden as he talks to Remy on the phone.

In the end, we decided to stay at Seven Mile Beach another few weeks, until the decisions about the house were finalized.

My husband might as well be a chained-up tiger. He's used to spending his days riding horses across wide-open fields, hunting and tracking his way through wild tropical rainforests, and fighting at some kind of level where (I've learned) the UFC tries to recruit you to compete but you're too busy.

It's safe to say choosing swatch colors isn't really his thing.

At least his combat skills have helped with the litigation. Turns out, between my family's brigade of lawyers and Wolf's cousin Dex, who's a big-shot prosecutor in Honolulu, they found out that Jericho had pilfered more than twenty million dollars from my family over the past ten years and put it into a bunch of different bank accounts all over the world. He was indicted and then arrested in record time. All the money he'd siphoned into his various trusts have been recovered.

Jett seemed to disappear without a trace. Wolf and Ash have both been digging into it to see if they could pick up a trail but there's been no sign of him.

It almost makes me nervous that he left so obediently. It doesn't seem like him. But I just try to be grateful that he's finally, after all this time, gone from my life. I never really realized how much the bullying had restricted me and held me back until I've been free of it.

Wolf had all the locks and security codes in the entire estate changed. He questioned the security team about their allegiance to Jett and made sure they understood the consequences of leaking information. Not one of them took up his offer to leave. They all accepted a raise, signed a contract and told my husband they never really liked their former boss anyway.

And Ash is the new manager of the charity foundation. He's the perfect person for the job. He's meticulous, enthusiastic and such a whiz with numbers that it makes everything easy to keep track of.

Ash and I only meet when Wolf is with me. It's our deal, so my husband doesn't lose his mind and/or control. It's easy to do because Wolf and I are basically inseparable. He doesn't like letting me out of his sight.

So, between the house renovations, the banking and theft fiasco and the reestablishment of the charities, there's been a lot going on.

It's been five weeks since our wedding.

Wolf is on edge. He wants to get back to Paradise and so do I. We've made a plan to leave as soon as we can.

Enzo and Silas are meeting about some of our families' co-owned businesses and Wolf and I are supposed to be joining them.

"Would you mind going without me?" I ask him.

I'm tired. We've been busy. And we often don't get a lot of sleep because my husband is so relentless about doling out orgasms like it's going out of style. I'm not entirely blameless either. All hell breaks loose inside me whenever my husband touches me.

"What's wrong?"

"I just feel a little … funny. Maybe I ate something."

"I'll stay with you."

"No, you go. I'm fine here, I promise. I might just take a nap."

"I'm not leaving you."

I'm in a strange mood. Maybe I'm hormonal. "You don't need to babysit me for the rest of time, Wolf. I can survive for an hour without you."

"I don't like the thought of you being alone."

"I *like* being alone sometimes. I've spent half my life alone. Up here, by myself. I'm safe here. I want you to go. I'm fine."

My husband is 6'4" and ripped. His posture and the way he stands, legs wide and with that hot alpha confidence, make it all the more heart-breaking that he's … worried. And so careful with me.

"You know they won't stop hounding us until one of us meets with them," I tell him. "This will keep them satisfied and then we can go back to Paradise and stay there."

Still, he won't budge.

"There are people downstairs, Wolf. Gabrielle. The design team. The contractors. If I need something, I'll get them to help me. Really. Go."

I finally talk him into it. He reminds me that there's a loaded gun in my bedside table. He's been training me.

Teaching me how to use some of the weapons he carries and showing me some self-defense moves. I keep telling him the threats are outside our walls now.

"I'll be back in thirty minutes." He's tense. Wary. "Then we're leaving for Paradise. Tomorrow."

"I can't wait."

After he leaves, I find a bikini. I can admit it feels strange to be without him. I miss him already and I'm almost regretting my little tirade.

*Get a grip. He'll be back in half an hour.*

So I try to make the most of the peace and relative quiet.

I reach for a white wrap-dress and put it on, tying it at the front.

Something's in the pocket. I pull out the knife Wolf gave me, that day on Lucky when he showed me how to use it. The sharp blade glints in the sun. On a whim, I slide it back into its holster and I strap it to my thigh, like he did.

And I grab my book and go out to the roof garden, which has new loungers, freshly potted tropical plants and a hot tub.

It's a beautiful day. The view out over the wall and down to the beach is idyllic.

Our plan is to extend the new wing's roof garden with a deck and stairs that lead down to the beach, to make better use of it. We'll replace the old gate that doesn't unlock with something more sturdy.

I lay on one of the loungers and open my book to where I'd left off.

I'm only a few paragraphs in when a shadow blocks the sun.

At first I think it's Wolf. "Why are you back so—"

But it's not my husband. "You didn't really think I would disappear that easily, did you, Vivi?"

*Holy fuck. It's him.* "H-how did you get in here?"

Jett holds up an old-fashioned key. "I took this a long time ago. In case I ever needed it." The scene is eerie and unreal, like a day-lit nightmare. My senses take in every detail, like my life is flashing before my eyes. Those uncannily dark eyes. His dark hair, cut in a military-style buzz cut. "It's the key to that gate right over there. The one that's not linked to the alarm system."

I didn't know that.

"Because I dismantled it. Just in case I ever happened to need a way back in."

I guess if you and your brother are embezzling millions of dollars from your so-called family, you might think to make contingency plans like that.

I scream but he must have been anticipating it because he's on top of me and his hand is over my mouth before I can move or speak. My scream is muffled and I can't breathe.

"You know what would be the worst thing that could ever happen to that prick of a husband of yours?" Jett seethes, straddling me, pinning me. He's holding my shoulders so I can't struggle. "For him to know that he's not the only man who's fucked his wife. It'll kill him. Every time he takes you from now on, if he even wants to, all he'll be able to think about is me. He'll be repulsed by you. Because you're dirty with another man's seed."

*"No. Get off me, you filthy——"*

He slaps me and grips me. I'm screaming and fighting him with everything I have but *he's so damn heavy.*

"I know you haven't had your latest birth control shot because I was tracking it. I know everything about you. It was me who put the tap on your phone. I've watched you all along. I've been obsessed with you for as long as I can remember, you little bitch. And all you've ever given me is grief. That hoity-toity disdain, like you're better than me. I was *never* good enough for you. But now I will be."

He tries to kiss me but I thrash violently and turn my face away. "You'll die for this."

"What if it's *me* who knocks you up?" He smells like sweat and doom. "What if your egomaniac husband has to live with *that* every day for the rest of his life? A child who isn't his. It would ruin his life. And yours."

I scream as loud as I can but he's gagging me, crushing me, fumbling with his pants.

No. No. This can't happen. I won't let it.

*My knife.*

He's distracted by what he's trying to do. His breathing is uneven and I almost wretch when I feel him tug at my bikini.

My fingers are somehow able to pull the knife from its holster. I hold it the way Wolf showed me.

I don't even hesitate.

*Gouge deep—and put some effort into it. Muscle is more resilient than you might expect. Up and in. Twist and slice.*

The blade is very sharp. It's easier than I thought it would be.

Jett reacts. There's commotion.

An animal growl.

A blur.

And a neat, deep red line across Jett's throat. Which bubbles and bleeds.

I watch the life leave his eyes in a ghostly, horrific shift.

And then his weight is gone.

"Vivi." It's Wolf, lifting me into his arms. Carrying me. Before I can tell him it's okay, I'm okay, I did it just like he showed me, I'm pulled under a deep, inky darkness that bleeds the world into black.

*COME BACK TO ME, baby. You're okay. I'm here now. You're safe. You were scared but there's nothing more to fear, my brave girl. Can you feel me? Wake up now, Vivi. Come back to me. I need you. I'm going to take you home. Please, princess. Wake up.*

My eyes blink open.

Wolf is holding me, cradling me in his arms. There are other people here, outside. Silas. Enzo. Malachi. Dealing with the aftermath.

"That's my girl." Wolf is gazing down at me with so much love and concern, I almost wonder if he's just a hopeful dream. Nothing can be this beautiful. "I'm taking you back to Paradise. We're going to have the most magical life. You and me. We'll swim and sail and have babies and I'll never leave you again. I could feel you. I could feel you were in danger and I came back. I'll never leave you again."

"Is he …?"

"Yes."

"Did you …?"

"You and me both. It's over."

*It's over.*

# 18

# Vivi

"IT SAYS TO WAIT TEN MINUTES." I place the small white plastic strip on the wide arm of the chair where Wolf is sitting.

"Come here, gorgeous." His voice is rasped and deep, growly with a subdued, manly excitement.

I climb onto his lap and Wolf leans me against his chest, holding me close.

We've been back at our house in Paradise for a week now. It took some time for both of us to recover from what happened. I was shaken but not hurt. Wolf was out of his mind with residual rage and a protectiveness that calmed only once we returned to our beach haven.

Enzo, Silas and Remy took care of the aftermath and all three of them have been checking in with us to see how we are.

I keep assuring them—and my devoted husband—that I'm fine. And I am.

Except for the nausea. And the tiredness. And the weird cravings.

My period is late. Which isn't actually that unusual. The shot used to mess with my cycle. But I haven't had a shot in almost five months.

I'm sitting on Wolf's lap, sipping pineapple juice from a straw. He's holding the glass, insisting I stay hydrated. We're out on the upper lanai and the light of the amber-hued sunrise paints his inked muscles gold. The ocean waves lap at the sand down below us. The early morning sky is the exact same color as my husband's eyes.

We both have a feeling we know what the results are going to be and our hopefulness wraps itself around us, binding us even more closely.

"Whatever the results of this test are," he says, tucking a strand of hair behind my ear, "I just want to tell you that you've changed my life."

I can't hold back a smile because I'm so damn *happy*. I hardly recognize myself. And because he's so earnest. Coming from my tough-guy husband, it's the most adorable thing. "Have I?"

His eyes narrow at my laughter but there's the mischief in him that's my absolute kryptonite. "You have. My whole life used to be dedicated to hunting and fighting. Providing. Growing our profits. Protecting. This is going to sound cheesy as fuck but I want to say it anyway."

"I'm listening." I let my fingers weave into his hair. He's

got the best hair. And by now I know that my husband is a sweet-talker. He's matter-of-fact about it though, like praising me is his job and his duty.

"There was something missing. Something monumental. I was doing all that because it's what I've always done. Which isn't really a reason. A lot of the time I was almost on autopilot, going through the motions. But now, because of you, I have a *reason*. My whole life feels like it's doubled in size. *You*. You're my reason. You and our babies are my reason."

"I love you," I whisper, kissing his lips. For all his hard edges, he has the softest lips. "There might not be a baby, you know."

"It'll happen. I have a breeding kink, you might have noticed."

"I think I might have one too."

"I know." He grins. "Your inner sex goddess is a fucking maniac, princess. I could see that about you when we first met." His thumbs glide along my cheekbones. "You were so gorgeous. You blew my mind with your sweet, fierce beauty. You're doing it now. You do it every time I look at you." He holds my head between his warm palms. "I love my wife." So carefully, with so much love, a tear leaks from my eye. He kisses it, licking it. "And the baby girl we're going to have."

"How do you know it'll be a girl?"

"I just do. We're going to call her Wilderness."

I laugh. "Wilderness? Wow. It's … unique."

"Wilderness Vivienne Sofia Fitzpatrick Ramsey. We can call her Willa for short."

"I love it," I whisper. *I love it. I love him.*

"Are you ready to look?"

"Okay."

"Okay?"

I nod, but I'm nervous. Because I want her so badly to be real.

"All right, then. Here we go." Wolf picks up the plastic strip. We both stare at the two vivid blue lines. "Wilderness is on her way."

# EPILOGUE

# Vivi

## *Fourteen months later ...*

OUR BEAUTIFUL LITTLE Willa was born a healthy seven and a half pounds, kicking and screaming and so perfect I can't believe she's real. She already has her besotted daddy wrapped tightly around her tiny finger.

Wolf *loves* being a father, as much as I love being a mother. I wasn't sure what to expect, since I never had a mother of my own, but my husband was so insistent all the way through my pregnancy that I'd be the best mother in the world that some of his encouragement slowly rubbed off on me. Now that I have Wilderness, I can't imagine life without her.

She has her father's blue eyes and my olive skin. She was born with a dusting of dark gold hair on her head as soft as feathers. She's the happiest, most enchanting baby I could ever have imagined. She has a feisty but sweet nature and she hardly ever cries. Possibly because she never gets a chance to. Wolf and I are, to put it mildly, doting parents. She falls asleep at my breast or in her daddy's arms. Not having known our own parents, we both felt that chasm in our lives deeply. Now, we're making up for it by loving our baby with everything we have.

Wolf had an addition put on our beach house in Paradise that's more than doubled the size of the house. It's where we spend most of our time.

We went to Italy for a month soon after we found out I was pregnant, while the renovations were being finished. We stayed in a luxury condo in Venice that looked out over the canals, rode on gondolas and ate a lot of outrageously good food. Then we went to Florence, Rome and Tuscany. We had a fantastic time but I was glad to get back to Paradise.

We spend time on Lucky, often sailing around to Pirate's Cove and spending long, blissful days just fishing, swimming and making hot, sweet, crazy love.

The Ramsey cousins built a new party house in the next cove over and we often spend evenings there, or up at the castle. The Ramseys are a close-knit family and they've welcomed me like one of their own.

Echo, Blaise and Cassidy have become my sisters and my best friends.

Echo and Cassidy started their own clothing label and between all of us and our various social media platforms, they've become some of the most sought-after designers in the world. They can't keep up with demand, so they've opened a studio and office in a new building in Paradise, which has become a sort of fashion hub for young, hip designers. They already have more than twenty employees and Blaise is helping them run and grow the business. They're thinking of opening an office in New York.

We see Cassidy and Knox all the time. They hang out here a lot, or we visit them at their beach house, which is a fifteen minute walk from ours. Their little girl Havyn is an adorable white-blond sweetheart, who's obsessed with her brand new cousin. Cassidy just found out she's expecting their second baby. Aside from my husband, I've never seen a man so obsessed with his wife as Knox Ramsey.

Blaise married Tristan in a beautiful wedding here in Paradise just two months after our wedding. Tristan is an artist whose paintings sell for huge money—and even more, now that he's married to a Ramsey. He also surfs. They divide their time between their house on the north shore of Oahu and their apartment in the castle.

With Wolf's help, I renegotiated all my contracts, choosing only the ones I really wanted to do. I still model and enjoy it a lot more than I ever did, now that I can do it on my own terms. Gabrielle is my assistant and has moved to Paradise. She's dating Wolf's cousin Hunter and things seem to be heating up.

It was more Wolf's decision than mine, but Lana and I parted ways. She moved to L.A. to try her luck in Hollywood.

Wolf took a selfie of us, with me sitting on his lap, that day we found out we were pregnant. We posted it on my

Instagram account and it went viral. A week later, I posted a heartfelt letter listing some of the causes our new charity supports.

I used to think I was being naive or idealistic by wanting to help people, but the results were actually sort of amazing. People responded in ways I wasn't expecting. The foundation has had so many donations we've been able to give full college scholarships to several hundred kids, fund a new hospital wing and support a lot of other charities Ash has been researching. We're actually using our following to making a difference and it feels more than good.

Ash has taken the foundation to the next level. He loves the job and he's very, very good at it. He and Thor moved in together, into a swanky condo in Waikiki with views out over the beach, a home office, a gym and a rooftop pool. It's not far from Seven Mile Beach and we see them when we spend time there.

Wolf and Ash have a stilted but not completely antagonistic almost-friendship. Ash teases Wolf and his reactions always make the rest of us laugh.

My mother's library is now a six-bedroom house. We spend a week each month there, or sometimes less, meeting with my brothers and the Kings about the various businesses we co-own.

Malachi and Aurora's marriage is a surprisingly happy one. They seem to have mellowed in a way that works for them and I'm glad to see it.

Wolf had a hard time forgiving Silas for his treatment of me, before my wedding. Wolf challenged Silas to fight, to get the grudge out of his system, he said. For the sake of his own pride, Silas accepted, but it didn't go well for him. He came away with two black eyes, several broken fingers, a new respect for my husband and a much kinder approach to his relationship with me.

Silas realized he'd been manipulated by our former cousins—who we rarely mention—and he's made an effort to be more caring to the people in his life. He's a father now, to a stunning little boy named Rocco. And his girlfriend Sasha, even though she hasn't managed to get Silas to the altar yet, is good for him. He seems happier in a way that's new.

Enzo King and I have become unlikely friends. He's shady as hell but he's got a wry sense of humor and a twinkle in those very-blue eyes. I heard he got roped into teaching a finance class at the university for a semester—some favor that needed cashing in. Apparently he's fallen insanely hard for one of his much-younger students. It's hard to imagine anyone hooking Enzo like that. I'm waiting for more gossip.

Perri is dating an astrophysicist who worships the ground she walks on. He's no MMA fighter, she said, but he's the kindest person she's ever met. Every time I see her, she's more and more smitten.

Tatum does what she's always done: works, travels and falls in love with one co-star after another. Last time I talked to her she was on location in London. She said she's thinking of writing and directing her own film.

As for Remy, he's the big brother I never quite had. He's

generous to a fault and loyal to his bones. We all think it's time for him to start dating again. Blaise and Echo keep trying to matchmake for him and he's slowly warming to the idea.

Remy, of all people, has suggested that we finally do away with the curse. He thinks we should commit to aligning our three families through businesses and real estate interests instead of marriage, since it basically has the same outcome. Which is what we're already doing. He doesn't think we should force our children into arranged marriages because of a superstition our great great great grandfathers dreamed up one night after probably having a few too many. He thinks the whole thing has gone on long enough. Bad things happen anyway, no one can control that. And we shouldn't try to.

I couldn't agree more, but some people are taking time to warm to the idea.

I'm just thankful *I* was forced into marriage. It's turned out to be the best thing that's ever happened to me. I can't imagine a better husband and I wouldn't change him for the world. For us, the curse turned out to be a dream come true.

Now, I'm sitting out on the upper lanai of our beach house, my favorite place in the world. It's dusk and the sun has just dipped below the horizon line. I can hear the soothing splash of the waterfall further along the cove that fills its own natural pool, and the lulling rhythm of the waves. The sky is glowing with fiery swirls of orange, lavender and pale pink.

Wolf appears in the doorway and comes to sit next to

me on the lounger. Like always, even the view can't compete with my beautiful, sexy-as-all-hell husband. He sets two glasses of champagne on the table next to me and pulls me onto his lap.

"What are we celebrating?"

"You."

"I'm still feeding Willa." I haven't had a drink in more than a year.

"One glass won't hurt. She's down for the night."

I take a small sip and he kisses my lips.

This man, who once seemed so cold and dangerous to me, has changed my life in every possible way, lifting me up and freeing me from a cage that was just as much about my own fear as it was about circumstance.

He's taught me how to value my life differently. He once said to me, *I'm going to give you the whole fairy tale. Your laughter, your safety and most of all your pleasure are my only priorities. I'm going to make all your wildest dreams come true. I'm going to lift you up until you're shining brighter than the sun.*

And he has. He's done all those things. My life fits me now, instead of fitting everyone else around me.

Even more than that, he's given me a sense of satisfaction in myself that I'd never experienced before. A sense of feeling comfortable in my own skin. A pride in who I am and what I'm capable of that I never saw until he opened my eyes and showed me.

His wild heart beats in sync with my own.

"So, about that breeding kink …" Wolf grins at me, with that dark hunger I know so well. I can feel the huge, hard ridge of him underneath me gaining momentum. "I bought you some presents."

"What presents?"

"They're in the drawer under the bed. You'll have to let me carry you inside to find out."

"Is that right?"

"This one will be a boy."

I wrap my arms around his neck as he lifts me. "What are we going to name him?"

"Phoenix Wolf Nathaniel Fitzpatrick Ramsey."

"That's quite a name."

"Come with me, Mrs. Ramsey. You're going to like this."

♥ If you enjoyed Wolf and Vivi's story, please consider taking a few minutes to leave a quick review or rating on Amazon for Wild Hearts. Thank you! ♥

Want to see what happens with Wolf and Vivi five years down the road? Read the bonus epilogue: https://BookHip.com/CKLPNXJ

**Xoxo,**
**Julie Capulet**

Please come join my Facebook reader group, <u>Julie Capulet's Romantics</u>, where I share cover reveals, insider info and we discuss all things romance!

Sign up for my newsletter for free books, updates, sneak peeks and exclusive giveaways!

# ALSO BY JULIE CAPULET

**I Love You Series**

XOXO I Love You

XOXX I Love You More

Max

**McCabe Brothers Series**

Hopeless Romantic

My Hero

Arrogant Player

**Music City Lovers Series**

Nashville Days

Nashville Nights

Nashville Dreams

**Paradise Series**

Devil's Angel

**Sexy Stand-alones**

Cowboy

Beautiful Savages

Julie Capulet is an Amazon top 25 bestselling author of contemporary romance. Julie writes about sexy, obsessed heroes who fall hard and fast and the sweet & sassy women who bring them to their knees. Her stories are inspired by true love and she's married to her own real life hero. When she's not writing, she's reading, walking on the beach, drinking wine and watching rom-coms ♥

For more books and updates, visit **www.juliecapulet.com**

Made in the USA
Monee, IL
24 February 2023

28595530R00199